A Family's Loss

A Family's Loss

Tim Barretto

Beech River Books
Center Ossipee, New Hampshire

BℝB

Beech River Books
P.O. Box 62, Center Ossipee, N.H. 03814
603-539-3537
www.beechriverbooks.com

LIBRARY OF CONGRESS CATALOGING-IN-PUBLICATION DATA

Barretto, Tim.
    A family's loss / Tim Barretto. -- First edition
    p. cm.
    Summary: "A novel set in New Hampshire about a family
    whose love for each other can be smothering or withheld,
    confused or improper, impulsive or passionless. This becomes
    a force that drives their fate through the tumultuous times
    towards the end of the Viet Nam War and leads to a
    cataclysmic loss in the climax" --Provided by the publisher.
    ISBN: 978-0-9839367-2-5 (pbk. : alk. paper)
    1.   Vietnam War, 1961-1975--Veterans--Fiction. 2.   New
    Hampshire--History--20th century--Fiction. 3.   Domestic
    fiction. I. Title.
    PS3602.A8368F36 2013
    813'.6--dc23

                                                    2012048988

Printed in the United States of America

For Mary, with all my heart—

Your love and support through the years
have made it possible to write this book.

Contents

Though I speak with the tongues of men and of angels, and have not love, I am become as sounding brass, or a tinkling cymbal.

—I Corinthians 13:1

It is sad not to be loved, but it is much sadder not to be able to love.

—Miguel de Unamuno

Chapter One

It's a Boy

The day-old infant sucked at her breast like some enormous leech. She knew she did not want it. Knew, too, that it was a shameful thing to admit even to herself.

The first had been easy. Five hours. Intense but mercifully quick, pushed out on the third good contraction. Though not the girl she had hoped for, Virgil was a beautiful healthy baby. But this *one. More than a day and a night of vomiting and diarrhea. Her strength gone and dilation stalled, they drugged her and cut her open.* Cut her open. *Still it would not have mattered. The thought had sustained her through the long months of retching and exhaustion and hot, sleepless summer nights, it had sustained her through the unbearably difficult and finally unproductive labor which had ended in her being cut, and it would have sustained her through whatever else was to follow:* her baby girl, Lydia, would make everything worth it. *She had known in the depths of her being that it would be a girl. The thought had pushed her through the nauseating smells of paint thinner to the completion of a pink-toned bedroom and a quilt her baby would be able to pass on to her own daughter.*

In the fog of anesthesia when the baby was born either she did not hear or they did not say the words she had been waiting for months to hear, the words she had exulted over more than once in her daydreams: You have a beautiful baby girl. *It didn't matter. She knew. No one had to say anything. Then she drifted into an airy, blissful sleep, a sleep distinguished not by absence of awareness but by an awareness so heightened in the distorted light of drugs and exhaustion and euphoria that she believed this must be what heaven was—this feeling of floating, of rocking on the most gentle of seas in this most golden light, the fragrance of roses filling the air. She dreamed that her own mother, whose abandonment of her when she was an infant she had never been able to confess to anyone, not even to Harry, came to see her, and she slipped her nipple into her baby's mouth and said without bitterness, forgivingly, "You see, Mother, this is how you care for a baby girl." Her mother smiled and nodded. Upon waking (they had transferred her from the delivery room while she slept) she told her roommate it was the most wonderful sleep of her life.*

Not even when they gave the baby to her early the next day and she put it to her breast did she realize her mistake. She saw only that her baby girl was taking the nipple as expertly as if she had been born with it in her mouth. It was only when, in a sort of half sleep, through the susurrant hiss of some nearby piece of hospital machinery, she overheard Harry talking with one of the nurses about plans for circumcision that she began to suspect something was wrong.

"Why are you talking about circumcision?" she asked.

"Oh, sweetheart. I didn't know you were awake," Harry said. "How are you feeling?"

"All right. A little groggy, I guess. But what's this about circumcision?"

"I was just trying to find out when they'd be able to circumcise the baby."

"I don't understand," she said, feeling a sudden chill deep inside.

"Well, I know we didn't discuss it, but I assumed since we had Virgil circumcised we'd do the same with this baby. We've really got

to find a name for him, though. It's terrible that we haven't picked one out already."

The chill blew through her heart and turned it to ice. "Him?" was all she could manage to say. She held her breath as she waited for the reply.

"Wait a minute," Harry said. The fear and confusion in his eyes informed her before his words could. She closed her eyes. "You didn't know he's a boy? My God—"

His voice seemed to be coming to her from an immeasurable distance, from a place where reality had proven mutable and deceptive. Her eyelids felt so heavily weighed down that she believed she could not have forced them apart even if she had wanted to; speech was out of the question. And even if she could speak, what good would it do either of them? Her words could only betray her. Her eyes could only become portals to the arctic cold in her heart. Better to keep it all inside until she had the strength to pray— because right now that too, prayer, could not rise beyond the level of imprecation: of God, of herself, of Harry, and most of all of this baby whose nine months with her had already brought her nothing but pain and disappointment.

"I think she's fallen asleep again," Harry said to no one in particular, then mused aloud softly, "I wonder if she was dreaming. She must have known."

I know now, Harry. Her abdomen began to throb where they had cut her. I know now.

Everyone told her that with his large, wondering blue eyes, downy blond hair, and perfectly shaped head he was a beautiful baby (one of the nurses, trying to ease the postpartum pain of her Cesarean, assured her that C-section babies, without the head molding of a normal delivery, were always the most handsome, and that this was especially true of her baby). But whether or not the compliments *were honestly offered made little difference to her. From the beginning he wanted more than she could give him.*

Even before her milk came in it seemed to her he was always at her breast, always rooting and sucking after something that was not there. And when the milk finally did come in her breasts grew so engorged and painful that she dreaded having the nurse bring him to her to be fed. His screaming seemed to her not the ordinary cries of a hungry newborn but the sentient recriminations of a child who already knew he was not wanted. She was terrified of his sucking lips, those voracious slivers of pink whose fervor to latch onto her nipple could deal her such terrific pain instantly. She knew he could sense this, knew it made him want to latch on all the more desperately. But even though she tried to nurse him, tried with honest and good intentions, she could not help drawing back from him. In time she gave up nursing him altogether and began using formula and bottles, which went against all that she believed in.

Even as Harry sought to find a name for the baby in the first days of his life she was planning for the next child. "How does David sound to you?" Harry would ask, "Or Michael?" She would shrug and say, "All right," or, "It doesn't matter; you pick it out." She was already looking ahead, reviewing girls' names in her mind to make sure that Lydia was the one she really wanted, vowing, too, that she would never set herself up for disappointment the way she had with this child. She would expect a boy next time and just continue having boys until she got what she wanted. At least that way, boy or girl, she could love the child. She wanted to love this one, too, this one whose name Harry finally decided would be Jake. Yet no matter how many times she searched her heart, she could never find anything for this baby but sorrow and disappointment. She would have to cover it up—and pray to God that somehow her feelings would change.

But within weeks of coming home from the hospital this baby whose name was now Jake proved himself just as difficult outside of the womb as he had been inside. He screamed, it seemed to her, incessantly. He woke screaming in the dead of night every night, and then somewhere in the middle of dinner each evening he would begin screaming again for at least the next three hours. He would draw his arms and legs in to his body with a tension so violent and strong it frightened her. Such power, such rage did not seem normal in one so small. She felt accused, found out, and tried everything she could think of to ease his pain. She held him, rubbed his belly, sang to him, tickled him, made soft shushing sounds, bounced him on her knee, handed him over to Harry, left him alone in his room. Nothing worked for long. Once, out of desperation, she tried offering her breast to him again—knowing her milk was gone and there was nothing for him to take—but even this did not slow the unrelenting fury of his cries.

"Colic," was what the doctor told her. "Unfortunately, there's not a whole lot you can do about it except wait it out and try not to blame yourself. It sounds a lot worse than it is. Believe me, one day it will just stop, and then a week later you'll think the whole thing was nothing but a bad dream. And don't worry—there won't be any lasting harm to your baby."

Easy for you to say, *she felt like telling the doctor.* You don't have him screaming in your ear and turning so red you think he'll explode.

Still, the doctor was right. In a couple of months the colic disappeared, though her own misgivings did not, for Jake continued to wake screaming in the middle of the night each night, usually more than once, and he did not always settle after she fed him. She knew—from reading and from talking with the doctor—that it was normal for even bottle-fed babies to wake during the night, but it was the tenor of the cries that disturbed her, sent the same chill through her that she had felt upon learning he was not her baby girl. The doctor could reassure her as he wanted, the books and the experts could do the same, but there was a message, a communication, in those cries that only she understood. And even though, in time, she trained herself to sleep right through his crying and could not have said, if asked, whether or not Jake still awoke in the night, she never stopped praying that she would be the only one to understand.

Chapter Two

Lydia's First Communion

As the smallest of the children making their First Communion (and probably the shyest as well—it had taken considerable cajoling from us to convince her she would not die of fright) Lydia was at the front of the procession, the very first girl. Which was, of course, where we believed she belonged.

There must have been fifty children making their First Communion that spring. The boys were scrubbed as fresh and clean as they would ever again be in their lives, homunculi with hair slickly combed and creased into straight white parts, all of them decked out in spotless white suits, dress white shirts and ties, and white oxford shoes with pink soles. The girls, sylphid in their white dresses and white patent leather shoes, had their hair done in radiant curls beneath white lace veils. I remember the children proceeding down the aisle with their hands before them in prayer and their heads bowed forward, noses to fingertips, as they tried to follow the instructions they had been given about not looking all around, about keeping their eyes ahead of them and their hearts on God. After all, they were about to receive the holy body of Christ for the first time in their lives. It was not a time to be giggling and showing off. And there at the front of this immaculate procession was Lydia, *our* Lydia. The very first to receive her wafer of grace, her communion with God.

Outside of our family Lydia was about as shy as a child could be. Even when someone she knew asked her a question she would cringe toward Mother (or another family member in the rare event Mother was not with her), wrap her arms around Mother's waist, and nuzzle there in speechless disregard of the question. Mother would always repeat the question and nudge her to respond: "Did you hear that, Lydia? Mr. Simpson asked how you are today. Can you answer him, please?" But Lydia would remain silent and Mother would answer the question for her. "She's fine, Mr. Simpson. Just a little shy today, that's all." Afterwards Mother would patiently explain how there was nothing wrong with feeling shy, but it was rude not to speak to a person who speaks to you. Lydia would always say she understood, and of course she did, but it never made any difference. The next time she would remain as intransigently mute as the time before. (I found it embarrassing and wished Mother would be more forceful with Lydia, but for whatever reason Lydia invariably received special dispensation.)

Anyone outside the family would have found it hard to believe this timorous little girl could be such a pixie at home. But that was Lydia—tyrant within the family, shrinking violet outside of it.

On the day of her First Communion the contrast could not have been more pronounced. At church it took all of her courage, I'm sure, to separate from us and lead the procession. At home she was irrepressible. In the space of an hour before dinner she had coaxed Grandfather into playing a card game of "fish" with her (which of course she let us all know she won), and then, safe in his lap, had wheedled him into telling her the story of the headless Indian chief (Lydia loved to be frightened) still occasionally reported to haunt Indian Rock, an enormous granite outcrop deep within a section of woods near our house; she had come up behind Father and jumped on his back several times, each time shouting, "Guess who?", and eliciting from Father his standard response: "How's my baby girl?"; she had scratched one of her many scabbed over insect bites until it bled and had pressed me into the service of fetching her a band-aid and placing it on the wound—so that her "concentration" in her game with Ben would not be broken.

She was the darling of the family (and knew it), it was her day this day, and she was going to play it for all it was worth. No one but Jake escaped her fancies (because he disappeared as soon as we got home from church), and even he was only safe until dinnertime.

In those days, for some reason Lydia used to tease Jake more than anyone else in the family—maybe because he seemed the least responsive to her teasing. Whether she made fun of his hair ("It looks like bats slept there," was one of her favorite lines) or chanted that he had "cooties," Jake usually ignored her. Once in a while he might say to her, "Why don't you go find a busy street to play in, Lydia," but usually if her taunting and her chatter got to be too much for him he would just lock himself in his room. She might pound on the door for a while and call out names, but he would never come out. On this day, though, despite family rules against it, Lydia began teasing Jake at the dinner table where he could not so easily escape her.

"See my dress, Jake? I'm going to get married." Lydia was sitting right next to Mother, directly across the table from Jake.

Jake said nothing.

"I'm going to get married but you never will, Jake."

Jake continued eating without looking up from his plate. He was sitting to my right. Grandmother was to his right, across from Mother. The adult half of the table seemed engrossed in something Grandfather was saying about aphids and mites destroying his garden last year.

"You'll never get married because you're too ugly, Jake."

"It always amazes me how critters so tiny you can hardly see 'em can cause so much damage," Grandfather was saying.

I could see that Lydia was getting to Jake even though he hadn't looked up at her yet (and even though, with his light brown hair and blue eyes, he was a remarkably handsome child—whom Lydia resembled in a striking way, as I came to understand later). His jaw muscles were tensed and the veins near his temple were beginning to stand out.

"I guess I've been lucky," Mother said. "I've never really had that problem. Isn't there anything you can do about them?"

Grandfather launched into his explanation just as Lydia said to Jake, "I'm going to get married but nobody wants to marry a pimple-face like you."

"Shut up," Jake said, not loud, still without looking up.

Those two words had always been taboo in our house. Lydia knew she had him at her mercy now. "What's the matter, Jake, don't like to hear the truth?" she jeered. Ben sat there smirking on her right. He and Jake, though not antagonistic, usually had little to say to each other.

"Shut up, you little bitch," Jake said, louder than before and this time staring straight at her. "You'll die before you ever get married."

"Jake!" Mother shouted, her face purpling with instant rage. "How dare you?" She broke off before betraying any more. But for me the damage was done, the truth revealed in her emphasis not on the word *dare* but on the word *you,* and in the look of loathing that flared up in her eyes like a flash of fire. It lasted only an instant, but the angle of my view was nearly the same as Jake's, and I saw it. What she had kept carefully hidden all these years had in a single moment of unbridled anger become suddenly very obvious to me. *Mother did not love Jake.*

She regained control so quickly that it almost made me doubt what I had just seen and heard. The only remnant in her voice of that apocalyptic rage was the grim evenness of her tone now. "You apologize to your sister," she said.

"For what?" Jake said.

"What's going on here?" Father said.

"Jake knows very well what's going on," Mother said. "I'm waiting, Jake."

"For what?" Jake said again.

"You know I will not tolerate those words in my house. I expect you to apologize to your sister first and then to the rest of us."

"Like hell I will," Jake said.

"Then you may leave the table and go to your room. I don't expect to see you down here tonight until we hear an apology."

Jake got up and left without another word.

"What was that all about?" Father said.

"There's no need to spoil the rest of the dinner by repeating what he said. I'll tell you about it later."

"I'm worried about that child," Grandmother said.

I was worried too.

Later, it occurred to me that if either Ben or I had not received communion earlier in the day Mother would have been much more upset than she had been about Jake. Even though I was fourteen at the time and had stopped believing in the Catholic Church, I had not stopped going through the motions. I still attended mass every week, went to confession occasionally (during which I would invariably lie to the priest in order to get off with a light penance), received communion, and mumbled all the appropriate and expected responses during the liturgy (except for an occasional profanity—in murmured cant—slipped in to pacify my conscience over this policy of appeasement: "Through my fuck, through my fuck, through my most grievous fuck"). Such deception was necessary because I knew what Mother's reaction would be—and it was definitely not a reaction I wanted to see. But it was also not the reaction Jake got.

The more I thought about this the more I realized it had been true in the past as well: Mother's responses to Jake's mistakes were different from what I expected—and different from her responses to my mistakes. There was the time she found him trying to sneak a Playboy into the house under his shirt. Jake must have been about nine or ten when it happened.

"What have you got under your shirt, young man?" Mother said as Jake tried to hurry through the kitchen after school one day.

He must have been fooled into thinking she was not home, as I had been upon arriving a few minutes earlier, when he didn't see her car in the driveway. (Mother's car was always there when we got home from school, but on this day, unknown to us, it was at the garage for repairs.) He must have started into the house figuring he had clear sailing to his room, suddenly found himself trapped, and shoved the magazine up under his shirt. Half the shirt was still untucked.

"Under my shirt?" Jake said, folding his arms on his chest.

I was sitting at the table with milk and cookies. It was so obvious he was hiding something that I had all I could do not to spray the milk and cookies in my mouth all over the kitchen in a sudden burst of hysterical laughter. But I did not want to give him away and I did not want to get in trouble myself, so I clamped my hand over my mouth and swallowed.

"Let me see," Mother said.

"See what?" Jake said. It was warm that day and the pale yellow short sleeve shirt he wore was very lightweight. If not for his arms being in the way you could have seen the cover girl's tits right through the material.

"Whatever is beneath your shirt," Mother said patiently.

Jake must have finally realized there was no way out. "You mean this?" he said, handing her the Playboy.

"Of course you realize I'm very disappointed in you," Mother said. "This magazine is nothing but smut." Jake just stood there with his shirt untucked. "Go to your room. I'll be in to talk with you shortly."

Later I asked Jake what she had said.

"Don't do it again," he said.

"That's all? No punishment? No lectures about burning in hell?" I asked, incredulous.

Jake shrugged.

"You lucky bastard," I said, thinking that if it had been me she would have cut off my allowance for about ten weeks and forced me to go to confession that same night.

Then there was the time he and some friends started a fire and had to have the fire department called in to put it out. It happened probably a year or so after the Playboy incident.

He and a couple of other kids from school had started what they called the "Smokers' Club." Each day coming home from school they stopped off at an old abandoned barn and smoked cigarettes they had stolen from the drugstore. When Mother asked him one time why he smelled like smoke, he told her he had been burning candles at a friend's house. She warned him it was dangerous to be playing with fire, and he assured her he knew what he was doing.

He tried once to get me to join the club too, probably figuring it would be safer for him if I were involved. I wanted no part of it. I knew if I got caught it would be a sin punishable, at the very least, by a lifetime without allowance. I told Jake I wasn't interested.

"Then just make sure you don't rat on us to anyone," he said.

It turned out there was no need of his worrying about that. In the first place anyone casually walking by the barn could have heard their voices and their coughing and seen the occasional wisps of smoke curling out through the cracks between the barn boards. And in the second place it was not long after the birth of the club that it died a fiery death when one of the members somehow lit the barn on fire. The fire quickly grew beyond what the Smokers' Club could handle, and by the time the fire department arrived on the scene the barn was mostly gone. Since it was an ancient structure to begin with, decrepit and dangerous, it was allowed to just burn to the ground. The sense of loss that the kids in the neighborhood felt at the destruction of what had been, at one time or another, a castle, a haunted house, a command headquarters for war games, and countless other incarnations of imaginative play was overshadowed by the allure and the excitement of the fire itself. The members of the Smokers' Club, unwitting firebugs that they were, were subsequently elevated by their peers to a kind of celebrity status and revered as heroes. The adults, secretly relieved that the worrisome old building was gone, still found serious lessons for their children to learn from what happened.

I was sure Jake was not the one who had started the fire—it was not his style. (Granted, he was caught that time with the Playboy, but it had been logical then for him to assume Mother was not home; generally, he was not so sloppy. In fact, it was probably this incident of the barn burning down that convinced him never to trust anyone but himself.) Still, I expected him to suffer some serious consequences for his actions.

But Mother (who was the lawmaker and enforcer in our family; Father was only the titular head) decided that the just punishment for Jake's high crimes of stealing, smoking, lying, and incineration of the barn was no television and no allowance for two weeks. *Jake hardly ever even watched television.*

"What is it with you, anyway?" I said to him. "If I did those things I'd be jailed in my room until I was eighteen."

Jake shrugged.

"Dammit, you're lucky," I said. "What did she say to you about it?"

"She hopes I've learned my lesson."

"Did she say it like that? Wasn't she pissed?"

"She didn't sound pissed."

"I don't believe it," I said, thinking there was no justice in this family and already planning my protests for the next time I did something wrong.

I began to think that Jake—at least as far as Mother was concerned—lived a charmed life. He could do no wrong. Or rather, when he did wrong—clear, indisputable wrong— somehow she did not treat it as such.

This suspicion about lack of justice was strengthened in me a few weeks later when I was caught skipping a history class (the first time I had ever done such a thing). For a whole week after the three school detentions I served, Mother forced me to come directly home from school and study (history, of course) in my room for two hours.

When I pointed out the discrepancy and—to my mind— obvious unfairness of my punishment versus Jake's, she told me that for every time I complained she would tack on an extra day. She also explained that "different people committing different offenses under different circumstances require different punishments."

With this I had no quarrel. But I failed to see how Jake's "different offenses" were less serious than my skipping a single history class. And the part about "different circumstances" didn't seem to apply: we were in the same family and born of the same parents, weren't we? How different could our circumstances be?

No. At the time, the only part of what Mother said to me that made any sense was that we were different people receiving different punishments. And though this made sense, it was not fair. Even Ben, even *Lydia* (Mother's "doll baby," as Ben sometimes referred to her), younger though they were, received stiffer punishments than Jake if they did something wrong. I began to think that Mother was showing favoritism toward Jake. For some reason, she loved him more than she loved the rest of us.

I pointed this out to Jake once and he scoffed at the idea. "For a whiz kid you're really a dolt sometimes," he said. I was a straight-A student in those days while he was a mostly C student, but he picked up words like "dolt" and "lackey," I think, from the comic books he read—and he enjoyed trying them out on me every chance he got.

It was not until dinner on the day of Lydia's First Communion that I finally began to put everything together and glimpse the truth of what was going on: Mother treated Jake differently not because she loved him more than the rest of us but because of just the opposite. *Mother expected Jake to fail.* And this was acceptable to her as long as his failures did not involve the rest of us. But when he attacked Lydia—however justified he might have been—it was something Mother absolutely could not abide.

Later, when Jake tried to run away and everyone wondered how he could do such a thing, I thought I understood.

Chapter Three

Filial Bonds

In the hours since dinner he had watched the May twilight diminish into full night knowing that he would do something. He had outwaited the ritual family gathering to watch The Ed Sullivan Show and all the subsequent goodbyes and noises of his grandparents' departure—the car doors slamming, the ignition fired, the crunch of gravel beneath the receding wheels, the final calls of farewell—and had waited further until all sounds of wakefulness had tapered into dark quiet. And then he had waited further still, knowing he would do something.

His first steps into her room were tentative and quiet, not like him. Not that he was incapable of being quiet or even of being surreptitious—because he was skilled at both—but that being tentative was not normal for him, who even in his most daring and clandestine prowls felt sure of himself, confident of his ability to observe undetected. But that was when observation was the sole intent of his stealth, and this time, although he was not certain what would happen and could not possibly have explained his own urgency, he knew that what he was doing went far beyond mere observation.

He took another step into her room and a floorboard creaked. He stopped, remained motionless, sought security from the darkness as if it were a warm blanket around him. He did not want to startle her and have her cry out. For years she had had a nightlight in her room at her mother's insistence, and the golden glow from it now made him pause, fearful that she would awake terrified at the sight of his outsized shadow on the wall near her.

He moved a step closer to her bed, barefoot, cat-quiet, alert as an animal. Even with his eyes now accustomed to the dim light he could barely make out her small shape beneath the quilt of sun and bright-colored flowers and smiling animals hand-stitched by their mother for her when she was an infant. A pillow would have been more substantial than the small swell before him. He could not even make out the rise and fall of her breathing.

His own breathing was shallow and quick, his heart beating with frightening force. When at last he reached the edge of her bed, the urge to wheel and bolt coming precipitately upon him, he saw that her head was turned toward him, her eyes wide and fearful, and he knew that he could neither leave nor follow now whatever murky impulses had led him here.

"Why are you awake, Lydia?" he whispered.

"I'm scared," Lydia said softly.

He sat on the edge of her bed and gently stroked her hair, his heart still beating with violence at the knowledge of his own compulsion and the uncertainty of her fear. "Of what?"

"The creatures," she whispered, shriveling more tightly into her fetal position.

"What creatures?" His heartbeat slowed with the thought that it was not his presence she feared.

"The ones that come at night."

He continued stroking her hair. "What are they? What do they do?"

Lydia clutched his hand in both of hers. "They're creepy. They move around the room like shadows and whisper to each other. I know they want to get me."

"How do you know that?"

"I just do."

"Do you want me to put out your nightlight?"

"No!" she said, tugging at his hand. "Don't. It would be too dark."

"Have you told Mom about this?"

"Yes. That's why I have the nightlight on."

His hand still in hers, he felt a tremor run through her. "How often do they come?"

"Every night."

"There aren't really any creatures, you know, Lydia."

"Yes, there are!"

"Where are they now, then?"

"You made them go away, I think."

"If they really wanted to get you, why haven't they got you by now?"

"I don't know, but they want to."

"It's the light that's causing the shadows."

She said nothing, unable to disagree.

"I'll put it out for you."

She tightened her grip on his hand. "All right. But you've got to stay with me, Jake. Just for a little while."

He left to switch off the light and then returned. Cupping her head in one hand, he resumed stroking her hair with the other, and it was not long before she fell asleep.

Each night after that he would go to her, late, when the others were asleep, and if she were awake he would turn off her nightlight and sit with her until she went to sleep, and if she were asleep already he would retreat to his own room and lie on his back in the darkness, waiting for the ebony balm of sleep to come to him too. His own demons were not corporeal, not in the sense that he feared their physical presence in his room, but they possessed a reality as terrifying as anything of his sister's. As he lay there in the darkness they sprang to mind unbidden and revolting in a series of lurid soundless flashes like the frames of a peep show, each image defined with startling sharpness and clarity: the piercing glint of the knife blade in his hand as he came upon the white expanse of his father's back from behind; the spurt of bright red blood as the blade, with surreal slowness, penetrated first the white dress shirt and then his father's flesh; the arch of his father's back and the desperate encircling sweep backward of his father's arms, which were never quite able to touch him. The images were not always of his father (sometimes they were of his mother, with Lydia in her arms, or of his grandmother when she gently touched his shoulder, or of his brothers gamboling in the woods with their friends), but the scenarios that played out before he could force the images from his mind were always violent, he himself always the avatar of violence.

He sought out her room then as if it were sanctuary, as if in her wild fears, real though they might be to her, there were a kind of escape or release for him. He would listen to her words and caress her hair with his fingers, and it was as if the listening and the caressing were rites of an exorcism performed not just for her but for him as well.

On some nights, she told him, she would fall asleep without any trouble, only to be awakened later by a bad dream. It was always the same dream, the one in which she started off chasing a white, pink-eyed rabbit the way Alice in Wonderland did—until they got to a large dark hole in the ground, whereupon the rabbit turned and said, "No, you'll fall down and hurt yourself," and began chasing her. The next thing she knew was that somehow she had been pinned to the ground beneath the rabbit's soft, furry white paws. The rabbit's great weight made it impossible for her to move, and when she looked up it was not a rabbit's face but the angry face of the Queen of Hearts and the voice of her mother screaming, "Off with your head if you go near that hole." It was at this point that she always woke up.

She was afraid to tell Mother about the dream because it might make her angry (or worse, sad); and Father always seemed so upset when anything woke him in the night that she didn't want to bother him either; so she just lay there in terror waiting for what seemed like most of the night for the memory of the dream to fade and the creatures to cease their murmurings and their shadowy darts about the room long enough for her to slip back into sleep.

On other nights, she told him, she could not get to sleep at all. The creatures would not leave her alone for even a minute, and if she began to get sleepy they would scream like fighting cats until she was completely awake again.

When he asked her what they looked like—trying to get her to see that her terrors held no substance and therefore no reality—Lydia would aver, all atremble, "I don't know what they look like, but I know they're out there."

He could not understand the amorphousness of her terror, because his own terror was grounded in such sharply real images, but he could understand terror, so he sat next to her and ran his hand through her hair and merely waited until she fell asleep.

Whether it was only a few nights or weeks or more than a month after the beginning he could not have said (he knew only that it was after her stay in the hospital), but at some point, without words or explanation, he began to lie down next to her, and without rebuke or question she accepted his presence as she would have accepted any other childhood talisman: a teddy bear, a special blanket or pillow, a favorite doll. He would lie on his stomach and fondle her hair—that shiny golden treasure nearly invisible to him in the dark, so prized by their mother—in his right hand. In his left hand he would clutch beneath him the erection he had kept hidden from her since the beginning. Desire for something—he did not know precisely what—throbbed in his hand and inside his heart so urgently that he believed she must be aware of it, must have felt the tension of it in his right arm across her small body and in his fingers touching her hair. But after a while, each night, she would drift into sleep and he would be left alone with it, the tension, the importunate yearning that diminished only slightly when he retreated to his room and masturbated.

In time it seemed to him she was falling asleep more quickly and easily each night, while the time he spent tossing and turning on his own bed afterward seemed to increase. One night when she was almost asleep and he was thinking of spending hours awake afterward, alone in his room, he rolled over onto his side. He took her hand and pressed it up against his erect penis. She pulled her hand away as if she had been made to touch the head of a snake.

"What are you doing?" she whispered. "What's that?"

"It's just me. It feels good when you touch me there."

She sounded fearful. "Why is it so hard?"

"I don't know," he said. "Just touch me, Lydia."

"I don't want to."

"Why? It won't hurt you."

"I'm afraid."

"It feels good when I touch your hair, doesn't it?"

"Yes."

"And it helps you to go to sleep, doesn't it?"

"Yes."

"Well it feels good to me when you touch me there." He took her hand again. She resisted momentarily but then allowed him to guide her hand back to the tight ache inside his pajamas. "Just move your hand up and down there for a little while. It will help me to go to sleep too."

"You won't go to sleep before I do, will you?"

"No. I promise."

But when it was over she was restless and could not settle back into sleep, while he wanted nothing more than to return to his own room as quickly as possible.

"What happened to you, Jake?" she asked.

"Nothing," he said.

"Something came out of you," she said, growing agitated. "Did you pee on me, Jake?"

He was afraid she might wake someone. "No," he whispered. "Shhh. It was just something that had to come out of me so I could go to sleep."

"Why?"

"Don't ask so many questions. Just go to sleep."

"I can't."

"Why not?"

"I want to know what happened."

He was quiet for a moment before he tried to explain. "You know how your creatures go away when I come into the room?"

"Yes."

"Well it's kind of like I have creatures inside me and you just helped them to go away. Do you understand?"

She did not answer right away. "I think so," she said at last.

But it took her what seemed to him a very long time to go to sleep, and when he was finally able to return to his own room he found that sleep would not come to him either. The old demons not only had not left but there were new ones now to haunt him, ushered in by the beginning of a thing he knew he could not control.

When the thought of running away occurred to him long afterwards he welcomed it, easing into sleep at last, as if the thought were a curtain someone had drawn across a very bright light shining in his eyes.

Chapter Four

In Search of a Peeper

After the dinner episode it did not surprise me that Jake never came down from his room to apologize or to say goodbye to Grandmother and Grandfather. Nor was it surprising that the next day, with no apology and no mention of the day before, Mother and Jake acted as though nothing had happened. Given the conclusions I had reached about their relationship, their behavior made perfect sense.

What did surprise me was Lydia's behavior. Instead of lording it over Jake for her victory the night before, she seemed almost contrite at the breakfast table.

"Would you like some juice, Jake?" she asked. Ben looked at me and winked as though he expected a resumption of the byplay we had seen last night.

Jake looked at her for a moment and then nodded.

Lydia took the orange juice out of the refrigerator, shook it a little, and poured a glass for him. Then she put the bottle of juice down on the table.

"What about me?" Ben said.

"I'm not your slave," she said.

From that day on I never saw Lydia tease Jake again. Ben and I received our accustomed portions of wheedling, importunate requests, followed by taunts if we did not do whatever it was she asked. But for Jake she seemed to have reserved a serious, even considerate side of herself. I never did understand this change in her.

Two days after her First Communion Lydia did not feel well and Mother kept her out of school. She developed a cough and a slight fever, her sinuses grew stuffed up, and she had trouble breathing. When she wasn't much better the next day Mother kept her out of school again. She fed Lydia aspirin, made chicken soup (though Lydia was not hungry and wouldn't eat), put cold cloths to her forehead, read to her, allowed her to watch her favorite TV shows, and generally tried to make Lydia as comfortable as possible.

But by Thursday Lydia's temperature had shot up to 104. She was having chills and shaking. Every time she coughed she grabbed her chest in pain and started to cry. "It hurts even when I breathe," she sobbed. Without anyone having to say it, we all knew that something far more serious than the common cold was wrong with our Lydia.

The whole family went with her to the hospital, Lydia curled up against Mother in the front seat of the car while Father drove. "It hurts," Lydia cried after each coughing spell, pressing the right side of her chest against Mother as though somehow Mother had the power to force the pain out. The three of us in the back seat all rode along in silence.

By the time we reached the fluorescent glare of the emergency room her cheeks were bright red and her breathing was so rapid it frightened me. Then, before Father could finish giving all the necessary information to the admitting nurse, Lydia lurched away from Mother's arms and sat rigidly upright. Her already too-rapid breathing became suddenly labored, as if she was having trouble getting any air at all down into her lungs. She was sweating profusely but now the flushed color in her face was changing to a kind of blue even as I watched.

"Help her!" Mother shouted. "My baby can't breathe."

"They're here too," Lydia said with a fearful expression on her face. She closed her eyes and shrank back toward Mother as though there were something before her she could not bear to look at. "Jake, make them go away. Jake, please. Please make them go away."

I turned to look at Jake. His eyes were trained intently on Lydia as she cringed towards Mother. He never even glanced at anyone else.

Mother pressed Lydia tightly to her side, stroked Lydia's hair with her free hand. "It's all right, sweetheart. I'm here, I'm with you. I'm with you." Lydia's eyes opened and she calmed down a little at that, although her breathing was still terrible to witness.

I could not tell by the shining, delirious stare of her blue eyes whether she thought it was Mother or Jake who comforted her.

Lydia was in the hospital for more than a week. She not only had the pneumonia Mother feared but also a collapsed lung suffered while we were waiting in the emergency room. Despite the doctor's assurances to the contrary, Mother believed that if she had been more alert she could have prevented the pneumonia and Lydia's lung would not have collapsed.

Perhaps it was out of this feeling of guilt, or a more acute sense of how fragile life is, how finely spun the thread connecting her daughter's life to her own, that Mother grew more protective of Lydia than ever before. Whatever her reason, Mother made it clear immediately when Lydia returned home that she would tolerate no "foolishness" around her sick child. No roughhousing (this might make Lydia want to join in, which was absolutely out of the question); no provoking Lydia to laugh too hard (this might collapse her lung again); no bringing food or drink in to her unless it was specifically authorized by Mother; no staying in Lydia's room for too long at any one time. Poor Lydia even had her own set of rules to follow: no getting out of bed except to go to the bathroom; no running or jumping under any circumstances; no shouting for help (she could use the bell Mother left by the bedside—Mother would always be near enough to hear it); no watching television or reading for more than an hour or two at a time without a rest.

"How are you feeling?" I asked Lydia one day as I breezed in and sat on her bed.

"Do you want the truth or do you want what you'd like to hear?" Lydia said. I was taken aback for a moment—but only for a moment. It was one of Father's favorite expressions, and Lydia, though only seven, already had a keen understanding of language.

"I guess I want the truth," I said with a laugh.

"The truth is I'm bored," she said, pouting.

"Why?" I asked, though of course I knew the answer.

"I want to go outside," she said. "I'm sick of staying in bed. I'm more sick of staying in bed than I am of pneumonia. I want to be able to run and play."

"Maybe I can talk to Mom about it," I said.

We were nearing the end of May and the weather was warm and sunny. Outside, all of nature buzzed and trilled the message that spring was here again, the ancient ritual of orgy and renewal upon us once more. It was as though the warm May weather had thawed the message from deep within every living thing: *Come. Come out into the sun. It is time again.* I could surely understand Lydia's desire to be outdoors.

"She'll never listen," Lydia said.

"Sure she will," I said, invoking more confidence than I felt.

But Lydia was right. When I suggested to Mother that it was a warm, beautiful day, and that Lydia hadn't been outside in a long time and might enjoy the fresh air and exercise, Mother abruptly vetoed the idea.

"It's out of the question," she said.

"Why?"

"Virgil, you just leave her care to me."

"But how long does she have to stay cooped up indoors?"

"Until I decide she's well enough to go out. Not before. Now mind your own business and be thankful you *can* go outside."

It occurred to me with a jolt that my seven-year-old sister knew Mother better than I did.

Which did not deter Lydia from rebelling. A couple of days after my failure, Lydia—with more than a little help from Jake—took matters into her own hands.

Apparently it all started when Jake (who deigned to stop in and visit Lydia for a couple of minutes every once in a while) said something to her about peepers. Lydia told him she had always loved the sound they make but had never actually seen a peeper. So the two of them decided to smuggle her out of the house and down to the swamp, where she might see one of the myriad little amphibians singing their fluty parts of the chorus—as they did faithfully every year—in the mad, ritual symphony of spring.

Our house sat at the end of a cul-de-sac that had been pushed into the woods during the late fifties, when even our fair city of Newtown was still nothing but a sleepy little burg. It was one of twelve nearly identical houses that lined the street, all split levels built with minor variations—a picture window instead of a bay window, an attached garage, a recessed front entrance with an ornate double door—to give each its claim to individuality.

Except for the too-frequent roar overhead of jets from a nearby air force base, the neighborhood was quiet and peaceful. Everybody knew everybody else on the street, and Mother was perfectly happy living there on the outskirts of a small, southern New Hampshire city; Father, who liked space and privacy, saw neighborhood living as a compromise made for the kids, but one he could live with because he had bought forty acres of the woods behind our house.

The woods were dense with underbrush, above which were young hemlocks and hardwoods, and above these an upper story of old white pines too warped and twisted to have been of commercial value when the land was last cleared for timber. The underbrush grew even more tangled and wild near the swamp, which sat deep in the woods at the back of our property and well out of view from our house. At the time, Lydia had probably never been far enough into the woods to even see the swamp. Mother had kept a tight rein on her even before her illness, although in this respect Mother was no different from the other mothers in the neighborhood, who kept their daughters closer to home than they kept their sons. The boys reinforced this sexual caste system by forming secret clubs and marauding bands that met in the woods and terrorized intruders, particularly young female intruders.

Ben and I were often members of these secret groups, but Jake, after his experience with the Smokers' Club, wanted no part of being dependent on others to find trouble. He could do that well enough on his own and could conceal the consequences far more easily. Probably because he was such a maverick, or because he wandered farther and spent more time in the woods than the rest of us, he knew them better than any of us did. Only Jake knew that if you went far enough in a particular direction along a particular path (which he would not divulge to us) you would come to a set of railroad tracks and, on the far side of the tracks, the river. He knew the network of paths and hideaways and secret fortresses carved into the dense woods so well, and traveled so quietly, that often in the midst of our most secret meetings he would pop up from somewhere close by and announce, "I'm out of here, this meeting is boring." Even when we fashioned a new, more camouflaged, more undetectable retreat he would find it that same day, or, with a cocky smirk on his face as he leaned against a nearby tree, he would be waiting there for us after school the next day.

So it was not surprising that Jake believed he could steal Lydia away in broad daylight for a brief visit to the swamp without anyone knowing it.

The first part of the operation was fairly well planned out. They would not leave until after Jake, Ben and I had arrived home from school and put in our customary time at Lydia's bedside. Usually after our visits Mother would insist that Lydia rest without interruption for an hour or so before Father got home from work. "Try to take a little nap," Mother would say, and then she would pull down the window shades and close the door to Lydia's room. This would be Jake and Lydia's call to action.

As soon as the door closed Lydia fluffed up her bed with the pillow just on the off chance that Mother might peek in on her. After that she slipped out the back window of her bedroom (making sure to pull the shade behind her), where Jake was waiting with a ladder and his stingray bicycle. (Jake was an artist on that bike. He used to be able to pull expert wheelies and ride around effortlessly for as long as he wanted—a feat that always filled me with envy because no matter how hard I tried I could never do it. "You're too much of a chicken to try what you have to do," he would tell me, which would only infuriate me all the more.) Still in her nightgown Lydia jumped on the banana seat in front of Jake, and off they rode like some knight-errant rescuing the fair young maiden.

In the woods behind our house there were many paths that led to the swamp, but the trick for Jake was to take one that would not lead him near any of the neighborhood gang who might be roaming about. He chose a path that wound its way up a slight incline and then descended rather steeply to the western side of the swamp—the far side of most of our forts and hideouts. A logical choice. But the glitch in the plan, of course, was Lydia herself. I'm surprised Jake did not foresee this. He should have had Lydia get off the bike and walk down the hill. On the other hand, maybe he did foresee the problem and just accepted it as part of the challenge, for beneath the canopy of gnarled old pines the steep path was studded with rocks and tree roots. It was not an easy trail to ride down, even for Jake, alone, and he must have known this.

Halfway down the hill Lydia started screaming. Whether it was with excitement or fear—or both—I'm not sure. Her screams were abruptly cut off by the roar of a jet overhead, although they were loud enough and lasted long enough for all six or seven of us on the other side of the swamp to hear them. We did not know who was screaming or what it was all about, but it sounded enough like an adventure to make us drop whatever we were doing and hurry right over.

When we got there I was shocked to see Lydia, dressed only in her nightgown, on the bike with Jake. The nightgown had pine needles on it and dark wet smudges at the knees, as though she had been kneeling in mud. Her face was flushed and she looked out of breath.

"What happened?" I blurted out.

"Nothing," Jake said.

"Then why was Lydia screaming?" said Ben. Normally Ben was a little frightened of Jake and would never have used such an aggressive tone, but I suspect his courage was bolstered by the presence of the gang.

Jake shot an intimidating look at Ben. "None of your business, half-pint."

"C'mon, Jake," I said. "What happened? You know as well as I do Lydia's not supposed to be outside."

"We were just trying to find a peeper," Lydia said, "and we got going too fast down the hill."

"*You were trying to find a peeper?*" asked Bucky Fulton, incredulous. "*On a bike?*"

Bucky (whose real name was Albert) was a skinny kid, maybe twelve at the time, with freckles and buck teeth. Jake looked at him as though he were something curiously and disagreeably subhuman.

"There are peepers at the swamp, which is where we're headed, bertbrain." Jake looked around at the rest of us defiantly. "Nobody tells anybody about this, you understand?"

I understood. Jake still had hopes of keeping this from Mother, although even as the gang members were silently nodding their heads we all distinctly heard Mother's frantic voice calling for Lydia. On this balmy May afternoon, the windows of the house opened wide, she must have heard the same screams we had heard and, after searching the house, deduced the obvious: the screams were Lydia's, and Lydia was outside.

At first no one moved. It was as though Mother's voice possessed the power to paralyze us all, transfix us to the scene of the crime until she could get there herself. "Lyyyydia… Lyyyydia… Where are you, Lydia? Are you all right? Lydia!…" A breeze must have come up, or perhaps it had been there all along and we had been oblivious to it, because between her calls we could hear the faint, random tinkling of the wind chimes Mother had hung from a tree limb behind the house, a discomforting sound that struck me—standing there in the woods—as discordant and unnatural.

After listening to Mother call another two or three times, accompanied by the strangely unnerving sounds of the wind chimes, Lydia finally broke the silence. "I think we better go back," she said.

Without a word Jake wheeled the bike around, with Lydia still on it, and began pushing it back up the steep hill.

For some reason Ben decided to tag along, which caused the rest of the gang, one by one, to follow single file behind him. Reluctantly, I brought up the rear of this curious parade. I remember thinking it was wrong for us to do this, we should allow Jake and Lydia the dignity to suffer in private whatever consequences awaited them. And yet I too, against my better intentions, followed the morbid compulsion to see what would happen.

Mother was standing near the clothesline behind the house, hands cupped around her mouth as she continued calling, when Lydia cut her off mid-syllable.

"I'm right here, Mom," Lydia shouted.

Under other circumstances Mother might have found the scene comical. She possessed a good sense of humor, complemented by the sort of honest, joyful laughter that made you want to join in with her. But this was a matter involving Lydia's health, and despite what must have appeared absurdly similar to a Norman Rockwell painting—the neighborhood renegade, already a legend in some ways, astride his mount as he returned the captive child to her home, behind him a motley brigade of admirers following in single file—she saw nothing in the scene to soften the grimness of her look.

"Lydia, where have you been?" she said in a stern, controlled voice. "No, don't shout. Come over here." She pointed to the ground in front of her. A wisp of her light brown hair, blown loose from the tight bun she nearly always wore, danced lightly in the wind upon her forehead, and together with the characteristic cheer of her red lipstick contradicted the severe knit of her brow.

We were still making our way towards her from perhaps fifty feet away, more slowly now because Jake, as if to show who was in control of the situation, had slowed the pace.

"*Now*, Jake," Mother said. Jake continued at the same pace. Behind Mother the wind chimes jangled louder than before with every gust of wind.

Mother's gaze was withering. From what I could tell it was fixed squarely upon Jake and no one else. At last Jake drew near and stopped about five feet from Mother.

"Lydia, you get over here right now," Mother said, scanning the soiled nightgown as she pointed down at the ground next to her. She gave Lydia no more than a cursory glare before returning her gaze to Jake. "The rest of you children can go home." She did not even look at the others as they sidled away, with hangdog expressions on their faces and furtive sidelong glances to see if anything would develop before they were forced out of range. Mother waited, without ever taking her eyes from Jake, until they were gone. Ben and I remained standing off to the side behind Jake.

Lydia had not yet moved from the bike. "*Right now, Lydia,*" Mother said.

Lydia slid off the bike and stood where Mother had pointed.

Mother put her hands on Lydia's shoulders and peered down at her. "Lydia, you nearly scared me to death. Now what's going on here?" She looked from Lydia to Jake, then to me, then to

Ben, and finally back to Jake. She slipped her right arm around Lydia's shoulder, unconsciously it seemed, and gently, protectively, gathered Lydia in to herself as though the three of us—Jake being the principal malefactor—had conspired to take her Lydia away.

Head up, still astraddle his stingray bike like some Hell's Angel on a Harley Davidson, Jake looked at her impassively. When she shifted her eyes to me for an answer I raised my eyebrows and shrugged. Then Ben said, "Don't look at me. I didn't do anything wrong."

Mother took a deep breath. Her anger was clearly growing harder for her to control as she began to realize, I suspect, that the facts might not come out. "What's your part in this, Jake?" she demanded.

There was silence again until Lydia answered for him, "He was just trying to help. I was going down to the swamp to see if I could find a peeper, and Jake asked me if I wanted a ride."

Mother stared at her unbelievingly. "What would possess you to ever do a thing like that when you've been so sick?"

"I've never seen a peeper before," Lydia said simply.

Mother looked at the ladder lying on the ground beneath Lydia's window. "How did you get out of the house?"

"I snuck out when you weren't looking."

"And you didn't have any help?"

"Nope."

Kneeling, Mother held Lydia at arm's length and tried to read from Lydia's face whether or not she could believe any of what she had been told. Mother must have felt trapped and betrayed, repulsed on all fronts by a conspiracy that included Lydia. She shook Lydia's shoulders gently. "Why were you screaming?"

Lydia seemed shocked at Mother's grip on her shoulders, gentle though it was. She looked as if she were about to cry. "Just because we got going fast down the hill."

"How did you get your nightgown so dirty?"

"I don't know."

Mother turned to Jake, who still sat unmoving on his bike. "Disregarding for the moment that you knew I wouldn't approve of your sister disobeying me, and ignored that, didn't it strike you as even the slightest bit dangerous to be riding two on a bike down a steep hill? Did it really never occur to you that if you fell Lydia could split her head open on a rock or a tree?"

Jake shrugged a little.

"You should be looking out for your sister, Jake, not putting her in danger." There was a coldness in her voice and in her aspect that made me suspect she saw Jake as deliberately trying to harm Lydia.

Mother must have felt some tremor in Lydia then. "Oh, Lydia," Mother said, shaking her head, knowing, undoubtedly, that important pieces were missing from Lydia's story, knowing too that without realizing how or why it had been waged, or even what the true nature of her own involvement in it had been, she had somehow lost a battle. "Don't you understand you're a very sick little girl? A swamp is the last place in the world you should be going to."

Lydia's blue eyes began to fill with tears. "I only wanted to get outside for a little while, Mom," she said, her voice breaking.

Mother hugged her tightly. "Oh, sweetheart," she said, "You've got to trust me to do what is best for you. I just don't want to see you back in the hospital away from us again."

Lydia was sobbing on Mother's shoulder as Mother picked her up and carried her back into the house. "Come on, let's get you inside," Mother said soothingly. "You've been out in your bare feet too long already."

Unless she managed to do it some other time, Lydia never did get to see a peeper.

Chapter Five

Into the Night

He had no carefully worked out scheme, no specific destination, no long-range master plan to underpin his flight and lend it a reasonable possibility of success, if success were merely the escape and everlasting separation from family and friends. He left home quietly, with little thought of the consequences. It was a thing, simply, that he knew he must do.

He made his way through the woods behind the house and began following the trail upriver. It took him more than half an hour of steady walking before he pushed into territory he did not recognize. Even then, with black flies and mosquitoes swarming about his head in the warmth of a late May day, he noted the fact not with the disquietude of some runaways—who, fully expecting to be caught, wonder fearfully upon reaching unknown ground whether they haven't made a terrible mistake—but with the self-possession of one often alone in unfamiliar settings. He noted that despite the meanderings of the river the railroad tracks to his west never left the river for long, and the trail he had been following since first reaching the river had narrowed but had not disappeared, although other trails veered off and abruptly seemed to vanish. He noted too an occasional fish leaping out of the broad, slow-moving river, a lone crow flying upriver overhead, a muskrat scurrying back to its hole in the riverbank, the calls of unusual birds that reminded him of the jungle in Tarzan movies he used to watch on television.

He registered all these things with an equanimity that had come about unsought through years of relying upon himself for all but the physical needs of his life. Now even those, the physical needs, were his alone to satisfy. He had brought along a canteen of water and a knapsack filled with sandwiches and canned food, a change of clothes, a blanket, a jackknife, some matches; but he had not yet put into words the meaning of these provisions: his life was now completely his own. *It would not have made any difference: having lived all his life with the knowledge of being alone, the matters of food and shelter would have struck him as unimportant details.*

He had left early in the morning, following Sunday breakfast. The rest of the family had gone to Mass, from which he had been excused after complaining that he felt sick to his stomach. He knew that his absence would probably not be detected until Sunday dinner sometime after noon, and probably not even then. It might not be until late afternoon that his mother entered his room, a step she had only taken when sickness prevented him from getting out of bed. "Leave Jake alone," he had often overheard her saying to the others, "he needs his privacy."

As the afternoon wore on he did not encounter another human being. On both sides of the river the unbroken line of trees and the dense underbrush crowding the riverbanks gave little evidence of human existence, a fact which—knowing as he did that farther down, the river cut through the heart of Newtown—at some level astonished but did not cow him. Only the thread-like trail he followed and an occasional culvert spewing raw sewage into the river suggested humanity must be near. Amidst the warmth and humidity of the day and the lush, primordial green everywhere, amidst the calls of the birds and the profusion of insect life swarming and buzzing all around, it was easy for him to believe that he had stepped into a world all his own.

*   *   *

The sun was descending as he made a little fire and ate a can of the beef stew he had taken from home. Camped near the river, through the chorus of birds and peepers and bullfrogs he heard the occasional plash of fish rising to insects and saw their telltale rings spread out in slow, concentric circles upon the surface of the water. He heard and then saw a great blue heron taking flight from a shallow stretch of river to the south, its piercing squawk and awkward, ponderous wings the atavisms of some flying prehistoric ancestor. He watched the brilliant golden light on the horizon gradually soften into the color of a rose and then, paling into lavender and finally gray, lose its quotidian struggle against the night. No thoughts of the future had as yet interjected themselves into the constant, unconsidered joy of his freedom. He did not even wonder, as he had earlier in the day, what the others must be thinking or doing, whether or not they had noticed his absence or called the police, who—if anyone—might mourn his loss. The sentient, conscience-riddled part of him had given way for a time to unthinking absorption in the moment, to that all-consuming existential terror/excitement which is both product of and generative force behind any leap into the unknown.

In the distance behind him a whistle sounded and then the slow rumble of a train approaching from the north. It struck him—only because he had been enjoying the sounds of night descending upon the river—that the train took an abnormally long time to come abreast of him, and then, having done so—the rumble and the occasional jarring shrieks of metal upon metal extinguishing all other sound around him, louder and closer than he had expected— the train took a long while to pass by before receding into the night sounds from which it had come.

He watched the fire and listened to the rising fish and saw night deepen across the sky as if the materializing stars were willing the *darkness for themselves, inventing it. Without a moon the stars grew more prolific in number than he had ever seen or imagined, and as he lay back against the earth, he wondered what it would be like to traverse space the way his comic book characters did. In the comic books it did not seem such an extraordinary thing to shuttle back and forth from planet to planet, but out here, alone, with the immense night sky and the countless stars above him at once so tangible and so coldly distant, it seemed a miracle beyond all miracles. If he could only be drawn up into it, if a spaceship could descend from the darkness this very instant and take him away forever, if he could somehow be given such a choice, he would do it without a second thought.*

He lay back gazing up at the night sky feeling comforted by it, kindred to it, and at the same time impossibly, inconsolably separate. At last, with the dew falling and the temperature dropping, he began to feel chilled and decided he would try to sleep. Earlier he had come upon an old lean-to with a tarpaper roof set back in the woods a couple of hundred yards from the river, near the railroad tracks, and he had decided to sleep there for the night. He had seen the charred remains of a fire and several empty cans lying about the site, but he had not stopped to consider how recent such spoor might be. It had never occurred to him—because there was within him yet a sort of trust in humanity—that there was any cause for alarm.

It was an oversight that in later years he would not make again—for as he made his way along the narrow dark path back to the lean-to, unconcerned about the rustling sounds he was making in the brush, he noticed the flickering light of a campfire, and drawing nearer to investigate, quieter now and more wary, he felt a sudden smashing pain at the back of his head that was indistinguishable in chronology from the flash before his eyes and the truncated what...*forming within his mind even as his body crumpled unconscious to the ground. It was an oversight that occurred to him even before he heard himself moaning and trying to open his eyes and finding that he could not yet do it, before discovering that he could not move his hands or his feet either, before the acknowledgement of the throbbing pain down below* in a place where there should not be any pain *(It was his head that had been struck, he should not be feeling pain there,* not there*), before the pain below had cohered into the certain knowledge that* something terrible happened, *and before the final mutation of that knowledge into a sense of violation and outrage and fear. An oversight, a mistake: he should have paid attention to those cans because they meant something, something which the hurt in his body and the mounting incomprehensible ache in his soul told him he should have known and feared and given wide berth to.* Should fear still.

He opened his eyes to the early morning light and his head began to throb violently. His vision was blurred at first but he could still make out the gray, bearded, rag-tag image of a man reclining, knees drawn up, across from him inside the lean-to. When he tried to move his hand to his forehead he realized that his hands and feet were bound. He closed his eyes, opened them again, and his vision began to clear. He saw the oozing sores on the milk-white flesh below the man's pant legs even before he looked up into the rheumy gray eyes.

"Always be the sucker-puncher, never the sucker-punched, is what Jacko says," the man said, cackling. He was holding an object that looked like a billy club between his hands. On his head was a hat that had holes in it as though moths or acid had eaten away at it. "Stick with Jacko and you'll be all right, boy. Old Jacko's been around." He cackled again and added, "looks like you ain't." Then he coughed, his whole body suddenly racked by a convulsion that went on for what seemed like minutes before it ended with his arms and legs trembling.

The rheumy eyes momentarily rolled and then focused, pupils narrowed into hard, tiny black holes. "Jacko's been feeling a little sick lately but you just wait, boy, you and Jacko's gonna have some fun."

He could feel his head throbbing and his vision beginning to blur again, and down below the unrelenting ache, the perversion, which his mind could neither comprehend nor accept but which his body registered with implacable certainty. The last thing he saw before he vomited and passed out was what he believed to be blood, dried now, at one end of the wooden object in Jacko's hands, which he no longer recognized as a billy club but as a crude wooden spoon.

When he awoke again he saw the hunched profile of the man stirring something in a small, steaming pot over a fire, the oversized wooden spoon in his hand absurdly out of proportion to the size of the pot. Every once in a while the man would let out a long, guttural moan and straighten out his back or one of his legs. He could see now that the man was small, his arms and legs nearly bone thin beneath the coat and pants that hung on him like rags on a moving scarecrow. He could see too that something was wrong with the man's ear, as though whatever had eaten away at his hat had moved down to the flesh of the man himself.

Quietly, surreptitiously, he began to move, first his hands, which were tied—not tightly—behind him; then his feet, which he drew forward without a sound so that he could see what bound him there. It was nothing more than a kind of frayed twine around his ankles, also not tied tight, as though the man either did not know or did not care what he was doing. He began working at the hands first, rubbing the twine against a corner board of the lean-to behind him and never taking his eyes off the hunched figure by the fire.

Suddenly the man's shoulders twitched upward and his head swiveled as though the unprovoked memory of something had struck him like a jolt of electricity. "So you're awake, boy. Must've been the smell of old Jacko's goor-may cookin'." The man stuck his head over the steaming pot and inhaled deeply. "Mmmm-mmmm," he said. "Jacko's got a reputation, boy. Greatest chef on the rail." The man scooped up some of the steaming brown gruel in the spoon and turned away from the fire. "Here, boy, try some."

For a moment he did not know if he was being asked to come forward, but then with one hand cupped under the dripping spoon the man began hobbling toward him. He faced himself forward and kept his hands out of sight behind him. The man drew near, grinning, stinking of decayed flesh, and placed the spoon before his lips. He turned his head away.

"That's not nice, boy. Jacko goes to all this trouble to make you a nice hot breakfast, and you turn your nose up. Here, now, you eat this." The man jabbed the spoon roughly at the side of his mouth, bruising him.

He shook his head and twisted it away. He could no longer see the man, refused even to look, but could feel him coming closer. Then he felt the sharp violation of bony, talon-like fingers wrenching his chin around so that he was forced to look squarely into those watery eyes now only inches away.

"Maybe you're just not hungry yet, boy." For a long moment the fingers did not relax, the miotic pupils never widened. Then the man winked, loosened his grip, and said, "Not yet, right?"

Some atavistic knowledge deep within warned him and he knew, simply, that he must nod.

The man cackled and released his chin, then returned to the steaming pot on the fire. "Jacko's gonna have to teach you some manners, boy."

He worked frantically now at his bonds, never taking his eyes off the troll-like figure before the fire. It did not take long. The twine around his hands was loose and rotting, the knots poorly tied—the slipshod work of a mind blasted by disease and a body no longer capable of performing the most ordinary physical functions.

As if having forgotten utterly that another living being was near, a being at once captive and potentially dangerous, the man never even glanced in his direction as he began untying the frayed twine around his ankles. Out of fascination and horror and a mounting sense of urgency, his fingers fumbling now with the remaining twine, tearing at it, he watched the troglodytic little man lose his grip on the spoon and fall precipitously in a twitching, fitful spasm which continued on the ground as though in some fetishistic ritual with the earth.

At last he managed to free himself completely, but for a moment freedom and fear paralyzed him and he continued to watch the writhing figure on the ground before him. Fearful, fascinated, he stood watching until the violation and the pain and the outrage welled up so powerfully inside him that they could no longer be contained, until the only steps he could take were not backward in flight but forward in a sort of spontaneous and all-consuming vengeance. "You fucking scum!" *he shouted when he reached the man's twitching, wasted body. He kicked the face as hard as he could and watched the head snap back, the dumb quivering lips turning instantly red with blood from the force of the blow. He waited a moment as if expecting some sort of reply, and when there was none except for the body's continued vellications and the blood dripping from the lips he kicked the face again, shouting,* "You queer fucking scum!"

The body went slack. As he stood there waiting for movement to return, ready at the slightest tremor to kick the face a third time, he found himself suddenly shrinking backward at the thought that the man might be dead, and any touch of that diseased flesh might infect him too. He began pawing at the ground with his foot, trying to wipe his foot clean in the dirt, until it occurred to him that even the air he now breathed was contaminated. At the thought of this he wheeled and fled without a backward glance.

He ran without direction or purpose or sense of time passing, without awareness that a fine spring rain had begun to fall or that his clothes were being torn and his flesh scratched by thick tangles of undergrowth. He ran as though the mere mechanical action of limbs propelling him were enough to satisfy and define the need inside him. He ran until at last, his body not mechanical but human and winded, he could run no longer. It was only then, with his heart pounding as he reclined against a large rock and sucked air down into his lungs, that he began to feel the rain and to understand not only that he had no destination but also that he did not even recognize where he was in the woods. He had lost the river and he did not remember having crossed the railroad tracks. For an absurd instant he wondered if he had been doing nothing but running in circles, and the thought of meeting up with the man again made him shiver. He remembered the man jerking uncontrollably on the ground and himself kicking that ravaged face, not once but twice, then the abrupt cessation of movement, and he shivered again at the thought that maybe he had killed him. He didn't care. The fucking bastard deserved it.

When the pounding of his heart had finally abated and his breathing returned to normal, he started thinking of what he should do next, but nothing came to him. He stood up and looked around, and in the instant that he spied the river through the trees, its broad dark waters moving back in the direction from which he had come, the image of his sister's golden hair came to him and he realized he wanted nothing more than to be able to touch her hair again.

Sometime after he had returned home and the turmoil over his running away had finally subsided, he entered Lydia's room late one night. She was not awake but as he sat on the edge of the bed her eyes opened and recognized him immediately. He reached out and gently stroked her hair.

"I was afraid when you were gone, Jake," Lydia said.

He continued stroking her hair but did not say anything.

"I thought you might die, or I'd never see you again."

Even in the darkness he could see that tears were forming in her eyes. In her voice was sadness and fear.

"Why did you do it, Jake? Why did you leave?"

He curled the ends of her hair softly in his fingertips. "I don't know," he said.

She was quiet for a moment, as though weighing his answer. Then she said, "Don't do it again, Jake. Please? Promise me you won't ever do it again."

He continued to stroke her hair without answering, and she grew agitated. "Promise me, Jake," she insisted, loud enough so that he worried she might wake someone. "Cross your heart and hope to die."

He bent forward and leaned close to her ear. "Shhhh," he whispered, "I promise."

Chapter Six

Coming Clean

I thought I understood why Jake ran away, given the realization I had made about Mother's relationship with him. What surprised me though was the timing. It would have made more sense right after Lydia's First Communion, or after the failed peeper mission, but a couple of weeks had passed uneventfully since then. There seemed no immediate or compelling reason for him to leave when he did.

Whatever his motivation, something in him was changed when he returned. He had never been much for conversation, but after he came home he almost never gave more than single-word answers to even the most open-ended questions. Once the commotion had finally died down the night of his return, I went to his room and sat on the floor near his bed. "Jake, tell me what happened," I said. "What was it like?"

Jake was lying on his back, hands under his head, staring up at the ceiling.

"Nothing," was all he said.

"Where did you go?"

"Nowhere."

"Come on, Jake," I said, "I won't tell anybody, I'm on your side. Why did you do it?"

He continued to stare at the ceiling.

"Were you afraid?"

No response.

"Jake," I persisted, "are you trying to make this into some kind of game? Because if you are, then I'm not playing." I stood up in a huff and made as if to leave.

"It's not a game," he said, pinning me to the spot with a dead-serious look.

I felt suddenly disarmed. "Then why won't you talk about it? I mean, people don't run away for nothing. You even had the police out after you, you know." He knew. Because shortly after he had walked in the door, soaking wet and scratched all over on his face and arms, Mother had belabored exactly that point, along with the fact that most of the neighborhood had also been out looking for him. As soon as I uttered that last sentence I regretted it, because without intending to I had drawn an unseen but palpable line between us, a line which placed me squarely in the adult camp of parents.

"Let's just forget about it. All right, Ace?" He went back to staring at the ceiling.

That was as much as I ever got out of him, and to my knowledge no one else ever got more. Mother and Father tried, I'm sure. The day after Jake returned they told the rest of us to stay in Lydia's room while they talked with Jake. A couple of days later they convened the whole family in the living room.

Father did all of the talking. He asked us to sit side by side on the couch while he and Mother pulled up chairs and sat in front of us. He told us that Jake's escapade had been upsetting to everyone, and that he and Mother did not want any of their children to feel running away was ever an answer. There was love in this family, he said, somewhat haltingly (he had never used the word with us before), and if there was love there was never any reason to run away. He urged us all to come and talk to them if we were having a problem, not to just assume there were no solutions and no one who cared. He said the worst thing a child could do in life—and here he stopped to point out that he was not singling out Jake, he was talking about any child—was to run away from those who loved him, "because without love…" again he faltered over the word, paused as though he did not quite know how to finish the sentence, before finally concluding, "we have absolutely nothing of value in this life." As if to underscore Father's words the grandfather clock began chiming the noon hour.

Then, almost as an afterthought, Father added, "And running away can be dangerous. Just yesterday the police found the body of an old hobo in the woods a few miles from here. They think he might have been killed. So please, come to us if you're having a problem. You never know what could happen to you if you run away." I don't think Father was making up this story, but whether he was or not it struck me at the time as the typical sort of scare tactic that parents had probably been using on kids since prehistoric days: "Don't wander too far from the cave or some nasty saber-tooth might get you." Jake fidgeted beside me on the couch as Father was talking, and I figured he must be sitting there muttering under his breath, "Give me a break."

When Father had finished he glanced over at Mother as though checking to see if he had said the right things, to see if she approved. Mother was strangely quiet and forlorn, hands in her lap, eyes downcast. She did not meet his hesitant attempts to catch her eye and did not say anything, but she looked as though she had suffered a great loss or defeat. She seemed older, too, although perhaps it was that I had never looked closely enough to notice the deep creases across her forehead and the crow's feet around her eyes that her makeup could not hide, or the gray beginning to show in her light brown hair (her hair was the same color as Jake's, a detail I must have noticed before but which had never seemed so apparent to me as in that moment).

"Do you all understand what I've been saying?" Father asked. I cast a sidelong glance at the others sitting to my left. At the far end of the couch Lydia and Ben were looking up at Father and nodding, as I was. Jake was gazing at some point below Father's feet as though he hadn't heard a word. "No one in this family runs away again, right?"

The three of us nodded. Jake seemed far removed from the rest of us, staring off into a world of his own, his face expressionless.

"Right, Jake?" Father said.

"Yeah," Jake said, without looking up.

In retrospect, I think that despite her silence and the way she looked that day with her head bowed—aging, tired, humiliated by all the frantic phone calling and the police being brought in and the neighbors out searching for Jake—Mother was less upset than Father was. If my assumption was correct that she expected failure from Jake, she could hardly have been surprised that at some point it would take the form of his running away.

Father, on the other hand, was a sort of naive Prospero, an idealist who thought he could somehow influence fate to the advantage of his children. I don't believe he had even the slightest suspicion, at the time, that a thing like this could happen in *his* family. It must have come as a shock to him, which probably explains why he did all the talking.

Years later, after his death, Mother told me why he had wanted to buy the forty acres on which our house was built. She said *she* had argued steadfastly for a house in a neighborhood, with lots of kids and other families around. But Father had grown up near Boston and had always wanted a place in the country, a place removed from the noises and confusions of city life and the pressures to conform of life in the suburbs. He wanted a place where his kids could be free, where they could hammer nails and build tree houses and holler like savages if they wanted without being concerned about what the neighbors might think. It also had to be a place where as parents they wouldn't have to worry about what their kids might find around the next block—he wanted freedom for them, but he wanted control, too. So when he discovered this new neighborhood being developed in southern New Hampshire, where young families—*though not too many of them*—would soon be moving in, a neighborhood with an end lot that had forty acres of undeveloped woodland behind it, Father saw an opportunity for a compromise between living in a more remote area, as he preferred, and a more populated suburb, as Mother preferred.

The strange thing about it all was that Father's work required him to be near a city—he worked for one of the leading defense contractors in the Northeast—and neither his previous life nor his work had prepared him for country living, although maybe that was the point. Maybe he wanted a clean break from everything he had known, a chance to create—or to orchestrate—the environment in which his children would grow up. In any event, he and Mother agreed upon the compromise of living in this quasi-suburb of Newtown, and I suspect he believed—until Jake ran away—that he was providing a lifestyle for his children as close to the ideal as possible.

He took me aside after his talk with the family and said, "Virgil, I want you to tell me the truth. I've been trying to get it from Jake but he won't say a word. Why did he run away?"

I could see the hurt and concern in his eyes, but there was nothing I could do to help him. "I don't know, Dad. He won't talk to me either."

"I just don't understand it," he said, shaking his head. He ran a hand through his thick brown hair and held onto the back of his neck. "What would drive him to do such a thing? Did he say anything to you—anything at all—that made you suspicious?"

His dark eyes searched my face for an answer even as I shook my head. "Jake and I don't talk all that much, Dad. He spends a lot of time alone."

He thought about this for a moment. "Then we're just going to have to change that."

I believe he was sincere. He wanted very much to be able to take Jake's pain—whatever it might have been—away from him. But I think he probably had no idea how to do it, and so the resolve of that moment disappeared into an intensified absorption in his work.

That too, his work, was a peculiar mix of contradictions. We were never sure just what he did, but he worked in a monstrous building six stories high and a couple of hundred yards long. When we were young we assumed Father ran the place, as though he were some powerful general commanding his fortress and protecting the country. But in later years, during the turbulence of the Vietnam War when there were protests in front of the building every week, the fact that this gargantuan structure whose principle *raison d'etre* was war-related could daily swallow up my father's existence struck me as an impossible paradox.

Father used to tell us how important it was to be an individual, to "step to the music" each of us heard (he was fond of Thoreau), yet here he was—along with two thousand other workers—stepping to the music of the company, which stepped to the music of the U.S. Defense Department. Granted, he was not a common laborer, he was an engineer of some significance to the company, but he was not an important general as we so naively assumed in our childhood, nor was he an owner or in any other way a policy-maker. He was a tiny cog in an enormous wheel turned by what many described as "the war machine." It was difficult to comprehend, never mind to accept, especially when he would look up at one of those deafening jets that so often roared overhead from the air base, wait until its repercussive thunder had finally passed, and say, "Somehow those things never make me feel safer when they go by."

He was an enigma in other ways too. He believed in simplifying life (the influence of Thoreau again—he even had a sign on his study door that served as reminder and admonition: "SIMPLIFY, SIMPLIFY..."); he believed in slowing down the pace of life, which he saw as far too hectic and barren of meaning; and he believed deeply in the value of family, his own parents and family having been, he used to tell us, "the single most important influence of my life." He constantly reminded us as children that what he hoped for most from us was that we be "decent human beings." If we could do that and nothing else he would always be proud of us. Yet he would spend long hours away from us at work, leaving our care and most of our discipline in the hands of Mother. To be fair, in this respect he was not much different from the other fathers in the neighborhood, those plodding warriors who would return home from the daily battleground of the workplace bone weary and beaten into resignation. If anything, though, he was probably less involved in our discipline than other fathers with their children since he absolutely hated punishing us. I do not remember him ever laying a hand on any of us.

These were things I realized only in later years. As a child in the halcyon fifties I was unaware of anything missing. I missed my father because I was crazy about him and wanted to spend time with him, but I never felt as though he was absent from my life, perhaps because he would blitz home sometimes on a Friday after work and exclaim, "All right, everyone, we're going to do something fun this weekend!" Then he would cart us all off to the bowling alley or take us to the beach for the day or lead us on a hike up a small mountain nearby that had a fire tower at the summit. Everyone but Father and Jake, who would scramble up first by himself, was terrified of climbing the steep, narrow stairs that zigzagged to the outlook at the top of the tower, but with Father's help the rest of us made it too and were always thrilled to be up there (whether we were thrilled by the view or by the residual terror of the climb I'm not so sure anymore; what counted most was that we were all together, and we were happy).

Once when I was probably about ten Father took us all camping in the White Mountains. I say took us all but the truth is that he took only me, Jake, and Ben. Lydia must have been around three at the time, and Mother was overly protective of her even then. "She'll have nightmares about bears," she complained. "And what if it rains? Maybe that's all right for you four hooligans, but I don't want my baby girl to catch cold."

The funny thing is that it did rain, but we had a great time anyway. We stayed inside the tent and Father taught us how to play poker. Then someone suggested we make it *strip* poker. Father saw nothing wrong with the idea and even added the condition that whoever had to strip down to his underwear first would not only be the loser but would also have to stand up and sing a song for everyone. Father, who had been winning quite regularly until the game turned into strip poker, was of course the loser (I always suspected him of deliberately losing so that none of us would have to suffer the indignity of singing half-naked). Upon shedding his undershirt he promptly bolted past the tent flap out into the rain, clad only in his boxer shorts, and with a bar of soap in his hand began lathering himself from head to foot, all the while belting out the lyrics to "Singing in the Rain" in his best, and loudest, tenor voice. The three of us watched from the dry confines of the tent and laughed at him with astonishment and admiration.

"Do we really have to call this guy our father?" I said to Jake. Jake just shook his head. "I don't know him."

Another time Father came home around lunchtime one Saturday after working part of the day and said, much to Mother's surprise, "Amusement awaits us at the park. Come on, let's go."

In no time we were on our way to Canobie Lake Park, where we stayed long into the humid warmth of a lovely summer evening. Jake wouldn't leave the rollercoaster, billed as the largest and most exciting anywhere in New England. He rode it again and again, alone, although Lydia clamored to try it and Mother wouldn't let her. "It will make you sick to your stomach," Mother insisted. Father was the only one to get on with Jake, and after their ride together his face was pale. "It's all yours, Jake," he said. "I've had enough." That verdict was the excuse Ben and I were looking for to pair up and seek our thrills elsewhere—pitching rings at impossibly large wooden pegs and throwing softballs at lead-weighted milk bottles—while Mother and Father took Lydia over to the merry-go-round and eventually to the Ferris wheel, which Lydia rode time after time sandwiched between the two of them, waving madly and calling out whenever she caught sight of us nearby. Dinner was hot dogs and French fries and a dessert of cotton candy, and afterwards, the summer night air descending gently upon us, warm and soft, we all took a long boat ride around the lake.

These times with Father were rare. They were like flashes of a light bulb—brilliant, signifying something memorable, but over in an instant, leaving us blind to the fact that he could be so completely absorbed in his work that we would hardly see him for weeks at a stretch, sometimes even months. We saw him at the dinner table, of course, but often after dinner he would retreat to his study to continue working there, and on Saturdays, too, he usually worked part if not all of the day. With Mother's insistence on church and church-related activities for us on Sundays, little time was left for us to be with him. Still, we saw him enough—and there was enough joy on those occasions when he did spend time with us—to feel that nothing was amiss.

Until Jake ran away, I think Father felt the same way. He loved his family; so much so, perhaps, that he could not conceive of anything wrong with it, certainly nothing of such magnitude that one of his children would run away. It was as if he believed that by loving his children no harm could come to them. When it did come, first to Lydia in the form of her illness, and then to Jake not long afterwards, I think Father was shaken to the core.

For a week or two it seemed he was always tapping lightly at Jake's door, checking to see if Jake was all right or if there was anything he needed ("a coke, maybe?"), reassuring Jake again and again that any time he wanted to talk "about anything at all" he should feel free to do so. Once I saw him try to put his arm around Jake's shoulder; Jake shrank away from the contact as though offended by it. Often Father would come up to me and say, "Has he told you anything yet?", as if every day I too tried to pry loose Jake's secrets. In time Father's excessive solicitude gradually waned as he immersed himself more deeply than ever in his work.

Mother essentially withdrew from everyone except Lydia. While Father made overtures to Jake, Mother spent time with Lydia, as though Lydia had been the one to run away and who therefore needed extra comfort and attention. Often when I passed Lydia's room I would see Mother, through the half-opened bedroom door, lying on the bed reading stories to Lydia or taking an afternoon nap with her, the two of them invariably snuggled up tight.

Lydia had experienced something of a relapse shortly after Jake ran away. Without warning she had suddenly started coughing and wheezing so badly that her face turned blue, and in the midst of everyone's concern over Jake, it seemed Lydia might have to be taken to the hospital again (later it was diagnosed as an asthma attack, one of the first of countless to bedevil her throughout her life). The coughing fit eventually subsided, although she continued the labored breathing—the excruciatingly long, wheezy exhalations we would all come to know so well—for a long time afterwards. To the extent that Lydia suffered during this attack she needed Mother's nursing, but she seemed fine as soon as Jake returned, and I wondered how he felt seeing the two of them nestled together as though they were the only people in the house.

Mother did continue to prepare meals and do the laundry and get the rest of us off to school or work each morning, but she didn't playfully pinch my ear or run her hand through Ben's hair the way she normally did, and she hardly spoke a word to Jake (whom she never touched, and who would never have allowed her touch). For perhaps two or three weeks after Jake ran away it was as though Mother trusted no one but Lydia. Then one morning as I was lying in bed I heard Mother singing in the kitchen the way she usually did in the morning, and I knew the storm within her had finally passed.

From that point on our family settled back into the routines of work and play I had always known without knowing I knew, although there were changes. Father worked more than was usual even for him. Mother paid more attention to the gardens she had neglected for several weeks. She loved gardening, and had both a vegetable garden out behind the house and numerous flower beds in front of the house. When she finally deemed Lydia well enough to be outside, the two of them could often be seen on their hands and knees—light, colorful kerchiefs on their heads and white floral-patterned cloth gardening gloves on their hands—pulling weeds or loosening the soil around the flowers and vegetable plants with hand trowels.

Mother also began to devote more time to church and volunteer activities. It was normal for her to be involved in such efforts, but after school got out it seemed as if she shamed one or more of us (except Jake, who flatly refused) at least once a week into helping her set up and tend a bake sale table or collect clothing for some charitable drive to help the poor and needy.

Still, it was not as though we never had time for fun. Mother and Father both loved the beach, and we took our normal two-week vacation in Maine around the Fourth of July. We rented a large beach house right across from the ocean, with Grandmother and Grandfather accompanying us as usual. The weather was marvelous, the air warm and dry, the sky clear blue except for a few puffy white cumulus clouds, the ocean that deep, cobalt color it gets when the humidity is low. With the tall beach grass green and glistening in the sun and the prolific bloom of rose hips along the ocean boulevard, their fragrance filling the air, it seemed an almost paradisal time. The whole family spent the long sunny days out on the beach, the adults talking or reading thick paperback novels; Ben and I bodysurfing or, if we could finagle the money from one of the adults, riding the waves on those canvas floats you could rent on the beach back then; Lydia, because of her fair skin relegated to the shadow-realm of the beach umbrella (Mother would only allow her out in the sun if she wore a hat and long clothing), reading Nancy Drew mysteries, playing card games and word games with anyone willing, and using a dinner knife or slender pieces of driftwood to carefully sculpt castles made from packed beach sand (no drip castles for her!); Jake listlessly frying himself on his towel a few feet apart from the rest of the family, in his hand a small transistor radio which Father had bought for him before coming to the beach and which was always close enough to his head for him to use the earphone.

At low tide some of us might draw a court in the hard sand and play handball games with a tennis ball. Occasionally Father would set up a net and we'd get a game of volleyball or badminton going, although Jake, unlike in previous years, never participated. The only real interaction Jake had with any of us on the beach was with Lydia, for whom—at her request—he would occasionally pile up and pack down mounds of beach sand or fetch water so that she could continue her sculpting. In the evenings we would feast—on lobsters and steamed clams that Mother would cook in huge pots on the stove, on steak or hamburgers and hot dogs that Father would broil on the grill, or on fresh seafood dinners at local restaurants when none of the adults felt like cooking. If not for the knowledge we all shared of Jake's running away, nothing would have seemed out of the ordinary, not even Jake's aloofness, which probably would have been dismissed as the normal behavior of an adolescent with a new radio.

Grandmother and Grandfather had been as upset as anyone by Jake's running away and tried, gently, to draw him out of his shell, which seemed to grow thicker in relation to the attempts people made to draw him out of it. A loving and affectionate woman, Grandmother would come up behind Jake at the dinner table—her hands alighting gently upon his shoulders—and whisper in his ear, "Would you like a piece of pie or some cookies for dessert, Jake?" Jake would say "no" and pull away from her touch or wordlessly get up from the table and get the pie or cookies for himself. Grandfather would ask Jake to go for a walk with him along the beach in the evening or play a hand of gin rummy or cribbage, but Jake invariably refused.

Except for Jake's unremitting detachment, the entire two weeks would have registered as just another pleasant summer interlude shared as a family, another shining pearl on the string of years that extended as far back into childhood as I could recall. Even Jake's remoteness might have faded from memory if Lydia hadn't almost died the day before we returned home, and if Jake hadn't been the one to save her.

Grandmother and Grandfather had decided to stay back at the beach house to get some packing done for the trip home. They had given Ben and me enough money to rent two floats for a few hours and had told us to try to get Jake to use one too. After using the floats for a while Ben suggested we take a trip out to the island off the far end of the beach, since we wouldn't be able to do it tomorrow, it was almost low tide now, and the only way to get to the island and back was to cross the tidal river as close to low tide as possible. Ben and I loved exploring the island. We would scavenge amongst the rocks for unusually shaped driftwood or other interesting pieces of flotsam that had washed ashore, such as lobster pot buoys still attached to their smashed traps by yards of rope, or broken sticks and seashells bleached white as bone by the sun. We'd look for sand dollars and stop at warm tidal pools to turn over rocks in search of starfish or crabs, or perhaps just sit there and marvel at the colors and the myriad subtle pulses of life in the limpid water. Any time we went to the island our imaginations were sparked by a sense of adventure and discovery, so I agreed with Ben that we ought to try one last expedition.

"Jake," I said before leaving, "Ben and I will be out at the island for a while. Why don't you use one of the floats? Gramma and Grampa wanted you to use one too when they gave us the money." Jake was lying on his towel, eyes closed. He had the earphone in his ear as usual but I knew he heard me. "Let's go, Ben," I said, assuming Jake would never touch the floats.

I couldn't have been more wrong, as I understood from the various fragments of the story later provided by Mother, Father, and Lydia.

Apparently, just after Ben and I left, Mother left too. She let Father know that she would be "back shortly," her code words for a trip to the bathroom. Father must have been dozing on the blanket because he swore later that he didn't even know she had gone.

At this point, according to Lydia, Jake grabbed a float, paddled out beyond the breakers, put his head down, and began drifting leisurely with the waves and the tide.

Here the truth of the story got a little hazy, to my mind. Lydia said she watched Jake for a while and began to worry that he had fallen asleep, because he was drifting out much too far, dangerously far. She went to the edge of the water and called to him but got no response, so she decided to use the other float to go out after him. The problem with her story was that Jake was a strong swimmer, while she was a very weak swimmer. Also, Father was lying down nearby, and if she had seriously thought Jake was in danger she could have roused *him* to go after Jake.

In any event, somehow Lydia got out past the breakers too. Up to that point, with her feet still on the ocean floor, she could control the float fairly well, but once she climbed onto it and got out to deeper water, she could not get enough of her arms and legs over the sides to direct the float (which Jake could do with ease). Worse still, the outgoing tide and the offshore breeze kept forcing her farther out. Very quickly Lydia the rescu*er* became Lydia the rescu*ee*.

When Mother returned to the beach she roused Father and said, "Where is everybody?" He had no idea where *anyone* was, so she began scanning the beach—without much concern at first—until it dawned on her that Ben and I had gone to the island and *both* of the floats were missing. At last she spied Lydia farther out on the water than she would have imagined in her worst nightmares. She began screaming frantically for Lydia to come back, and then as she fought her way through the breakers, with Father just behind her, she watched in horror as Lydia fell off the float and disappeared beneath the surface of the water. She was still a considerable distance from Lydia when this happened.

Later, Lydia insisted to me that she was fine until she heard Mother screaming—a little frightened, perhaps, but not so far from Jake that she felt beyond help. When she heard Mother's panicked cry and saw Mother splashing through the waves faster than Lydia had ever seen her move before, she grew terrified and lost her balance. Then an unexpected swell tipped the float and sent her into the ocean, which was way over her head so far from shore.

When she surfaced she found herself separated from the float. A weak swimmer to begin with, she had never been in ocean water over her head and was shocked to reach down with her feet and discover that she could not touch the bottom. Disoriented, having lost sight not only of Mother but of the shore itself, she heard Mother's cries as she went under again. She surfaced moments later and felt someone's arm encircling her from behind, then began thrashing and tearing at the arm as if she were being attacked rather than rescued. "It's me, Lydia," she heard at last through her own splashing frenzy. "It's Jake. Calm down or we'll both drown."

She did calm down at that and latched onto the float that Jake had paddled over on. The two of them clung to the side of the float as Jake directed it slowly back to shore, though Mother and Father met them well before they reached land. Mother hugged Lydia tightly and said over and over again, "My baby, my baby. You could have drowned." Father put his arm around Jake and said, "I'm proud of you, son." For once, Jake did not pull immediately away.

Later that evening, when the story was being recounted for perhaps the hundredth time, with Father lauding Jake once more as the consummate hero, I noticed that Mother, who held Lydia in her lap wrapped in a blanket, said nothing, and I realized then that from the beginning she had not said a single word about what Jake had done. She seemed reserved, almost wary, as though she suspected Jake of having intentionally drawn Lydia into danger.

No matter how much Father played it up and Grandmother and Grandfather, beaming, offered encomiums at the appropriate points in the narrative, Jake the hero refused to bask in the glory. He seemed to get more uncomfortable with each new superlative, until at last, when Father concluded the story and put his arm around Jake's shoulders as he had done earlier in the day, Jake stiffened and said, "I think I'll go for a walk."

"I want to go, too," Lydia blurted out as she sat up in Mother's lap, the blanket falling from her shoulders.

"You'll do no such thing, young lady," Mother said, shaking her head. "We've had enough excitement around here today without your catching pneumonia again." She wrapped the blanket around Lydia once more and gathered her in tight.

"Don't go, Jake," Lydia said.

Jake looked at her for a moment before walking off into the cool summer night alone.

Another incident involving Jake happened shortly after our stay at the beach. It signaled the end of my involvement with the neighborhood gang, and with that the end of my childhood. I understood none of this at the time, of course. We never understand the turning points of our lives until long after they have occurred, if we ever understand them at all, but I am convinced now that it was Jake, however unwittingly, who ripped away my final adhesion to childhood as though it were some rotting umbilical cord and shoved me wholly, irreversibly, into the anxiety-ridden netherworld of adolescence.

I was already in my early teenage years and had started taking an interest in girls, and I was being invited over to friends' houses for parties, which were usually held in some finished basement where we could listen to music, dance, and "make out" without the unwelcome intrusions of parents or younger siblings. The parties invariably started off for an hour or more with the boys on one side of the room and the girls on the other, laughing and gossiping amongst themselves while listening to the Beatles or the Beach Boys, knowing what would eventually happen and waiting—with secret anticipation and a sort of bated inner excitement as evening waxed into night—for the one or two daring boys who would end the separation of the sexes and usher us all, yearning, into the darkened realm of petting and soft kisses.

But I still met with the gang occasionally after school. Being the oldest member, I had been feeling awkward and uncomfortable about these meetings for some time, but I had not yet found the requisite honesty or courage—or whatever it was I needed—to leave that part of my childhood behind. One thing we used to do every so often was hold a "come clean" meeting. The object of the meeting was to get each member to reveal one of his "deepest, darkest secrets." "Coming clean" usually involved such mundane stuff as spitting in your sister's milk when she wasn't looking, or pinning your brother on the ground and farting in his face. But there were times when someone would tell the gang a story that was truly exciting, if not disturbing. A freckle-faced, red-headed kid named Jimmy Miller once told us that when he was little he often had to attend big family get-togethers, and every time he went there was this one uncle—who was popular with the rest of the family and whose breath always smelled of Canada Mints—who would hoist him up in his arms and to the delight of Jimmy's parents and everyone else present waltz around the room with him; but later on the uncle would always manage to find Jimmy alone, unzip his pants, and proudly hold "this big ugly purple dick in his hands," as Jimmy put it. He said he hadn't told his parents because he figured they'd never believe him.

Another time Bucky Fulton told us the true reason for the black eye and broken nose he showed up with at school one day. At school he told everyone his stupid younger brother had swung a baseball bat when Bucky was standing right behind him and Bucky had caught it across the bridge of the nose. Later he told the gang he'd just seen the episode of *Leave It to Beaver* on television that involved Beaver giving himself a haircut that created several bald spots and forced him, in trying to hide the evidence, to wear a stocking hat at all times, even to bed at night. Bucky decided it wasn't really believable that Beaver would do such a lousy job on his hair, so he decided to try it on himself. Bucky didn't leave any bald spots but naturally he butchered his hair, and when his father came home from work that night and saw it he called Bucky a "stupid son of a bitch," smashed him in the face, and told him if he ever tried anything that stupid again he would cut off every last hair on Bucky's head and make him go around totally bald for awhile.

Then there was Johnny McDougall's story of his precocious sexual exploits. Johnny was a scrawny little kid, small for his age, with scruffy brown hair, brown skin and a wide, cheerful grin on his face most of the time. He was only about eight or nine when he told us how he had been walking home from school one day, taking a shortcut through the woods and minding his own business, when Candy Dube, who was walking some distance behind him, began making fun of his size. As a sixth grader Candy was taller and bigger than anyone else in grammar school, but her true claim to fame was that she had already pushed forth a pair of round, full tits that were the object of every boy's fantasies and every girl's envy. Johnny's story involved an elaborate scheme by which he managed to trick Candy into showing him her tits, "*all of them.*"

"So what were they like?" someone asked him.

I don't know if we were expecting a sort of detailed anatomical description, but about all Johnny could say, over and over again, was "big and juicy."

Such stories sent nervous tingles of excitement along my spine, and I, like all the gang members, eagerly anticipated "come clean" meetings while dreading having to actually "come clean" myself. Unless you were divulging something you could boast about, as Johnny did, it was almost like being inside the confessional, except that the gang members would occasionally reject your story because it wasn't good enough or wasn't believable and would demand to hear another. I used to assume most of us lied or exaggerated, although over the years, as more and more reports have surfaced of children being abused and molested, I've come to suspect that the tamer stories we heard were probably cover-ups for the more truthful ones that happened far more often than I would have believed. After all, in my family—long before experts began preaching the gospel of non-violent parenting in vogue today—our parents had disavowed corporal punishment and never hit any of us, so the stories other kids told of their parents' drunken, violent behavior struck Ben and me as difficult to comprehend.

After Jake ran away, when it was Ben's turn to "come clean" he told the gang his brother Jake had run away, the police had been out looking for him, and no one knew why he had done it. The rest of the gang agreed it wasn't good enough—Ben wasn't telling them anything new. They wanted details. Had Jake been caught stealing from our mother's purse? Had our father beaten the shit out of him before he left? Was Jake just trying to prove who was boss in the family? What happened to him while he was gone? Why did he come back?

Even when I came to Ben's defense and pointed out that nobody knew the answers to those questions except Jake himself, and he wasn't talking, they weren't satisfied. They said if we didn't know the answers we should try to get Jake to come to the next meeting. I refused outright, but they kept pressuring Ben, who finally said he'd try to talk Jake into coming.

It was a foolish idea, which I'm sure Ben understood right from the start, but he did tell Jake that some of the gang had been asking about him and wondering if he would come to the next meeting. Ben said Jake gave him that weird look that makes you feel like an insect, and said, "I've got better things to do than hang around with a bunch of queers."

Just hearing that secondhand through Ben made me feel uneasy and ashamed, not because of the word "queers" but because I had a sense that Jake was somehow superior to me in his solitude—stronger, more mature, above such childish confession games. Unfortunately, not only did I ignore those feelings and go to the next meeting myself, but Jake went too, and he went, as always, without anyone knowing he would be there.

After the gang had finished ridiculing Ben for his explanation of why Jake wasn't there, a couple of the other kids gave their "come clean" stories. One of the stories—the last one I ever heard as a member of the gang—was a grisly tale by Donny Fletcher. Donny was one of the older kids in the gang, blond, clean cut, and very bright in school, but he was a kid I always wondered about because he had such a dark, sadistic streak in him. Probably the only reason he wasn't a bully in the neighborhood was that he was not particularly big or strong, but with insects or small animals it was a different story. He started telling us about his "experiment" with a bullfrog he had recently hung upside down from a tree branch using some fishing line tied around one of the frog's legs. He wanted to find out two things: what would happen to the frog right after being strung up, and what would happen after it had been left that way for a day or two. Donny had finished giving us the gory details (he referred to them as "funny") about the frog's initial violent, absurd attempts to jump free of its bonds as it dangled in midair, and had just started to tell us what the frog looked like the following day, when Jake's voice abruptly cut in from somewhere outside our meeting, which was being held inside a bower we had fashioned out of deadwood and leafy boughs propped against an enormous bull pine far back in the woods. We could not see Jake but we could hear him clearly.

"Torturing frogs. What a gang of pansies and chickenshits."

When I heard his voice something inside me froze. The others immediately began filing through the thatched entrance into the open woods as I found myself paralyzed, not wanting to move, not wanting to go outside and be identified as one of the "chickenshits" accused of torturing frogs. It felt as if I were about seven years old and being called to account by an adult, not by my younger brother. I was the last to leave.

Outside it was very bright and I had to squint just to see Jake. He was standing a few feet away, thumbs hooked into the front pockets of his jeans, gazing disdainfully at each of us as we emerged like insects from a hole.

"Jake," Bucky said, excited, oblivious to the humiliation of Jake's words, "how come you ran away? Everybody's been wondering."

"None of your business, asshole."

Ben was confused. "I thought you didn't want to come today, Jake."

"I had to see for myself what this 'come clean' bullshit was all about. Now I know."

Jake fixed his gaze squarely on me. "What the fuck are you doing here, Virgil?"

The question pierced me like a knife in the heart. What *was* I doing here? I felt exposed and guilty, guilty of a sin whose specific nature I did not understand—though it was certainly not the torturing of frogs—but guilty nevertheless. For the first time in my life I saw clearly that Jake was somehow wiser than I, as though he, not I, were the oldest in the family, while I was nothing but a vain and silly little boy. Shamed, I could find no words to answer him and finally just gave a weak shrug.

"What a waste," Jake said, then wheeled and left. I did not know if he was referring to all of us in general or to me in particular. But it was the last time I ever met with the gang.

The fights began in earnest during the next school year. Jake and I attended the same junior high school, Jake in the eighth grade,

I in the ninth. We did not see each other very often during the day because we had different classes and different lunch periods, but word of the fights got around. Most of them took place before or after school, away from school grounds, so I was able to see two of them myself.

Jake had been in fights in grade school, probably more often than most kids his age, but those were no more than a series of headlocks and wrestling holds, and they hadn't happened often enough to cause real alarm. I overheard Father telling Mother once after such a fight that it was a fairly normal thing for young boys, and that he had been in several fights himself when he was young and never suffered any great harm. He assured her it was just a stage some boys went through. But while most eighth grade boys were busy passing triangular-shaped love notes to girls in the hallways, Jake was bludgeoning other males with his fists.

The first fight he was in that year happened during the second week of school, and *everyone* heard about it, including the school administration.

According to second- and third-hand reports (Jake, of course, told me nothing), Jake was standing in line outside after the morning bell had rung. One kid jokingly pushed another kid—someone Jake did not even know—who in turn bumped into Jake from behind. It was an accident, from everything I heard, but Jake suddenly went crazy and started beating the shit out of the kid, punching him in the face and kicking him when he was on the ground. The principal, Mr. Dickson (alias *The Dick*), called home to inform Mother of what had happened, and said Jake had given no explanation for his behavior. Just shrugged whenever he was asked about the fight. *The Dick* warned Mother that even though Jake had not been suspended, he would be if he was caught fighting again.

"What do you know about this fight Jake was in, Virgil?" Father asked me that night.

"The only thing I heard was that someone bumped into him accidentally from behind," I told him. "But I don't really know any more than that."

Father put his arm around my shoulder and said, "Talk to him for me, will you? I can't seem to get close to him. He won't let me." Father shook his head in that sad, bewildered manner of his whenever he talked about Jake. "I just don't understand him."

I didn't understand him either, but I said, "I'll try, Dad."

After school the next day I went to Jake's room and knocked on his door.

"Yeah," came the reply.

Jake glanced up at me as I opened the door and walked in. He was lying on his back reading one of those pulp magazines whose covers always depicted a commando rescuing some helpless, wild-eyed female with big, bulging breasts and a dress in tatters. I wondered if Mother knew about this. She used to give each of us an allowance, and I couldn't imagine her permitting the money to be used this way. If she had seen me with such a magazine she would have grabbed it away in disgust and cut off my allowance immediately.

Jake had returned to looking at the magazine. "Good reading?" I said.

"Not bad."

"Hey, Jake, I was wondering about that fight you got in yesterday." I had planned to try to ease into the subject, approach it as though out of a kind of casual curiosity.

"What about it?" He flipped a page of the magazine.

"Randy Whittier says you creamed the kid."

"So."

"Is that true?"

"Maybe."

I moved a little closer to see what Jake was looking at. Some sort of battle was going on between an American commando and Nazi soldiers. The American was firing his machine gun at the Nazis and behind him, cowering, was the half-naked female from the cover.

"What did the kid do?"

Jake glanced up at me again. "What do you mean?"

"I mean, how come you creamed him. What did the kid do?"

Jake began looking at the magazine again. "The kid was an asshole, that's all."

As always, Jake's answer left gaping holes and no room for questions. But Father had asked for my help, so I tried again. "Randy says the kid bumped into you."

Jake wouldn't take the bait.

"Is that what happened? Is that why you did it?"

"Like I said, the kid was an asshole."

We were going around in exactly the way I had hoped to avoid, so I tried making a joke of it. "But what made him an asshole? Did he try to goose you or something?"

Jake screwed up his face and turned toward me. "What's it to you, Virgil? Why are you asking so many questions?"

"I was just wondering. You really destroyed the kid, from everything I heard."

"Yeah," Jake said. He had driven us full circle.

A couple weeks later Jake got into another fight with a different kid, older than Jake and a known bully. It happened during the lunch recess, so again I did not see it, but I found out it was broken up quickly by the teachers on duty. This was probably a good thing, because even though Jake was of better than average height and possessed the thin, wiry strength and speed of a coiled spring, the other kid was bigger and stronger. I had seen the kid out on the playground before. He looked to be about sixteen or seventeen, muscular as an ape, and he had straight, oily black hair and a pock-marked face. He used to run around the playground like a berserker during chase games with his cronies at recess, smashing into circles of kids and then bolting away, leaving in his wake two or three kids struggling to get up off the ground. He had done this the year before to a group of kids I was standing with, and one kid in the group shouted, "Watch where you're going!" The bully grabbed the kid's shirt collar and said, "You want your *fucking* head punched in?" then threw the kid aside and resumed his chase.

I imagined Jake in that situation. He would have gone running after the bully until he'd caught him, then probably would have called him a fucking moron and started swinging.

Whatever happened out there that day, Jake got a three-day suspension for it. Mother and Father must have been at wit's end by this time with Jake running away and being in two fights within the space of only a few months. I know they called the school and made an appointment to talk with *The Dick* and Jake's guidance counselor. Father took part of the day off from work so that he and Mother could meet with them, but as far as I could tell nothing much came of it. The guidance counselor probably didn't even know Jake's name, and *The Dick* was one of those scowling martinets who, if not for the praise he all too often lavished on the jocks and cheerleaders at pep rallies, would have appeared to despise everything about adolescents. *The Dick's* advice to Mother and Father, other than taking Jake out to the woodshed for a sound beating, would probably have been to put up a basketball hoop in the back yard and buy Jake a pair of high-top sneakers.

The only effect I observed in Jake afterward was that he learned not to fight on school grounds. Because he did fight again, many times, but he was never caught on school property and never went before another school administrator.

His fights were always with kids I didn't know, tough kids with reputations as bullies or dirty fighters who made me worry about how Jake was spending his time, how he even came into contact with them—although there was one time when the circumstances were quite clear. Jake had a class with Bucky Fulton, who was actually a couple of months older than Jake despite being so small and scrawny that he looked like he should still be in grammar school. They were both in the eighth grade and were in the same woodworking class, for which one of the projects was to saw, chisel and sand various pieces of wood and dowels into a lamp shaped like a water pump with a spout and a trough, then shellac the whole thing before being graded on the finished product. Woodworking was something Bucky excelled at, which was presumably why Frank Egner, another kid in the class, switched his lamp with Bucky's and told Bucky he'd better keep quiet or Frank would see him after school. To emphasize the point Frank gave Bucky a quick, sharp punch in the arm while the shop teacher, feet up on his desk, was reading one of the racy paperbacks he'd become famous for amongst the junior high boys. When Bucky's short yelp attracted the shop teacher's attention, Bucky told him that he had just absent-mindedly walked into a vice and jabbed himself in the side.

But Jake had seen the punch and went over to ask Bucky what it was all about. Bucky admired Jake and was probably more afraid of lying to him than of telling the truth about Frank, so he told Jake what had happened. According to Bucky, Jake—keeping his eye on the shop teacher, whose feet were still resting atop his desk and who had once again immersed himself in the

dirty novel which he held, two-handed, in front of his face—
went right over to Frank and said, "What's this about switching
your lamp with Bucky's?"

Frank ignored Jake and glared at Bucky, "So you're a fucking
rat besides being a fucking twerp. I'll see you outside after
school, asshole."

"You'll see me outside too," Jake said.

"I've got no fight with you," Frank said. "It's *him* I've got the
fight with."

"Wrong, asshole. It's me you've got the fight with now."

Bucky said Frank didn't look too happy about that but said,
"If that's the way you want it." Frank narrowed his eyes then and
stared at Bucky. "I'll get you too, you fucker."

Bucky didn't say anything.

"Out behind the church," Jake said.

"I can't wait," Frank said.

By the end of the day word had spread that there would be
a fight after school between Jake and some other kid. When I
heard about it my first thought was *Jake, don't do it!* Words like
"reform school" and "sent up the river" ran willy-nilly through
my mind and made me fear for my brother—not some kid from
the wrong side of the tracks but *my own brother.*

Twenty to thirty kids were out behind the old brick church
that afternoon, a place used for fights because it was off school
grounds and out of view. I had never been back there to see a
fight myself, but I would often see kids excitedly heading down
the alley that led to the rear of the church. I never followed
them. On this day the boisterous group I trailed warily down the
alley, a safe distance behind, contained Jake's adversary (I did not
know this at the time) and three or four of his cohorts. Jake was
already waiting behind the church with Bucky standing slightly
behind him like some feeble second when we all arrived.

"I didn't think you'd show," Frank said, clearly feeling brave with his buddies behind him. One of them squawked out a chicken call and they all guffawed.

Jake didn't say a word. He merely stood and waited, staring.

For some reason that I cannot explain to this day, I stayed back and tried to keep out of view behind a couple of other bystanders, so that Jake, who was completely focused on his antagonist, probably never realized I was there. I could see from where I stood that he and Frank were about the same size, and as I watched, my heart pounded as though I were about to be involved in the fight myself.

Frank moved up near Jake, his buddies tagging close behind. "It's not you I want, anyway. It's this little fucking rat behind you." He tried to reach around Jake to grab at the flinching Bucky, but Jake shoved his arm aside.

Frank threw a wild punch at Jake, missed, and took a knee in the midsection. He doubled over in pain, the wind knocked out of him, while Jake stood his ground and waited for the next attack. It came soon enough. "All right, you asshole!" Frank said, and suddenly sprang at Jake like a cat. Jake was ready for it. He smashed Frank in the face and stopped him mid-leap, then watched Frank crumple to the ground in front of him. Frank was on his hands and knees now, groggy and bleeding from the nose and mouth. I craned my neck to see as Frank shook his head and sprayed drops of blood on the pavement.

Then with an unexpected burst of speed he lunged for Jake's mid-section like a football player going after a tackling dummy and shouted, "Get him!" The others closed in quickly and Jake went down hard against the pavement. Bucky started pounding on the back of one of Jake's assailants, who, as if reacting to the bite of a fly, straightened, found the source of his irritation, and swatted Bucky with a vicious backhand that sent Bucky reeling backwards.

The last thing I saw before I ran away—to my everlasting shame—was the moiling scrum of bodies, below which was my brother Jake, and the flail of fists arcing high above him.

When Jake arrived home later that day I watched him move quickly past Mother to his room. His face was a mess, all bruised and swollen.

"What happened to you, Jake?" Mother called after him.

"Nothing," Jake said.

"Come on, now. With a face like that something had to have happened." She had moved from the kitchen to the near end of the hallway, but Jake had already disappeared into his room and closed the door. "Jake?" There was no answer.

She turned to me. "Did you see?"

I nodded.

"Do you have any idea what happened?"

I shrugged quizzically, although my heart was going haywire and I felt suddenly nauseated and vile.

Mother just raised her eyebrows and shook her head as though at some mystery that was entirely unfathomable to her.

Jake's injuries could not be dismissed quite as easily as he might have liked, however, because one of his front teeth had been knocked out in the fight and there was no way he could hide that fact for long. His only explanation for it—and he stuck to the explanation with stubborn disregard for its implausibility—was that he had fallen off his bike and tumbled down an embankment. He hardly ever rode his bike anymore by this time, but with no one coming forth to contradict him (Bucky had fabricated something similar to his parents in order to explain his own injuries), the story remained the only solution to the riddle of Jake's battered face. Mother saw to it that the dentist did all the necessary orthodontic work on Jake's mouth, and that—except for the guilt I have carried with me ever since—was the end of it.

It was not the end of Jake's involvement with Frank Egner, however. According to Bucky, after the fight Jake kept close watch until he caught Frank walking home alone after school one day and "beat the living piss out of him." Jake warned him that if he and his gang ever tried to get any kind of revenge against either Bucky or himself, they better be ready to kill, because that's what Jake was going to do to Frank if he ever tried anything again. When I asked Bucky how he knew all this, he said simply, "I just do."

"Were you there?" I asked, and he said he wasn't.

"Did Jake tell you all this?" I asked, and again he said no. Jake had only told him he met Frank again and Frank wouldn't be bothering him anymore. Soon after, Frank gave back the lamp and never said another word to Bucky about it.

"Why else would Frank change his mind if Jake didn't threaten to kill him or cut off his balls or something?" Bucky argued.

Even as a ninth grader inured to the grisly language of baby jokes, I found Bucky's words, or perhaps the possibility of their truth, revolting, but I had no answer for him. Unknown to anyone but me, I had seen the evidence of Frank's cowardly brutality with my own eyes. I too wondered what inducement— other than the sort of intimidation which, issuing from absolute fearlessness, sends an absolute message—could have any effect on Frank's hyenoid brain.

The only other time I witnessed one of Jake's fights, Jake knew I was there. Before any punches were thrown, squared off as he was before his opponent, he saw me and I called to him, "Jake, don't do it. It's not worth it." I had in mind that this time I would redeem myself by jumping in and somehow stopping the fight, but Jake never gave me the chance. As soon as he heard me he turned and went after the other kid with a frenzy I had never seen in him before. So furious was his attack that the kid—who was certainly no smaller than Jake—fell before it in a matter of seconds, then limped away bloody and humiliated while Jake, his back to me, stood and watched him go.

It was as though my words had been the trigger to Jake's rage, my very presence an exacerbating force in his assault. Numbed by the experience, speechless, I turned and began walking slowly home alone, my mind reeling, my heart flooded with emotions too diverse and confusing to make clear sense of anything I was feeling. The only thing I understood for sure was that Jake's life had become violent and dangerous, and I had no idea where that was leading him—or *any* of us in the family.

Chapter Seven

A Secret

"No one can ever know about this, Lydia," he whispered. It was dark and quiet, the others long ago asleep, she herself awakened to the darkness by his body slipping in next to her beneath the covers, his fingers lightly searching out and tracing the furrows of her innominate softness. "You know that, don't you?"

She nodded.

"No one would understand."

She knew that too, for she did not understand either except that he said it helped him, and even through the confusion over rectitude which swelled her young heart to the point of bursting she saw that to help him—whom she wanted to help; who drove away her terror, her creatures; whose own creatures were incomprehensible to her although she understood his need to be free of them—she must keep quiet, she must submit to what he asked and keep quiet.

"It will always be our secret," he whispered, and she nodded again, sensing the truth of his words more profoundly than he could ever have guessed since there was no one she could tell even if she wanted to. She could feel her eyes welling with tears in the darkness.

It would always be their secret.

Chapter Eight

Separation

After moving up to the senior high school in tenth grade, where I had even less contact with Jake than before, Bucky Fulton informed me with unmitigated admiration that Jake was getting laid by some sleazy ninth grade girl. Bucky could offer no convincing proof, but even the rumor of it confirmed my sense of Jake moving irrevocably away from the rest of us in the family into his own grim and frightening world. To imagine Jake rutting in some darkened alley with a girl grown whorish before her childhood years had ended was shocking enough to whatever Catholic sensibilities remained in me, but to envision also—as I could not help myself from doing—her possibly diseased flesh and Jake not only touching it but entering into it made me cringe inside. I had no way of ultimately confirming or denying Bucky's story, but the truth of it struck me with a sort of visceral certainty.

By this point my own path in life was becoming more defined all the time. I was in upper level college prep classes, a course of study which resulted not so much from choice as from a kind of invisible set of expectations—an ineluctable momentum generated by the entire system of school, parents, and community—which herded me and all of my friends through courses such as Latin or French that we professed to despise. Mine were the ilk who joined the track team in the fall, the ski team in the winter, and the golf team in the spring, who became members of the debate team or the student council or the French Club, who belonged to enough groups and amassed enough extra-curricular activities to impress even the most jaded and selective college admissions officers. We were the ones who would join the anti-war, anti-establishment, anti-materialism forces in the country and years later trade in the bandanas, patched jeans and VW bugs for Vuarnet sunglasses and Volvos. Yet in our midst—or perhaps it was the other way around, perhaps we were in *their* midst—was an entire underclass whom we never noticed despite their populating the same hallways of the same school, kids deprived of life's opportunities through the inheritance of ignorance or poverty or violence or plain bad luck, indistinguishable beings tracked into a future of obscurity and failure by those same invisible forces that tracked us into college. It was within this shadowy underworld that Jake had somehow learned to move about most freely.

Ben, on the other hand, was becoming quite an accomplished athlete in the clean-cut, mainstream world of sports. He had never been more than a slightly better than average student, but by seventh grade his reputation as a prodigy in baseball and basketball had already preceded him to the junior high school. Whatever stain Jake might have cast upon the family name through his fighting was more than washed clean by Ben's presence on the sports teams. Bucky told me he had seen *The Dick* in the hallway one time smiling and talking to Ben, who was backed up against the wall and fidgeting as if he was afraid *The Dick* would "slap a make on him right there." Ben was one of those kids whose athletic talents and general optimism, whose unreflective enjoyment of life—seasoned with just enough caustic wit to protect him from the label of "stupid jock"—made it easy for people to like him.

Since her pneumonia, however, Lydia had grown more chronically sick and dependent on the family, especially Mother, than ever before. Early in the fall she suffered another sudden, violent coughing attack in school one day. The teacher, in a panic, called the school nurse, who went to the classroom immediately and was able to calm Lydia, but Lydia had to leave school and remain in bed at home for a couple of days.

During that time Mother took her in to see her regular pediatrician, who immediately suspected asthma and suggested testing to see if it might be caused by allergies. Mother and Father were shocked to think their little girl might be asthmatic but decided the prudent thing was to find out once and for all what was bedeviling her, so they took Lydia to the hospital to have her pricked and scratched with antigens. The tests were generally inconclusive but indicated she might be having at least a mild reaction to things like dust and animal dander.

In those days we had a cat, Caesar, so named by Mother because she realized not long after taking him in that he acted with imperious disregard for petting. When he showed up on the doorstep a few days before Jake was born, apparently abandoned by someone, he was a fuzzy little ball of entirely black fur. Mother didn't have the heart to send him to a shelter, and keeping him as a family pet seemed like an excellent idea: he would make a wonderful companion for the new baby. It turned out that not only was Caesar stingy with his affections, but as Jake made his way through infancy and toddlerhood he tormented Caesar incessantly by chasing him about the house and pulling on his tail. It didn't matter that Jake received scratches and bites for his reign of terror—he was relentless. Caesar grew so fearful of his intended lifetime companion that he bolted away whenever he saw Jake. It was only when Lydia was born a few years later that Caesar deigned to allow someone to touch him, someone he did not also have to fear. It was as though he had been waiting for a female child before he would bestow—or allow to be bestowed upon him—any affection, because in truth Lydia was the only one in the family who cared a whit about that cat. Even though Mother knew how much Caesar meant to Lydia, I think she was secretly pleased when the doctor told her it would be a good idea to eliminate from the household any pets or feather pillows or wool blankets or any other objects that might contain the kind of antigens presumably causing Lydia's attacks.

Caesar was quite old and nearly blind by this time, and generally more crotchety than ever before with everyone but Lydia. He had lost control of his bladder and leaked spots of cat piss wherever he curled up to sleep. Lydia, of course, saw no need to part with him. She put up a terrific fight to keep Caesar at home, alive, but Mother would not give in this time. I'm sure she remembered all too well how she had given in to Lydia on a matter of health once before with disastrous results. She would not make that mistake again no matter how much Lydia cried or argued about it. Caesar would be taken to an animal shelter and that was all there was to it.

"Don't you care whether he lives or dies?" Lydia screamed at Mother. "They'll kill him there, you know they will."

"I care more about you, Lydia," Mother said. "I'm sorry." That was the end of Caesar.

Unfortunately, it was not the end of Mother's battles against Lydia's illness. She waged a relentless campaign to learn as much as possible about asthma: she bought medical textbooks like *Gray's Anatomy*, which became a fixture on the living room coffee table; she went to the library frequently and mailed away for pamphlets; she called Lydia's pediatrician whenever she couldn't answer questions through her own research, and if he couldn't answer them she would press for the name of a specialist who could.

As a result she grew fanatical about keeping the house clean—vacuumed and dusted every day, often more than once. When the weather was good she made us take off our shoes on the throw rug inside the door; when the weather was bad we had to take them off before we could even enter the house. Either way, she shook out that rug at least twice a day.

One weekend, armed with oversized bottles of ammonia, Mr. Clean, and an almost frightening array of pails, sponges, and bristle brushes, she tore through the house on a cleaning rampage that left no corner or closet of the house unmolested by the scourge of her reddened fingers. She even scoured the walls. And all during this assault against the invisible enemy within—those heinous antigens that preyed upon her little girl—Mother threw out anything that might have mildewed or gone moldy, anything that could conceivably have been a repository of animal dander or dust, even items we never thought she could part with. Like a terrible avenger she cast off dolls that were heirlooms from her grandmother, stuffed animals, feather pillows and even, to Lydia's horror, the infamous First Communion dress.

"Mother, what are you *doing*?" Lydia said when she saw what was happening.

Mother had a black plastic garbage bag next to her and was hunched over a lidless box of clothes in the hall closet where we used to find Caesar, if the closet door had been left open, curled asleep atop the clothes, his shining ebony coat a striking visual contrast to the uppermost article of clothing upon which he rested—Lydia's First Communion dress.

"I'm trying to make this house safe for *you*, Lydia. So I'm getting rid of anything that might cause an asthma attack."

"But I don't *want* you to get rid of my dress. I don't *care* if I have asthma attacks. *Just don't get rid of my dress.*"

"But look at it, Lydia. It's covered with Caesar's hairs, it's stained, it smells—it's a mess."

"You can just wash it then," Lydia said, her voice quavering, tears welling up in her eyes.

"Sweetheart, you'll never wear this dress again."

"But I can *pretend*," Lydia insisted. "I can pretend it's my wedding dress. Or I can wear it for Halloween and pretend I'm Glinda, the Good Witch of the North."

Mother shook her head sadly. "Lydia, honey, the dress doesn't even fit you anymore. Why don't we wash it and try to spruce it up a little and give it to the Salvation Army? That way maybe some poor little girl who isn't as lucky as you are can get some use from it."

"It does too fit me!" Lydia shouted. "I'll put it on right now and show you."

She began tugging violently at the dress that Mother held in her hands.

"Lydia, please stop," Mother said. "You'll rip it." She did not raise her voice but neither did she let go of the dress; her grip tightened as Lydia pulled harder.

"I want it!" Lydia shrieked, yanking at the dress and wildly jerking it from side to side. "It's mine, let me have it!" With her left hand still on the dress, she began clawing at Mother's hands and arms with her right hand like some ferocious little animal.

"Stop it, Lydia," Mother cried, but with one final, two-handed attempt to wrench the dress free Lydia tore it from the neckline to the hem.

For a moment they froze, each looking at the other while still holding onto a torn portion of the dress. It was as if the sound of the dress tearing—a sound at once portentous and ludicrous—had left them not quite sure how to respond, whether to laugh or cry.

It was Mother who spoke first as she took back the ruined garment from Lydia's suddenly unresisting hands. "Look what you've done," she said sadly, turning the dress this way and that. "Now no one will be able to use it."

Lydia gazed at her own empty hands for a moment, then fixed Mother with a terrible look. "I hate you! I hate you!" she shouted, then wheeled and fled upstairs to her room.

Lydia spent such an inordinate amount of time indoors that reading became an obsession with her, which is probably why she excelled in school. One night at the dinner table when Father asked her how school was going, she boasted, "I'm the best reader in the second grade!" It was not an idle boast. Halfway through second grade Lydia was reading at fifth grade level, and her teacher, Mrs. Albright, called Mother in for a conference to discuss having Lydia skip a grade. She had already read everything in Mrs. Albright's second grade library more than once, and to keep her interested Mrs. Albright was having Lydia read books from the school library or—Mrs. Albright found this remarkable—*write her own stories,* which Lydia really seemed to enjoy and which were far more sophisticated than anything her classmates were capable of writing. Lydia's spelling was superb (100's on all spelling tests, always the winner in spelling bees), and even her math—which Lydia said she did not like—was quite advanced. Mrs. Albright thought the idea of moving her up a grade was worth considering because Lydia might get bored if she continued in school so far ahead of her peers.

After hearing all of this Father grew excited and argued that Lydia should not be held back, which in effect was what they would be doing if they did not follow Mrs. Albright's advice. He wanted Lydia—just as he wanted for all of his children—to go at her own pace, however fast or slow it might be. The important thing was to keep her interested, challenged, excited about learning. Mother believed that having Lydia skip third grade altogether was not a good idea. She conceded it might be more beneficial intellectually for Lydia to leap ahead, but emotionally it might not be. Lydia was small for her age, and to put her in with kids who were not only a year older but also physically bigger and more mature seemed to her a serious mistake. Mother did not want to call more attention to Lydia than necessary. Placing her in a situation where she was unmistakably different from everyone else in the class would single her out, and kids could be cruel. They might make fun of her, call her names, ostracize her. In the long run it might be more damaging to Lydia, even intellectually, to be treated as an outcast—or worse, as a freak—in an advanced class than to be treated as a prodigy amongst her peers. Also, Mother believed it was not only possible but obligatory for the child's family to provide what the school could not. In this respect, although certainly not in most respects politically, Mother was a diehard New Hampshire Yankee. She believed in taking care of her own.

At the time, Lydia knew nothing of these adult conversations regarding her fate. None of the rest of us kids knew anything either. In fact, much of what I know of the past I've learned only in recent years through conversations with Mother, who, searching herself ruthlessly for answers, cannot help from recalling certain memories and asking for my opinion. Her telling and retelling of particular stories reminds me of the way—at home, seated in the overstuffed chair in which she and Lydia were so often curled up; or kneeling in the front pew of the church, to which I must now drive her—her fingers relentlessly turn the dark beads of her rosary. I know what she is searching for. In one way or another she often asks me. It is the same thing I am after myself. But I have no answers. I can offer no salvation.

Eventually, Mother convinced Father that the best alternative was for Lydia to stay right where she was in school. Mother would work with Lydia at home to make sure she was being challenged and also work closely with Lydia's teacher to plan an effective strategy and monitor her progress. To my knowledge, Lydia never once complained of school, which makes it difficult to accept Mother's retrospective misgivings. Whenever she asks, "What do you think, Virgil, should we have allowed her to skip a grade? Do you think she felt held back?" I bristle a little and say, "Mom, she loved everything about school. Don't torment yourself."

She especially loved reading and writing. By the time I got home from school she would be hard at work with pen or pencil in hand, or so absorbed in a book that she would hardly look up when I said hello. Often she would be working with Mother at the kitchen table, but many times she would be lying prone on the oriental rug in the living room, her face about three inches above the open pages of a book. Or she would be sitting on the couch, knee-socked legs drawn close to her chest to prop up the black and white speckled notebook in which she kept her "secret diary." She started keeping a diary at a young age and filled up many volumes over the years, but unfortunately none of them remain. She was always covetous of their secrecy, and must have taken them with her when she made that fateful trip, years later, to visit Jake.

One of her favorite books was *Charlotte's Web*. I remember coming home from a high school golf team practice one day on a warm, sunny spring afternoon and finding her curled into an almost fetal position in the overstuffed chair in the living room. Tears were streaming down her cheeks and her face was flushed.

I didn't see the book at first, or somehow didn't make the connection between the book and her tears.

"What's wrong, Lydia?" I asked as I hunched down near her, instantly concerned.

"It's so sad," she said.

"What is?"

"This book."

"Oh," I said. "What is it?"

"*Charlotte's Web.*"

I had never read it and knew nothing about it. "Why is it so sad?"

"Because she's dying."

"Who is?"

"Charlotte."

"How do you know?"

"Because I've read it before."

I resisted the urge to ask her why she was crying when she already knew what was going to happen. "Who is Charlotte?"

"A spider."

"You're crying about a dying spider?" I said. I could imagine someone like Donny Fletcher observing what happened each time he plucked a leg from a daddy longlegs. I had probably even done the same thing myself as a young boy. "Why?"

"Because she does so much for Wilbur. She saves his life, and when she dies, she's all alone. Nobody knows what she's done except Wilbur, and even he doesn't really understand."

"Who is Wilbur?"

"He's the pig she saves by weaving her webs into words."

"A spider named Charlotte saves a pig named Wilbur by weaving webs into words?"

My baffled tone must have sounded too flip to her, because she quickly retorted, "Leave me alone, Virgil. You're wrecking it."

"I'm sorry," I said, "It just sounds sort of funny when you don't know what the story is about." I tried to make amends by peering over her shoulder to read along with her, but she would have none of that.

"Go away," she said. "I want to finish it by myself."

"I just wanted to understand, Lydia. I wasn't trying to hurt your feelings."

"Well you can't just read the end," she said, not about to let me off the hook so easily. "If you want to read it, you'll have to wait until I'm done and read the whole book yourself."

"I *have* read the book, Lydia," I want to tell her now. "And it's a wonderful book." But so long after all that has happened, I know that too would sound foolish and patronizing to her.

Mother saved all the stories and poems Lydia wrote. Even the earliest ones, dating back to second grade, show remarkable sensitivity, imagination and flair for language. And Lydia did not write about the subjects one might expect from an eight or nine year old girl—no dolls or birthday parties or Christmas presents for her. Instead she wrote about *words:*

> I like the way words trip out of your mouth sometimes,
> Like an accident, or a fall;

or *chickadees:*

> Chickadees are the bravest birds of all
> Because even though they are very, very small,
> They stay with us through the whole year,
> Through winter, spring, summer and fall;

or *shadows:*

They dance around the room at night,
With hopes of giving a terrible fright,
But they cannot live without a light,
So I flip the switch and say, "Good night…"
And "Good riddance!"

When she was a bit older she wrote a sort of cautionary tale called "Snowstorm" that describes snow falling worldwide day after day, "relentlessly and mercilessly," until the whole world is buried beneath so much snow that people can no longer breathe and everyone finally dies. And the snow keeps falling even beyond that, until the entire world is white, so that someone gazing from space would see nothing but a pure white ball. Then after eons the snows melt, people come back onto the earth, and this time they take care of it and are good to each other. There is no more pollution and no more war.

Just after Jake left for Vietnam Lydia wrote a poem called "Separation." It is a poem I have read again and again until I know it by heart:

Separation

My brother is gone to Vietnam and I don't know what I'll do.
He is gone to fight for his country, his home and family too.

He says he will come back to see us again.
He says he is not sure when.

But I am afraid of where he is going.
For I have no way of knowing
What will happen to him.

Before he left he said he would write.
But will he?
I can't be sure.
I'm afraid he will die first in a fight.

I pray to God for him every night,
Because my brother is brave and good.
But even the brave and the good, I fear,
May die before they should.

I will not rest at all even if I could,
Not until my brother returns, safe with us back here.

The poem is achingly beautiful to me, not because I share Lydia's naive faith in Jake's motives, her sense of him as an intrepid hero, but because of her fear and doubt... and her love. I envied Jake for that poem—for Lydia's uneasiness, her sense of foreboding, her loyalty to him and her implacable, tunnel-visioned concern about his fate. "My brother is gone to Vietnam..." *It was as though she had only one brother.*

Jake enlisted in the military during my freshman year of college. He turned eighteen in February and signed up shortly afterwards. He did not even finish his senior year of high school.

When Father found out sometime in January of 1970 what Jake was planning to do, he telephoned me at school and asked me to come home to talk with Jake. As always, I told him I would try my best but that I'd never had much luck in convincing Jake of anything. He already knew this, of course, but I could tell he was desperate.

A drizzly freezing rain was falling when Father picked me up at my dorm, and he had to drive so slowly that the normal hour ride home must have taken us two hours. He kept his eyes glued to the road as he told me about his conversation with Jake.

"He just came up to me one night last week and said, 'I'm signing up with the Marines when I turn eighteen. I thought you'd want to know.'" Father shook his head in disbelief. "That's exactly the way he said it, too, as if he was telling me he was taking the car out to get gas and he'd be right back. Can you believe it?"

There were melted drops of freezing rain glistening in Father's thick dark hair like limpid jewels. Inexplicably they filled me with a sudden, poignant awareness of Father's mortality, of his frailty as a human being who—even though he was my father—possessed no more protection against loss and sorrow, no greater assurance of invulnerability, no finer or more divine understanding of life's enigmas and absurdities than I or anyone else in this world possessed. The realization swelled me with such an intense sympathy for him—such love and disappointment all jumbled together—that I could not say a word.

"My mouth must have dropped to the floor at that point," Father continued, "but I finally gathered my wits and said, 'Jake, why in God's name would you want to do that?'

"'Somebody's got to do it,' he said.

"'Got to do what?' I asked him.

"'Defend this country,' he said.

"'Against what?' I said.

"'Against communism,' he said.

"'My God, Jake,' I said, 'do you really believe all those damned lies? The Vietnamese people don't want us there. Who are we to decide what kind of government they should have?'"

"What did he say to that?" I asked.

Father turned up the defroster fan because freezing rain was beginning to congeal on the windshield wherever the wiper blades didn't reach. "He called me a hypocrite because I work in the defense industry and I'm arguing against the war on communism."

"So how did you counter that?" I asked, wondering about it myself.

"I told him that working toward the legitimate defense of this country is one thing, but fighting an offensive war against people who don't want us there is another thing altogether."

"Then what did he say?"

"Nothing. So I told him none of us wanted to see him die, not ever, but certainly not in a war that's wrong and that will probably be over soon anyway. I tried to get him to see how dangerous it is, how brutal, how war isn't anything like what the movies show, especially not this war. None of it seemed to make even the slightest impression on him."

"Has Mom talked to him at all about it?" I asked.

"No, but she feels the same way. We talked about all this before *you* turned eighteen."

I wasn't as sure as he was about Mother, so I said nothing.

"What are your thoughts?" he finally asked. "All of a sudden you're very quiet."

"I don't think there's much I can say to Jake that you haven't already said. He's a very stubborn, private person."

Father sat stiff and erect behind the wheel, leaning forward a little to peer through the windshield and never taking his eyes from the road. "Why does he want to do this?"

It was silent in the car except for the sound of the defroster's struggle against the elements and the metronomic click of the windshield wipers.

"I don't know," I said at last. "I haven't understood Jake for a long time now."

Father thought about this for a moment. "Why is that, I wonder?" I thought he meant my lack of understanding, until he said, "I mean, what makes a child so remote, so unfathomable?"

The question hung there between us, resonating, but I did not want to attempt an answer.

"What did Mom say when you told her about Jake?" I managed to venture after a while.

"She was upset, of course, but she said he's always been different from the rest of you, always someone who keeps to himself. Even as a baby he never wanted to be picked up, never wanted anyone's help or interference. She seems to have a better handle on him than I do … or at least accepts him more for who he is."

"Do you think she'll try to convince him not to do it?"

"I don't know," Father said. "I expect she'll talk with him, but I think as soon as I told her about it she began resigning herself to the fact that Jake will do what he wants."

"What about Ben and Lydia. Do they know anything about it?"

"Ben does. I've talked with him already. But I don't think Lydia does. I haven't wanted to upset her until the waters clear. I for one haven't accepted Jake's enlisting as a certainty yet. That's why I asked you to come home. Maybe together we can get him to listen to reason."

I didn't say anything then, but I remember thinking all during the ride home afterwards, *Dad, you'd* better *start accepting it as a certainty, because Jake's as good as gone already.*

That night we asked Mother if she wanted to speak to Jake with us. She demurred, said it was a male subject and would be best for us to speak to Jake without her. She also said Lydia had suffered another severe asthma attack earlier in the day that had forced her home from school again, and Lydia really needed her attention (Lydia did not look well at all when I arrived home, but she had been very quiet and hadn't told me about the attack).

There was no answer when Father knocked on Jake's door, although in a moment we heard Jake's off-key, *a cappella* voice blurting out, "I can't *get* no"—and I knew Jake was listening to the Stones with his headphones on. The door was unlocked, so Father gently pushed it open and said, "Do you mind if we come in for a minute, Jake?"

Jake shrugged, and Father stepped aside for me to enter first before closing the door behind him. A small pink cone of incense burned on the night table next to Jake's bed and sent a thin stream of smoke up into the air, filling the room with its cloying sweet scent and masking the faint trace of the other scent, the one that I—and most of my generation—knew well but that Father probably wouldn't have detected.

Jake had begun to grow a mustache and goatee since the last time I'd seen him a couple of weeks earlier. They were the only two areas of his face where anything darker than peach fuzz sprouted. His light brown hair was as long and shaggy as it had ever been. Behind him on the wall was a huge day-glo poster of Mick Jagger with his tongue sticking out.

"What are you listening to, Jake?" I asked.

"*Aftermath.*" I'd already noticed the album cover clearly visible next to him on the bed.

"An oldie but goodie, huh?"

"The Stones are still the best," he said. Then he looked me in the eyes and cut right to the heart of the matter the way he always did. "How come you're home again so soon, Ace?"

Father answered before I could. "I asked him to come home, Jake. I thought we should talk some more about your decision to enlist."

"There's nothing to talk about," Jake said. He was reclining against the headboard of the bed, the headphones circling his neck and emitting a steady but muted stream of sound. There were no chairs in the room so Father and I stood there looking down on him, his gaze at once impassive and defiant. I felt as though we were inquisitors intent not on asking questions but on compelling the heretic, backed into the corner, to accede to our righteous demands. With only a few feet separating us and without his having traveled anywhere yet, Jake already seemed an immeasurable distance away.

"I thought it might be a good idea for you to at least talk with Virgil about school," Father said. "I know your grades haven't been all that great and it might be difficult for you to get into a school, but before you make a decision you might regret for the rest of your life, or that might even *end* your life, God forbid, I think you should consider the alternatives. Virgil has only been away for one semester but I'm sure he can tell you a little about what you could expect."

"This is pointless, Dad," Jake said. "I've made up my mind. I'm not interested in school."

"Just listen for a minute, Jake, will you?" Father said. "That's all I ask. Just listen for a minute. Go ahead, Virgil."

Father had taken me completely by surprise. I had known, of course, that he wanted me to try to persuade Jake not to enlist, but I had expected to be talking about how many men—boys, really—had died, how corrupt the Thieu regime was, how much mendacity existed in American policy in Vietnam in general and in Richard Nixon in particular. When it became clear that my mission was to present the merits of school to Jake, who had never shown any interest in school at all, I found myself suddenly tongue-tied.

"Um—" I stumbled.

"Don't bother, Virgil. It won't make any difference anyway," Jake said.

"Well…the thing is, Jake, I don't know if you're thinking you might as well join because you could be drafted anyway, but if you go to school you can get a deferment—I'm sure you know that already—and the war will probably be over by the time the deferment has ended."

"I'm not looking for a way out, I'm looking for a way in."

"But *why*, Jake?" Father interjected. "That's what I just don't understand. What would make you *want* to go to Vietnam?"

Jake just looked at Father without saying a word. The silence was uncomfortable.

"Jake, you like Hendrix, right?" I said, suddenly inspired by a new tack. Listening to and enjoying Jimi's music was one of the few things Jake and I had shared in high school. We had even gone together to see him in a concert once. "He served in the army. Did you know that?"

Jake shook his head.

"You know that version of the Star Spangled Banner he plays, the one with all the sounds of bombs dropping and exploding? Well it's about Vietnam. He hates the war. You listen to the lyrics of his songs—'Purple Haze,' 'Manic Depression,' 'Come in from the Storm'—they're about being really fucked up by war—excuse me, Dad, but it's true."

"He served his country, though, didn't he?" Jake said.

"Yeah," I said, beginning to heat up, "but he hated the army. He was dishonorably discharged from it. And he hates the war because it really screws people up. Look what happened to Calley and those guys at My Lai. Why do you want to do that to yourself?"

"Everybody's screwed up," Jake said.

"Jesus, Jake, you could be *dead* screwed up if you go over there, and what's the point?"

"I'm gonna die sometime anyway. I could be dead on the highway tomorrow."

"I don't believe this," I said, shaking my head. "You're not making any sense, Jake."

"Tell me what does make sense, Ace. You've been a good, sensible boy all your life. Does it make sense to run away like a coward?"

"Nobody's running away."

"Then why do all you college boys get to stay out of the war? Why don't you go to jail?"

"Because I'm not about to get raped in prison because I don't believe in killing people."

Jake didn't say a word then. He just looked at me.

"Shit," I said, and threw my hands up in the air. "I don't know what to say to him, Dad."

"Don't say anything. I didn't ask you to come in here."

"Jake," Father said quietly, "what about the rest of us? Have you thought about that? How do you think your mother and I feel? You're our son. We don't want to see you die, or come back all 'screwed up,' as Virgil was saying. And what about your brothers and sister? Don't you think they'll be worrying about you all the time, too? This is a family, a close family. We're all affected by what happens to any one of us. Surely you can understand that."

"Yeah, but it's my life, Dad. I can't live it for everybody else."

"Oh, Jake," Father said, shaking his head sadly. His voice was beginning to crack. "Yes, it's your life, but you can't just throw it away like this." Father opened the door then and said, before he left, "Just promise me one thing, Jake."

"What's that?" Jake said.

"Promise me you'll think about the rest of us before you make a final decision, okay?"

Jake nodded and put the headphones back over his ears. I left with Father.

That night before going to sleep, while lying on our beds in the darkness, Ben and I talked a little about Jake's plans to go to Vietnam. "I wonder how Lydia will take it when she finds out," I mused aloud.

"She already knows," Ben said.

"What do you mean? Who told her?"

"I did this morning, before we went to school. I didn't realize no one had told her anything and I just happened to say something about Jake going into the Marines."

"Didn't Dad tell you not to say anything to her?"

"He might have. I don't remember."

"Jesus, Ben, you're a big fucking help." I remembered with sudden and forceful clarity that Lydia had had a serious asthma attack at school earlier in the day.

"What's the big deal? She had to find out sometime."

"Not from you."

"What's the difference?"

"Forget it. It's not worth arguing about."

After a moment Ben said, "I wonder if he'll have to kill anybody."

I had been thinking the opposite way, not what he might do to others but what others might do to him. I had been thinking about boot camp and all the horror stories I had read and heard about its power to dehumanize, and booby traps and steamy jungles with ticks crawling everywhere and faceless, half-crazed Viet Cong waiting in ambush to slit his throat. There was a certain lunatic courage in Jake that gave me, against all sense and rationality, a peculiar admiration for him and made me just a little uncomfortable with myself. I couldn't imagine being able to endure what Jake would have to endure, and I couldn't even begin to fathom why he would *want* to put himself through such a hell.

"I don't know, Ben," I said finally. "Maybe he'll decide not to enlist after all."

But true to his word and the unflinching, intractable nature of his will, as soon as he turned eighteen Jake quit school, enlisted in the Marines and shipped off to boot camp at Parris Island. In eight weeks he wrote perhaps two letters home—about such general and unrevealing subjects as the weather and the mess hall food. For Lydia, on the other hand, Jake's enlistment precipitated a frenzied letter-writing campaign which, over the course of Jake's military service, probably did more for her literary development than all the books she read.

One day while Jake was at boot camp I asked Mother about his enlistment. She was sitting in the living room with her feet up on a hassock, flipping through an issue of *Better Homes and Gardens* in what was, for her, a rare moment of relaxation.

I was home from college early because protests against the war had forced the university to close weeks ahead of schedule. I suppose I caught her off guard when I asked her point blank if she had tried to talk to Jake about his enlisting. She gave a quick glance up from her magazine to say "No," but I noticed her outstretched legs tensing up on the hassock.

"Why didn't you talk with him?" I asked. She wouldn't look at me—which was unusual because Mother had always seemed confident and self-assured to me, someone who rarely backed down from anyone or anything (in this respect, ironically, Jake was much like her).

"Jake has always gone his own way," she said, flipping pages and gazing steadfastly into her magazine. "I knew as soon as I heard his plans there would be no changing his mind."

"You wouldn't have treated any of the rest of us that way," I said, treading on ground I had never been on with her. I did not know what to expect, but I had come home from school with a head of long, bushy dark hair, a belief in the need to take "existential leaps" into the unknown (along with a grab bag of dictums: "seize the day"; "not to decide is to decide"; "not to act is to act"), and the brash confidence of a nineteen year old who in 1970 had just completed his freshman year of college. I wanted answers, or at least I thought I did.

"Jake is not like the rest of you," she said, without looking up from the magazine.

"What makes you say that?"

"Because the rest of you need coddling. Jake doesn't, and never has."

"Oh, and I suppose you think I still need 'coddling'?"

"Of course you do, Virgil." Mother had not looked up yet, although I noticed the tension dissolving as she refolded her legs comfortably on the hassock. She appeared to have found something engrossing to read in her magazine.

"But Jake doesn't, so it's okay for him to go to Vietnam," I said, trying to regain my footing on this shifting, unexpectedly slippery ground. "Jake knows what he wants—which just happens to be killing or being killed—so he doesn't need any advice or 'coddling.'"

"Whatever I might have said or done would have made absolutely no impression on Jake," Mother said, in a voice that would clearly brook no argument. She was looking straight at me now. "It never did before, and it wouldn't have in this situation. So why torment myself that way? Of course I don't want him to go to Vietnam. He's my son. But Jake will do what Jake will do. That's the way he's always been. There's nothing I can do to change it."

When she finished speaking she continued to look at me without any apparent heat or anger, almost patiently, as though she were waiting for my dull brain to catch up. Behind her, the grandfather clock began chiming eleven times. I stood there speechless, struck dumb by the knowledge that even as I searched for ways to refute what she'd said, I mostly agreed with her.

Then she turned her attention to the magazine again and said, "There's an interesting article here about ways to protect your roses from Japanese beetles."

Whatever advantage the element of surprise had given me at first had now disappeared completely. Mother was in total control of herself again, while I, having been routed from what I thought was the moral high ground, felt myself in inexplicable retreat.

Jake came home on leave for a time after boot camp. I hadn't found a job yet, so I was in a routine of sleeping late and soaking up the sun in the back yard. The weather was abnormally hot for a spring day and all I had on was a pair of cutoff jeans, but I was still sweating profusely as I lay on a chaise lounge reading *The Armies of the Night*. My hair was tied back in a pony tail, and in those days I wore granny glasses—nothing unusual by the standards of the world I had been living in for the previous eight months, a world of ponytails and Afros, of bandannas and patched, motley clothing, of young men with unkempt facial hair and bra-less young women with hairy legs and armpits; it was a world where questioning authority was the standing order of the day, where traditions were held in contempt and institutions dismantled, where ROTC—"rotsee"— was a force of pure malevolence, and where nothing could be accepted at face value, especially nothing involving the U.S. military.

So when Lydia began shouting, "Virgil, Jake's home! Jake's home!" and Jake, rounding the corner of the house, walked towards me in full sunlight, it came as a shock. Here was my brother sharply dressed in uniform, his shoes shining in the sun, his head shaved beneath his cap. The wispy facial hair he had grown not so long ago was completely gone. His face was tanned and there was a whitish scar just below the corner of his left eye. If it hadn't been for the familiarity of those blue eyes, I would not have recognized him, even here at home.

We shook hands, and his hand felt dry and calloused. His steely grip was so tight that within it my own sweaty hand seemed as weak and soft as a small animal caught in a trap.

"How are you, Jake?"

"All right, Ace. How are you?"

"Okay, okay," I said, unable to shake the sense that a stranger stood before me. It was not just the shaved head, though, that dramatically altered my sense of Jake. It was also the associated images that abruptly appeared in my mind's eye— the tonsured Buddhist monk who had immolated himself in the streets of Saigon, the wacked-out Hare Krishnas that accosted me on campus and in airports—and the odd bumps and depressions of Jake's skull that should have been hidden by hair. And it was the fact that somehow my gaze was drawn more unerringly than ever before to those icy blue eyes of his, which had a way of boring into you with such riveting force that you could not look away. "What happened to your eye?" I asked.

"Just had to have a few stitches."

His eyes revealed nothing and he offered no further explanation.

"Jake might not have to go to Vietnam," Lydia blurted cheerfully. She had gone with Father to pick him up at the airport and was standing beside him now, looking up at him. Mother had gone to Ben's baseball game.

"Is that right?" I said.

"It's possible," Jake said. "Right now they're trying to cut down on troops over there so my orders are to stay stateside, but I'm trying to get that changed."

"Don't, Jake," Lydia said. "We don't want you to go. Right, Virgil?"

I did not want to rehash old arguments so I merely nodded. "How was boot camp? Was it as bad as everyone makes it out to be?"

A faint smile curled out from the corner of his lips. "Nah, it wasn't so bad."

My face must have betrayed some form of skepticism as I reexamined his shorn head, because the smile on his lips widened. He ran a hand along the side of his head in an affected manner and said, "You like my new style?" There was a kind of leer in his expression.

Jake had always been curt and uncommunicative, but never arrogant. Something new was revealing itself here that I did not like at all.

"What did they do to you, Jake?"

"Hah!" he laughed. "They like to think they made a man of me."

"I think they're right," said Father, who had been standing nearby all along. "Anyone who can stand out here in uniform in this sun without being drenched in sweat has to have something going for him. Come on, let's go inside and get a cool drink."

Jake turned to Father and said with a laugh, "This is nothing compared to where I just came from." Then he shot a look at me, sweating in my semi-nakedness, and said, "And it's nowhere near as hot as where I'm going."

In that moment, as I looked into Jake's cold blue eyes and saw something flash there, I thought I had the answer to the question I had just posed to him. Father may have been right—they may have made a man of him as Jake had so facetiously suggested. But from where I stood they had done something else to him as well: they had made him a killer.

Eventually Jake did get himself shipped over to Vietnam, and as with boot camp, he hardly ever wrote letters. When he did, they were short, with virtually nothing in them for us to grab hold of. Except once. That letter ended with the words, "Cong firing—will write again." Below this last line his name was partially obscured by a rust-colored blotch which we all assumed was a drop of dried blood. By the time we received the letter we knew that if anything serious had happened to him we would already have known about it, but the unintended closing served to remind us, perhaps more forcefully than anything Jake might have written, that while our lives progressed as usual, his was in constant danger.

Still, if not for Lydia it might almost have seemed, with the passing of time, as though Jake no longer existed. It was Lydia who thought of getting a map of Vietnam to check on place names mentioned in the news. "Look, Quang Tri!" she might exclaim while the rest of us were finishing up dinner. "Here it is on the map. "It was Lydia who made sure we gathered in the living room when Father turned on the evening news each night. "Come on, Ben, come on, Virgil, the news is about to start," she would say. And it was Lydia who wrote to Jake most faithfully. She was always writing to him, it seemed, and always admonishing the rest of us for not writing more often. "How would you like it if you were ten thousand miles away from home and people were shooting at you and your own brother didn't write to you, Ben?"

Summer came and I took a job with a furniture moving company. I learned (or perhaps I should say I was humiliated into learning) from that job how to drink coffee without three teaspoons of sugar and how to drink beer at any time of day under any circumstances. I learned how to sit in the cab between a drunken truck driver and an ex-con with a switchblade and pretend that leaning out of windows to ogle bra-less females and to hoot vulgarities at them was just about the most natural thing a man could do. In the evenings I got together with college friends who held equally menial summer jobs—in factories or on construction crews—and we went out to pubs to drink more beer, or drank beer as we cruised around town and listened to music cranked up on the car stereo: Deep Purple, Led Zeppelin, Jimi Hendrix, The Allman Brothers. We almost never talked about Vietnam. Vietnam was on the other side of the world, we did not have to worry about going there, and the war was probably going to be over soon anyway. It made infinitely more sense to talk about getting wasted on booze or dope, or relationships with hot chicks, or rock concerts, or even the latest failures of the Red Sox.

I followed the war pretty closely—much more closely than any of my friends did—because of Jake; because the seeds of interest and social responsibility planted by a couple of my high school teachers had taken root; because of the nightly family ritual of watching the evening news before dinner; and because of Lydia's ceaseless efforts to remember Jake. And although I would never have traveled to Washington or put myself in a position to be arrested, I occasionally attended anti-war protests. I thought about the war and Jake often, but mostly in the abstract. Neither possessed any sort of concrete reality in my day-to-day world. For years now Jake and I had been distant. For years now he had existed in what seemed a parallel universe possessing its own reality and its own set of rules. I could observe this universe, sometimes from what seemed close range, but I could never really touch it or be a part of it, nor could it touch me.

Ben was young enough and apolitical enough that he wouldn't have given Vietnam any thought at all if not for his brother. He had just completed his sophomore year of high school and had started the first job of his life that summer with the school's groundskeeping crew mowing lawns part-time. After an outstanding baseball season on the varsity squad, he was still deeply immersed in his final season of Babe Ruth as a member of the All-Star team playing in the state and regional championships. If he wasn't mowing lawns somewhere he was at a practice or a game. Ben's baseball activities—which involved games that many of us attended and always required someone to drop him off or pick him up—had a more direct effect on everyone and occupied more air time in family conversations than Jake's being in Vietnam.

Father was not very good about writing letters but he often talked about Jake. It fascinated me how he could rail against the war but change his tone 180° whenever he spoke of Jake. Gone were all references to Jake as a confused adolescent with mixed-up priorities. Instead, Father spoke of him now with pride: "I wonder how our warrior is doing today," he might say; or, "No matter what anyone says, it takes courage to do what Jake's doing"; or, "I have to admire Jake's loyalty and self-sacrifice—not many people have such strength of conviction these days." Still, I always had the sense that beneath the surface of pride was an undercurrent of doubt and rationalization. Father would not have tolerated anyone second-guessing Jake, but he himself seemed constantly to be searching for reasons and justifications, as though he were befuddled by it all and needed his own words to buck himself up. Even his rituals of watching the nightly news and reading *Time*, as I look back upon them, seem to have been his attempt to find order within chaos, to find answers—and perhaps a measure of relief—to what was unrelentingly inexplicable to him.

Mother, on the other hand, had little to say about Jake. Like clockwork she wrote to him for one hour every Sunday morning after she and Lydia had returned from eight o'clock Mass, but I never heard her wonder aloud, as Father and Lydia did, just what Jake might be doing or where he might be at a given moment in time, and she offered no judgments about his bravery or his moral courage the way Father did. She seemed neither troubled nor uncertain about Jake's being in Vietnam. If anything, as I consider now how many hours she spent diligently tending her roses with Lydia by her side, her white gardening gloves on her hands and a brightly colored kerchief upon her head; as I recall the way she used to sing *Que Sera, Sera* with such airy and melodious freedom; and as I reflect upon how much more energy, how much more *joie de vivre* she seemed to possess in those days as opposed to the days following Jake's attempt to run away, I can't help but think that even though his departure meant a tour in Vietnam, she was relieved somehow that Jake was gone.

Chapter Nine

Night Patrol

He could see them hanging on the wire, some without heads or arms, some without scalps, some with everything intact except that their ears had been cut off, could see them clearly although he did not know how since it was night and he was moving outside the wire: mama-sans and papa-sans and gook kids, some maybe VCs but you couldn't tell, NVAs too, hanging there like trophies and bobbing slightly as though in a breeze, a random, hollow sound like the clinking of dog tags coming from somewhere, although none of this made sense either because there was no breeze, only unmoving inescapable heat and the smell of burning human flesh, which did not leave him even after he had moved deeper into the jungle and left sight and sound behind him. Then he could feel the darkness pressing in on him heavy and thick: quiet, animate darkness in which he knew he was not alone—ubiquitous, ancient, compound-eyed darkness, life all-seeing and unseen everywhere and nowhere at once, more than a match even for him: which he had come to understand and respect and fear, his own life granted reprieve from extinction only by the absence of one brief muzzle flash which he would perhaps see but would not even have time to hear if it were aimed well enough, one small blip of light from an AK-47 which would wed him to the darkness forever. Hunter and hunted coexisted in him as he moved through the night stopping and listening, moving on again, then stopping and listening, not knowing if death awaited in motion or in motionlessness, the adrenalin of fear and of killing indistinguishable inside him, outsized gook faces suddenly springing forth from behind trees like giant jack-in-the-boxes, too near and too lurid to be real and yet grinning a murder that could not be ignored: you or him, him or it—whatever, just waste the fucker and don't ask questions, questions will kill you. Then the whining of a child somewhere behind him down low in the bushes—an infant cry of abandonment or a gook trick?—don't ask questions, don't ask questions, waste the fucker and don't ask questions. Night thickened around him into absolute obscurity, the darkness congealing so completely and so palpably it was like a living voracious thing feeding off anything visible, sucking all light and all objects of refraction, however large or near, into its enormous maw: the nebulous canopy of night sky, the murky outlines of leaves and tree trunks, the indistinct silhouette of his rifle barrel, the blackened fingers of his own hand held right before his eyes, until, seeing nothing at all and no longer certain whether his eyes were open or closed, whether or not he had somehow gone blind—he felt a sudden uncontrollable urge to create light, those blinding staccato bursts of light which issued so freely from his rifle at the press of his finger, but even as he was about to press the trigger the flickering golden aura he knew he must follow appeared in the distance before him like the will-o'-the-wisp, alluring, elusive, irresistible, the gun began to sear the flesh of his hands, and he awakened in camp to the blistering sun beating down upon him and the curious dried-flesh stink of his ear necklace.

Chapter Ten

A Hero Comes Home

After the shootings at Kent State and the closings of colleges and universities around the country, pressure to withdraw troops from Vietnam increased tremendously. As far as our family was concerned, complete withdrawal of all forces could not happen soon enough. We watched with satisfaction, albeit warily, as troop reductions and Nixon's "Vietnamization" continued through the remainder of 1970. By the end of October the weekly death toll—the most significant fact of all for us—was the lowest it had been in five years. Jake was still involved in combat, but we began to believe he just might get out of Vietnam alive.

Then we received a letter from Jake's platoon leader notifying us that Jake had been hit by shrapnel from mortar fire and had been hospitalized. During the shelling, which was very heavy, Jake showed "heroic disregard for personal safety" in helping to rescue fallen members of his platoon. As a result he was wounded himself, but he "bravely continued to aid his fallen comrades" until he lost such a significant amount of blood that he collapsed in the field and needed to be helped himself. Because of such "uncommon valor" Jake was to be awarded the Bronze Star and the Purple Heart.

The news filled us with mixed emotions. On the one hand we felt thankful and lucky: he was alive, and his wounds were not life-threatening. We felt relieved, too, that he would not be involved in combat for a while. And I believe everyone felt proud of Jake, not just for his courage—which I think we all knew he possessed—but for his willingness to help others, to sacrifice himself. Reading the letter sent chills along my spine. Jake had done something for other human beings that I didn't know if I had the inner strength to do myself, and I found it a humbling thing to realize.

Even Mother, although she did not say much, smiled when she read the letter, and I saw her rereading it later on in a quiet moment when she must have thought she was by herself. Father and Lydia were thrilled, of course, and often boasted about having a hero in the family. Lydia was so inspired that shortly after we got the news she wrote another poem about Jake—"The Hero"—which she promptly mailed off to him. She told us that in school her teacher asked her to stand up and read it to the class, and although she was afraid at first to get up in front of all her classmates, she remembered how brave Jake had been and decided the little bit of courage required of her to read the poem aloud was the least she could do for him.

On the other hand, as proud as we all were, we were also angry that Jake had been wounded at all. The war was winding down, and virtually everyone agreed we were no longer trying to win it. The anger turned to shock—and then outrage—when Jake wrote to inform us he would be heading back to combat as soon as he finished recovering in the hospital.

During the summer of 1971 I was in a pub late one night drinking beer and eating peanuts with some friends. About twenty minutes before last call a guy in a wheelchair came in, a skinny guy with long, thin scraggly hair. Both of his legs were missing from above the knee. He looked familiar, but he also looked quite a bit older than the person I had in mind.

"Bucky?" I said.

The guy turned his head. "Virgil! Hey, how you doing, Virgil. It's good to see you."

I left my friends and went over to shake hands.

Bucky was one of those people who could never seem to catch a break. He had always struggled in school, so college was not really an option for him. Then he pulled a low number in the lottery and was drafted right after Jake went into the Marines. I'd heard about all this even though Bucky's family had moved from our street, but I hadn't seen Bucky in a couple of years and had no idea that he'd lost his legs.

"I wasn't sure it was you at first," I said, and immediately felt stupid for saying it. "It's been a long time."

"Things change, don't they?"

Bucky was waiting in front of the bar to catch the bartender's attention. He looked bleary-eyed and drunk, as though he'd already been drinking before coming into the pub.

"Two beers," he said when the bartender turned to him. "What are you drinking, Virgil?"

"Schlitz draft."

"Two Schlitz drafts," Bucky said.

The bartender poured off the beers.

"Let me get it," I said.

Bucky was very adept at getting his wallet from his back pocket. "Nah, I've got it."

We made our way to an empty booth. I slid in to one side while Bucky sat in his wheelchair at the end of the table. I could not believe how much older he looked than the last time I had seen him. There were creases in his brow and dark circles beneath his gray eyes, which possessed a kind of weariness far beyond his years. It was as though he had skipped what remained of his adolescence and young adulthood and leaped ahead into middle age.

Bucky took a drink of his beer. "So how've you been, Virgil?"

"Not bad, not bad." I hesitated. "How about you?"

"Hey, except for getting my legs blown off in Nam and a few months of fun and games at the VA hospital, I can't complain." He lifted his mug in a mock toast and took a long drink.

I took a drink myself and began cracking open peanuts. "Want some?" I asked, pushing the bowl towards him.

"Nah."

"I heard you'd been drafted but I didn't know you'd been sent to Vietnam."

"Some people just have all the luck, I guess," he said, and gave a short laugh. "But hey, fuck that. It's ancient history. What're you up to? Still at school?"

"Yeah. I'm working for the summer, but I'll be going back in a few weeks."

"You must get into some pretty hot pussy up there. Are you in a fraternity?"

"No, not me."

"But you're getting laid, I hope."

I smiled, embarrassed, and looked into my beer. I had been seeing a girl from Rhode Island for the better part of the school year, but she'd gone back home after school and we'd left it that we should both be free to go out with other people during the summer.

"Come on, Virgil. Don't give me this shit that you're not getting laid. I mean, that's more of a waste than my fucking legs being gone." Then he laughed. "Come clean, remember?"

I laughed too at the memory of our childhood game. "Everybody gets laid up there. You can't help it. It's like it comes along with registration, Free Love 469."

Bucky grinned cheerfully, the way he always used to. "All right. That's better, that's what I like to hear. You had me worried there for a minute."

"What about you?" I said. "Have you been able to find work since you got back?"

"Shit no. Are you kidding? About the only thing I'm good for now is a freak show. But the fairs don't start until the fall."

Bucky had always been one to laugh at himself, the kind of kid who—despite his general awkwardness, his ineptitude—had learned to fuse self-ridicule and cheerfulness into a sort of irrepressible optimism which made almost everyone like him. It was more of a jolt to see that this optimism—under the influence of alcohol, at least—had turned to hard and self-abusive irony than it was to see the physical changes in him.

"Maybe you could apply where I'm working. The place manufactures stereo speaker cabinets. You always liked working with wood, and I know there are jobs you could do there."

"Yeah, maybe. I'm pretty good at drinking beer these days. Do they pay anyone there to sit around and do that?"

"Hey, that's no joke. Every Friday night some of us pack a cooler with beer and ice and pretty much just drink for the last two or three hours."

"What's your job?"

"Sanding the cabinets. The only thing I have to watch out for is that I don't sand too hard and go through the veneer. Otherwise there's nothing to it. It's simple."

Bucky looked impressed but unconvinced. "Who runs this place? Aren't there any foremen around?"

"Sure, but they're good guys. They don't give a shit as long as production doesn't fall off and we don't fuck up the product. They'll drink right along with us. I've never seen the owner of the place myself, but they tell me he's some political big-wig in New Hampshire."

"That explains everything," Bucky said with a knowing nod of his head. "Fucking politicians."

"I'm telling you, Bucky, if you want a job it's a good place to try."

"Maybe I will," Bucky said, but I knew from the way he said it that he never would.

A waitress came by and informed us it was last call. "Two more Schlitz," Bucky said before I could open my mouth. She brought the beers.

"This time it's mine," I said.

"No way, Virgil. It's good seeing you, man."

I did not want to argue with him.

After he paid the waitress he watched her move away and took a drink of his beer. "Too much pussy on the brain," he said. "That's my problem. That's how this happened." He gestured disdainfully at his absent legs. "Stupid fucker that I am I took R&R as soon as I could. In no time at all I was out of Nam and staying in a fancy hotel fucking my brains out. Bought a different chick every day. It was like I'd died and gone to heaven for three days. Next thing I know I'm back in country on a sweep, supposed to watch every fucking step. Only that wasn't where my head was, you know what I mean? My head was still underneath clean sheets eating pussy. That's probably what I was dreaming about when I stepped on the booby trap." Bucky was no longer seeing me. A sort of glazed, self-absorbed look had come into his gray eyes.

I could think of nothing to say so I took a drink of beer and cracked some peanuts.

Then Bucky turned to look at me again. His eyes were watery and he was having trouble focusing them. "I still got hands, I still got a tongue. I can suck off some chick if I pay enough. But what the fuck good is that? I got a dead pecker, limp as fucking cooked spaghetti. And for what? Nobody thinks you're some kind of hero. They see you coming and you can just tell they're saying to themselves: 'Oh, oh, here comes another one of those fucked up Vietnam vets.'"

I took another drink, struck dumb by the irreconcilable knowledge that this was Bucky—a neighborhood friend from my childhood days, younger than I was and still a kid, really, at only nineteen or twenty—not some grizzled old veteran of a war fought before I was born, not some stranger whose life had been forever altered, his future literally blown away, in a time long before my own. This *was* my time, my friend, my past, and yet none of it seemed real.

Bucky rescued me. A light came into his eyes and he said, "Hey, I'm surprised you didn't know I was over there. Didn't Jake ever mention we saw each other?"

"You saw Jake?"

"Yeah."

"When? I haven't seen him in over a year."

"Just before that R&R I told you about, in Da Nang. We bumped into each other there."

"How was he doing?"

"Same old Jake, except tougher. Harder. Like fucking Nam was made for him."

"What do you mean?"

Bucky's watery gray eyes looked at me steadily now. "Lots of guys over there write shit like 'Born to Kill,' 'High on War,' on their helmets. There's nothing on Jake's helmet but it's there anyway, like it's written on his forehead. You can see it in his eyes." Bucky paused for a moment and took a drink of beer. "You know what Jake does? You have any idea?"

"Not really."

"Of course not. Stupid question. Nobody knows, especially nobody back in the World. Jake's a fucking Lurp, Virgil. Lurps are guys that do long-range recon. They go out at night, they go out alone. It's bad enough humping hills in the day over there. But these fucking guys go looking for VC at night. You gotta be royally fucked up or have balls of steel to do what they do—or both. Lurps are some crazy fuckers, Virgil, believe me."

Bucky finished up his beer. I wanted to know more. I wanted to ask him a hundred different questions, and yet I did not know what to say to him, which questions to ask, which questions he might find offensive, did not know if I even wanted answers to some of the questions. Images of My Lai, of slaughtered women and children sprang to my mind unbidden, and some indefinable thing amounting to terror turned language itself into a divide between us.

The waitress came by and told us it was closing time. I chugged the rest of my beer.

"I guess we better be leaving," I said. "Do you need a ride, Bucky?"

"Nah, I got a special rig outside that the old man coughed up the dough for. It cost him a fortune but I think it makes him feel good, like even though he can't stand the sight of me he's really not such a bad guy."

"Why do you say that?"

"What, that he can't stand the sight of me?"

I nodded.

We made our way outside into the hot, steamy summer night.

"Because of this," he said, gesturing at the condition of his being in a wheelchair. "And even more because of this fucking bag," he said, grabbing onto the bulge by his waist. I hadn't noticed it until then, and although at the time I had never seen or considered such a thing, did not even have a name for it, I figured out pretty quickly what Bucky was talking about.

"He was all gung ho before I went, but when I came back like this I could tell the second he laid eyes on me I'd disappointed him somehow. You know, like you're supposed to go over there and kill gooks and win the war and nobody ever really gets hurt. Hell, you're an American, right? And they're only gooks. Bad things aren't supposed to happen to Americans."

Tears were forming in Bucky's eyes. I looked at him and couldn't say a word.

"Aw, fuck," he said, and shook his head violently. "I'm sorry, Virgil."

"It's all right," I said.

"No it isn't," he said. "It sucks. You see a friend you haven't seen in a long time and you fall to fucking pieces."

I stood and watched quietly, sorrow filling my heart, as shudders wracked his thin, maimed body. Then he took a deep breath and shook himself again. "I'll be all right," he said, his shudders gradually subsiding. He closed his eyes and took another couple of deep breaths. "The worst thing of all is when I start feeling sorry for myself."

"Can I give you a hand getting in the car?" I asked, groping for something to say.

"No, I can do it. I'm all right now." He wiped his eyes on the sleeves of his shirt. "But hey, if you got nothing better to do why don't you follow me home? We can get another drink. They close these fucking places when the night is still young."

I thought about it for a moment. "I think I better get going. How about a rain check?"

"Sure, Virgil. My mother goes apeshit when I drink at home anyways."

"Take care of yourself, Bucky. And thanks for the beers."

"No problem."

"See you."

"Yeah. Good seeing you, Virgil."

I watched him wheel himself around and make his way down the street. He turned and called back to me, "Hey, Virgil. Tell Jake I said hello."

"I will," I said. "I just hope he gets back here alive."

"Don't worry about that. Trust me, it's like Jake has a charm around him or something."

"Maybe," I said, thinking that if Jake had any sort of charm around him it must be a bad luck charm. "He was wounded a while back, you know."

"Doesn't matter. Jake always lands on his feet. He's like a cat. He's got nine lives."

"I hope you're right."

"I am," Bucky said. He spun around again and I watched him wheel himself down to a shiny red Mustang parked along the street. Before I could see how he managed to get himself in, I turned and headed back to my own car.

"Come now, Virgil, surely you're not afraid of giving a little blood," Mother said.

I was home on spring break, which unfortunately coincided with one of the volunteer activities Mother had been involved with for years: helping the Red Cross at local blood drives.

"Of course I'm not afraid."

"Then why don't you join us tomorrow afternoon?" Mother said.

"I haven't figured out what I'm doing yet."

"Well that's the point, isn't it?" Mother said, smiling with amusement. "If you haven't got anything planned, there's no reason why you can't come along."

At school some of my friends had reported seeing rugged football-player types pass out from giving blood, which only fortified my conviction that it would happen to me. Irrational scenarios played out in my imagination: after the nurse stuck the needle in I would be abandoned, forgotten, while an unstanchable stream of blood flowed from me and drained my life away; or as I lay there so vulnerable on the recliner, someone just passing by would inadvertently catch the tubing and twist the needle ninety degrees inside my arm.

"I'd do it if I were old enough," Lydia chimed in from the living room. She was sitting in the overstuffed chair reading *Huckleberry Finn*.

"Sure you would," I said.

"It's true. I want to now but I'm not old enough." Lydia was three months shy of thirteen at the time, still very small and thin for her age. Unlike other seventh-grade girls, who had clearly reached puberty, Lydia appeared not to have rounded the corner of fourth grade.

"Hey, this is my spring break. What I really should be doing is lying in the sun on some beach in Florida, getting a tan like everybody else I know, not lying down in the Moose Hall watching blood drip from my veins."

"Don't be a hypocrite, Virgil," Lydia said. "You're just afraid and you won't admit it. And another thing, not everybody you know is getting a tan on the beach. What about Jake? Think *he's* relaxing on the beach? Think *he'd* be afraid to give a little blood to help out other people? No, because he's already done that."

"All right, all right," I said.

But Lydia would not let me off the hook, or the needle, so easily. "Jake had to be given a lot of blood after he was wounded. What if there hadn't been enough for him? What if it was Jake who needed the blood and everybody said they'd rather be out on the beach getting a tan?"

"All right, already. You don't have to crucify me to get my blood."

So I went to the blood drive with Mother and Lydia, who had accompanied Mother on so many of these missions of mercy that all the nurses and staff at the drive knew them both.

"So you're one of Rose's boys," said the craggy-faced old nurse taking my blood pressure.

I nodded.

"You're a lucky young man to have a mother like her. She's an angel. I don't know what we'd do without her. And your little sister too. She's quite a girl, that Lydia." I could see Lydia behind a table across the hall, flitting back and forth to serve food and drinks to people. Mother was escorting people to the table after they had finished giving blood.

"Thanks."

The nurse squinted a little and looked at me closely. "You're not the one who's been over in Vietnam, are you?"

I would have thought my pony-tail to be a surefire giveaway. "Not me," I said, shaking my head. "I'm Virgil. It's Jake you're thinking of."

"Jake. That's right." She wrapped the cuff around my arm. "Well that little sister of yours talks about Jake all the time. He was wounded a while back, wasn't he?"

"Yes."

"Is he all right now?"

"As far as we know. He should be coming home in a couple of months."

"That's wonderful." The old nurse inflated the cuff until my arm felt as though all life had been crushed from it, then listened intently through her stethoscope as she slowly released the pressure. "Your blood pressure is within normal limits, though the numbers are a little high for someone your age. Are you feeling nervous or excited about anything today?"

"I've never given blood before."

"Well that probably explains it," she said, unwrapping the cuff. "Don't worry, you'll do just fine." She gave me a pat on the arm and allowed her liver-spotted hand to rest there for a moment. "Thanks for coming today, Virgil."

I started to get up but she held onto my arm. "And Virgil," she said, smiling kindly. "That's quite a family you've got there."

"Thanks," I said, and moved on to the next station.

The old nurse was not the only one to comment on Mother and Lydia that day. Everyone who noticed my name on the form I carried from station to station sang their praises.

"Your sister is my little darling," said a plump woman working at the food table with Lydia. Lydia blushed as the woman encircled her with a fleshy arm and gave her a squeeze. "She's always helping."

"She's a saint," said the nurse who drew my blood, speaking of Mother. "Frank," she said to a man also giving blood at her station, "this is Rose's boy."

Frank was a balding, middle-aged man dressed in a green uniform that had his name stitched above the shirt pocket in yellow letters. The shirt sleeve that had been rolled up to allow him to give blood exposed a dark-skinned arm thickly forested with curly black hair. I imagined him wishing he could transplant some of the hair on his arm to his head. "Let me tell you something," Frank said, turning to me. "It's because of people like your mother I keep coming back here every eight weeks. She's a gem, a real lady."

It was a strange afternoon. In some ways I found it more difficult to respond to all these well-intended compliments about my family than to have the nurse stick me with a needle. To this day I am not sure why, but with every new word of praise for a family member I felt more and more uncomfortable.

Perhaps it happened because when a total stranger seems to know someone we love in a way we do not, we grow a little jealous or uneasy. I had been aware of this public side of Mother—and by extension Lydia—for years, but I had never seen it from quite such close range as at the blood drive. That a fleshy and jovial fat lady could know my sister and a hairy-armed man named Frank could know my mother in ways that I did not was unnerving.

Or perhaps the discomfort arose because whenever someone presents an ideal vision of a person we love, reflexively we begin to compare that vision to what *we* perceive as real. When the two don't align, we see something as being out of focus, as if we're looking at a double exposure. Far from being the reincarnation of Florence Nightingale, Lydia could be a demanding little minx at home. On a hot summer day she might say to no one in particular, "Could you set up the fan for me?" while she sat reading or writing in the living room. If any of us replied, "You can do that yourself, Lydia," she might whine and complain and accuse us of not loving her. With everyone but Jake she used the line, "You don't love me," or, "If you loved me you'd do it," with outrageous frequency and effectiveness, and no apparent sense of conceit.

Or perhaps at some level I sensed there was a hidden element to Mother's volunteer work that made it not quite as pure or as altruistic as people thought, as though it were the mask to a face she did not want anyone else to see, or as though, like the moon, there was a luminous side, bright and open to all, and a dark side that never came into view even under the most intense scrutiny. Over the years she spent countless hours working to organize bake sales and clothing drives; rounding up toys at Christmas for children whose parents couldn't afford them; helping to raise money for countries where legions of people were starving; collecting canned goods, baking bread and preparing meals for the local soup kitchen; vending popcorn or manning a booth at PTA functions; chaperoning school trips to concerts or plays or museums; and, of course, donating her time and her willingness to serve, not to mention her own blood, to Red Cross blood drives. I have no doubt her conviction about the need to help people less fortunate in life was sincere; her energy and her vitality were truly prodigious. And yet... there was something awry: a desperation in her, perhaps, that people mistook for unalloyed enthusiasm.

I did not get this sense, this feeling, from knowledge of her past, because her past was largely a blank canvas to me. I knew from Father, who said she had always been extremely private about her past, even with him, that both of her parents had died when she was very young in some sort of freak train accident. After the accident she had been raised by her mother's parents, who died before I was born. They were devout Catholics and very strict with her. Beyond these meager details I knew virtually nothing. It was a subject Mother never talked about and none of us asked her about.

So I cannot truthfully say my sense of her desperation came from any knowledge of her past. But I felt it, nevertheless. It possessed the same zealous intensity with which she purged the house in hopes of controlling Lydia's asthma. Just as surely as guilt over Lydia's illness seemed to drive her to keep the house immaculate, especially following an asthma attack, so too did something—I do not know what, exactly—seemed to drive her to do volunteer work.

There is one thing I know with certainty, however: her volunteer work increased as we drew closer to Jake's return. She even had to cancel out on a commitment to help the church with a day-long event for handicapped children at the Crotched Mountain Center: it fell on the same day Jake would be arriving home.

A week or so before Jake returned I was home alone and had about half an hour to kill before a friend came over to pick me up, a girl named Jill whom I had gone out with for a while in high school and who was also home from college for the summer. We'd had an on-again off-again relationship in recent years, usually on in the summer and off during the school year. We were planning to see the Jane Fonda movie, *They Shoot Horses, Don't They?*

While I was waiting for Jill I happened to notice the family photo albums on a bookshelf in the living room. I hadn't looked at them in years, so I decided to flip through them until Jill arrived. The first album I opened contained pictures from 1954 to 1955, all of them black-and-whites. As I sat there gazing at the pictures I initially felt the usual sort of mild astonishment and disbelief at seeing myself as a three or four year old and my parents as two people who were thinner and younger-looking than I had ever known them to be. It occurred to me as a kind of marvelous absurdity that when these pictures were taken my parents were only slightly older than I was sitting there, and I chuckled at the incongruity of it all. But what totally confounded me for an instant was the thought that there existed in this album a sort of warp in the chronology of our family. The flaxen-haired toddler who sat beside me in so many of the pictures—the child about whom a distant part of me had been asking as I flipped through the album: why is she in *all these pictures?*—was not Lydia but Jake. It took a moment for this to sink in. I'd been so focused on my parents and myself that I scarcely paid attention to the other child in the pictures, and he registered as Lydia rather than as Jake. I had never considered the two of them in juxtaposition as young children, but there was a *remarkably* strong physical resemblance between Jake and Lydia, or at least between them when they were approximately the same age.

I hadn't seen the pictures in a long while and had forgotten just how fair-haired Jake was in those days. He looked to be nearly a tow head in the old black-and-white pictures. Over the years his hair had darkened to the same shade of light brown as Mother's, while Lydia's hair, although it had darkened a little, remained very light and fair. I began flipping through albums rapidly in order to trace Jake's and Lydia's development. I wanted to see if the resemblance was real or simply the result of an overly active, if not traitorous, imagination.

By the time I reached Lydia's birth in 1958, however, the albums had given way to slides. It was inconvenient to dig out the projector from storage, but I felt an inexplicable compulsion, as if my own identity somehow rested on the results of my investigation.

I closed the shades in the living room and switched off all the lights. The first tray was dated 1960, and even before focusing the picture I recognized the scene before me. It was a scene from Storyland, where Mother and Father had taken us once when we were all young. The shot was taken by Father, who was the only one missing from the picture. The "story" behind this particular scene was Jack and the Beanstalk. The fallen giant, probably twenty feet long, lay on the ground supine. Ben and I were sitting on the giant's midsection, smiling, while Mother stood just to the side of us holding Lydia, who was probably about two, in her arms. Mother was also smiling but Lydia was in profile to the camera and leaning, arms outstretched, as though she wanted to get out of Mother's arms. Jake was standing alone atop the giant's bulbous nose. What I remember most about the picture is that just before it was taken Mother had been trying to get Jake to come down, and Father had said not to worry about it, it made for a neat shot.

In years past the whole family (Grandmother and Grandfather too) used to gather in the living room for an evening of watching slides, many of which—along with the same, unvarying narratives provided by adults—were fixed so securely in my memory that they possessed an almost liturgical reality, as faithful and dependable to a child as the bars of his crib.

But what if the child grabs the bars and hauls himself up, leans against the railing, and the entire side of the crib gives way, leaving him to land face first on the floor? What if we find, upon rereading *Crime and Punishment*, that Raskolnikov is not a murderer at all, that someone or something else kills the old pawnbroker and her sister? What if we suddenly learn that we've had it wrong all these years: the dish really runs away with the knife instead of the spoon?

Such was the effect that viewing the black and white pictures, and then the slides, had on me. I discovered it was not just my imagination that Jake and Lydia looked astonishingly alike as two-year olds—it was the truth. What's more, both of them more or less resembled Mother, while Ben and I, who were dark-haired, resembled Father. I had never even noticed this split in our family before; and I had always assumed that in the Jack and the Beanstalk picture Lydia was trying to get down from

Mother's arms to sit next to me and Ben on the giant. Her leaning body and outstretched arms clearly give this impression when you look at the picture quickly. But upon closer inspection it becomes obvious that her gaze is fixed on Jake. She probably wanted to get down so that she could join Jake atop the giant's nose—which was why Mother wanted Jake to get down. And Father, peering through the camera lens and trying to get what he thought was the best picture of the family, probably didn't realize what was happening.

Patterns that I had been unaware of before also began to appear. As the family photographer, Father was hardly ever in the pictures. Ben and I were usually seated or standing next to each other. Jake, even in pictures taken during the first years of his life, was almost never smiling, while Lydia's face, especially when she was very young, was nearly always lit up with an effervescent smile and a cheerful twinkle in her blue eyes. You could easily tell them apart by the presence or absence of a smile. Jake was often either standing slightly apart from the rest of us or, with his head turned, gazing at something other than the camera. Mother was usually holding or touching Lydia.

The doorbell rang and I hurried to open the front door. The sight of Jill standing there smiling in the light sent a shiver of relief through me. Her clear green eyes, red hair and freckled face, pleasing to look at, seemed reassuringly warm and open and familiar, with nothing to hide. She was dressed in cut-off jeans, sandals, and a sleeveless white top that immediately made me want to slip the straps down and caress the smooth white curve of her freckled shoulders.

I held out my arms and she came forward into my embrace. We kissed.

"I didn't think anyone was home," she said, drawing back. "Why was it so dark in here?"

"Come on, I'll show you." I took her hand and led her up the stairs to the living room.

"When you suggested seeing a movie I didn't think you meant *home* movies," she said with a roll of her eyes at the sight of projector and screen.

"I didn't. I was just glancing through some old family photo albums when I noticed Jake and Lydia looked a lot alike when they were little. I'd never noticed that before, so I wanted to check it out and see if I was just imagining things."

"Were you?"

"I don't think so. But you can decide for yourself. My mother is holding Lydia in the picture up on the screen." I turned on the lights and handed her one of the old photo albums. "Now take a look at these pictures. The blond in here is Jake."

"You're right, they really do look alike," Jill said.

"Isn't it amazing?"

"Well, I wouldn't call it amazing, exactly. I mean, they are brother and sister."

"I know, but still. It would be hard to tell the two apart if you didn't know the dates."

Jill looked at me curiously. "Why is this so important to you?"

I thought about the question for a moment. "I guess it's not, really. I just found it kind of surprising. They're so different in so many other ways."

"If it's not important why did you go to all this trouble?"

"It wasn't that much trouble. Besides, I hadn't seen the pictures in years. I thought it would be kind of fun to look back."

She smiled and gave me a wry look that seemed to say, "Do you expect me to believe that?" But then her expression softened and she said, "You want to look at some more? We can always go to the later show."

"Sure. Why not. Some of these are pretty funny." I took my wallet from the back pocket of my jeans and removed a joint. "But before we get started, let's get in the proper mood to appreciate them." Jill smiled and arched her eyebrows in approval.

We smoked and giggled foolishly as we traveled back to a time and a history that seemed impossibly distant and naive. Not only were there slides from Storyland but also from places like Santa's Village, Plymouth Plantation, Sturbridge Village, and Disneyland, where the entire family had once gone for a week. There were pictures of vacation trips we'd gone on to the mountains and the lakes and the ocean, pictures of us swimming, under sunny skies, in the blue pools of motels where we had stayed.

Jill laughed out loud at one set of pictures I had nearly forgotten about from a place called Frontierland. In one picture the whole family was about to ride a stagecoach, with Jake, Ben and me on top next to the driver, and Mother sitting inside the stagecoach with Lydia. What I remembered most clearly about that stagecoach ride was the terror I felt when we were attacked by outlaws, whose gunfire sounded so real that when our driver slumped over I really thought he had been shot. I sat there sort of frozen with fear. I don't know what Ben did—he was still pretty young—but Jake got his guns out and started firing away at the outlaws, one or two of whom fell off their horses as though Jake had hit them. In a different sequence Jake, garbed in a dark brown cowboy hat and shirt and wearing a gun and holster tied down on his leg, was involved in a mock gunfight with another boy (who must have worked for Frontierland) on the dusty main street of the town. There's a picture of Jake drawing his gun and the other boy falling, and then later a picture of Jake behind bars in the town jail, with his cowboy hat still on, his hands gripping the bars of the cell, and a red bandanna covering all but his eyes, which peer out at the viewer with a kind of menacing and defiant stare.

"You really did a lot of fun things with your family," Jill said. "You're lucky."

"Yeah, I guess we did do a lot."

We were sitting next to each other on the floor and I had my arm around her. I was sort of playfully slipping one of the straps of her top from her shoulder.

"It must be hard on your family to have Jake in Vietnam," Jill said. "You seem so close."

I didn't say anything. She was not wearing a bra, and I slid my fingers down along the smooth slope of her chest, found the tender bud of her nipple and softly began to caress it.

"When is he due home, anyway? It's pretty soon, isn't it?"

"Mmmm," I said, nuzzling her neck. "Next week." I could detect a faint, sweet smell of perfume mixed with her own pleasing odor. I covered her mouth with my own.

"This is not a good place," she said, backing away slightly.

"Why not?" I whispered close to her ear.

"It's too open. What if someone comes home?"

I could feel the tender flesh of her nipple responding, growing firmer, between my fingers. "Then let's go to my room," I said softly.

She kissed me. "All right."

I helped her up and held her hand to lead her away.

"Shouldn't we take care of the projector?" Jill asked, with a tug on my hand to stop me.

I looked at the image on the screen of Jake the gunslinger, behind bars, staring out from above the border of his red bandanna. "Later," I said.

As I led her out of the living room it occurred to me that Jill had never been to my room before, and a strange and inexplicable impulse came to me: I might, if I wanted, lead her to Jake's room. It took only an instant for the idea to percolate through the filter of objections and thrill me. Would Jake, or anyone else, be likely to know about it? Would Jake be likely to care even if he did know about it? Is there any other good reason not to do it? I never thought to ask if there was any good reason *to* do it, any good reason why it should be exciting to me. The pounding of my heart was reason enough without any further examination of motive.

The window shades were drawn and the room was very dark when I closed the door behind us, but I did not want light. Usually I wanted to see Jill, wanted to be on a picnic blanket with her off in some pasture—in full daylight—to enjoy the visual pleasure of her freckles and her lovely green eyes, her small breasts and almost baby pink nipples, her sparse little beard of pale, curly orange hair down below where she loved for me to kiss her. But tonight the darkness and the knowledge of where we were acted as an aphrodisiac that daylight could not match.

I slipped her top over her head and caressed her naked shoulders, kissed her neck and ears and traveled down to her breasts where I kissed her nipples and took each of her small breasts almost wholly into my mouth. She moaned a little at this and I felt strangely powerful, in control of a dark universe where I was the compassionate, pleasure-giving master. I undid the snap of her cut-offs and, kneeling now, lowered them to the floor, hooked my fingers beneath the elastic of her panties and slid them down her legs. She stepped lightly out of the clothes at her feet, touched my hair with her hands.

"You too," Jill whispered. I stood up and she kissed me as she reached down and began pulling up my T-shirt. She undid my belt buckle and unzipped my jeans, dragged them down to the floor until I too was completely naked. With my hands on either side of her head I guided her to the erection that throbbed so intensely it seemed to be sending out signals, angry pulses of urgency that she must surely have sensed. My hands caressed her hair as she began to move back and forth on me in the darkness, making me believe for a moment I was a god, the god of darkness, and she the most generous and loving of goddesses. I remembered again where we were and my legs began to feel rubbery, a shiver of excitement raced along my spine, I moaned aloud. I could feel myself beginning to come, and without realizing what I was saying blurted into the darkness, "Oh God, take it from me, please take it." Jill slowed her own rhythmic movements and waited for me without pulling away, with what seemed such patience, such merciful understanding that I felt suddenly humbled. A powerful wave of love and gratitude washed over me, and for the first time since I had known her I wanted to tell her I loved her.

Instead I reached down to bring her up to me again and with my arms around her backed her toward the end of Jake's bed. I kissed my way up along her belly, all the while holding myself above her in the darkness, the only contact between us the press of my lips against her skin. Feeling powerful again and holding myself away, I reached her lips at last and kissed her in the very moment I pushed into her.

Jill drew back from my kiss and whispered, almost as a kind of question, "You're still hard." Even in the darkness I could tell that her eyes were open and searching me.

I did not say anything. No longer possessed by the mindless importunity of the first time, I was even more conscious of exactly where I was, and of Jake's impending return. Drawn back now at full length, poised above her, I could feel my earlier tenderness for her, my gratitude, ebbing away, being replaced by something less desperate perhaps but harder and more driven, more selfish, as though something that hadn't yet been established or proven needed to be.

"Don't you want to?"

"Yes," she said, answering with an upward thrust of her hips. I held myself from moving to meet her. "You just surprised me," she whispered, "and I didn't know if we would have time." She gave a few quick thrusts as if to prime the pump that for some reason had stopped operating.

"I'm full of surprises," I said, and gave an abrupt, almost violent thrust in return. As Jill wrapped her legs around me and dug her heels into my back, I had the absurd thought, which made me want to laugh although I refrained from doing so aloud, *We've got plenty of time. Jake won't be home for another week.*

We saw the flash of headlights on the window shades and heard the car pull into the driveway while we were putting our clothes back on in the darkness of Jake's room.

"Perfect timing," I said with a laugh.

"You're a sly one, Virgil," Jill said, cupping my balls through my jeans.

By the time Mother and Lydia had parked the car in the garage and come into the house, Jill and I were back in the living room looking at slides.

"What's going on in here?" Mother called out from downstairs. I could hear the jingle of her keys coming closer to us. "Is that you up there Virgil? I thought you were going out to the movies." The light came on and Mother and Lydia appeared on the stairway. "Oh hi, Jill."

"Hi, Mrs. Goodwin. Hi, Lydia. How are you both?"

"Fine," Mother and Lydia said almost in unison.

"We were just looking at some old slides," I said. "I haven't seen these in years."

"What about the movies?" Mother asked.

"We got kind of caught up in this and decided to go to the later show." Mother eyed me suspiciously, or it so seemed in my slightly paranoid state of mind. Jill and I had not had a chance to wash up at all, and I could still smell her aroma on my face. Maybe the whole room reeked of sex, and the conversation we were having was nothing but pretense, the truth too obvious for anyone not to know. Yet here we all were standing around as though nothing out of the ordinary had happened. Jill, smiling almost demurely, was especially convincing.

"Virgil and I were just talking about how much you and Jake look alike in your baby pictures, Lydia," Jill said. "Has anyone ever told you that before?"

"No, I don't think so," Lydia said. A moment of awkward silence followed.

"Have you ever noticed it, Mother?" I asked.

Not even the faintest shadow of doubt crossed her face. "No, I can't say I have. Other people have commented on it, but I've never thought they looked at all alike."

"Huh. I couldn't believe the resemblance," I said. I turned to check the grandfather clock behind me. "We'd better get going," I said to Jill. "I'll just put these things away first."

"No, don't," Lydia said. "I want to look at the slides too. I'll put everything away."

"Why don't you let Virgil do it, honey?" Mother asked. "The screen and projector are too heavy for you to lift by yourself. Besides, wouldn't it be better to see the slides sometime when the whole family can look at them?"

"No, I want to look at them now."

Mother shrugged and shook her head. "Suit yourself."

"Thanks, Lydia," I said.

"Bye, Lydia. Bye, Mrs. Goodwin," Jill said. "It was nice seeing you both again."

Mother and Lydia said goodbye as the clock rang out its half-hour chime.

I left the house wondering what conclusions Lydia would come to, because it seemed clear she was after more than a frolic through the past. She too was after some sort of truth, and I wondered if she would be ready for it if she found it.

On the day Jake was to arrive home, Grandmother and Grandfather waited back in Newtown while the rest of us piled into the car to meet him at the airport. Everyone seemed just a little nervous on the car ride down. Father and Ben listened to a Red Sox game and spent much of the ride analyzing the Sox' chances of winning the pennant. Ordinarily I got involved in such discussions myself, but I didn't feel much like talking. I was too busy worrying about how Jake would look and act, trying to imagine what I could say or do beyond offering the perfunctory "How are you?" with a handshake. I wondered how he had changed, what the war had done to him, what it would be like to have him back home again, how it would feel to be sitting in the car next to him, my own brother, when he had undoubtedly killed people. Must have *had* to kill people. The question was, did he enjoy it? Bucky's words kept coming back to me with a virulence I had not felt in the pub that night: "It's like fucking Nam was made for him."

For some reason I had never really dwelled on these questions until that car ride to the airport. Now that Jake was coming home he was bringing with him a Pandora's box of things I had clearly not wanted to think about. *Had not expected to have to think about.*

It occurred to me with a start that this was the truth, this thought that slipped into my mind like a stiletto to the heart: *I had not expected to have to think about these things because I had not expected Jake to return home alive.* And why was that? *Why was that?*

Lydia was sitting in the front seat, as always, between Mother and Father. She was engrossed in Tolkien's *The Return of the King,* which she had been reading nonstop for a couple of days. Every once in a while Mother would make an observation to her or ask her a question which Lydia would dismiss with a terse, don't-bother-me sort of reply.

"It looks like you need to have your hair trimmed again, Lydia," Mother said as she ran her fingers through Lydia's long blond hair. "The ends are starting to split."

"Mmm," Lydia said, without glancing up from her book.

"Would you like to try a new style? Have it cut shorter, maybe?"

Lydia shook her head.

"I know straight hair is in these days—the straighter the better—but don't you think it would look nice with some waves in it?"

"No," Lydia said.

Later Mother tried to draw Lydia into a conversation about redecorating her room. "What about tomorrow after church? Want to go shopping for your room?"

"I don't think so," Lydia said. "Jake will be home."

That was the first and only direct reference to Jake until we reached the airport. It was as though each of us had decided to use the drive to the airport to make our private, individual preparations to meet him. Even Lydia, who had written to him so religiously for more than two years and spoken of his return so often in recent weeks, seemed content to withdraw quietly into herself. Only the day before, in an almost frantic state of excitement and anticipation as she flitted about the house making signs and stringing crepe paper streamers, she had had another asthma attack, the first really serious one in quite a while.

It wasn't difficult to spot Jake. His plane had arrived ahead of schedule and he was standing between his bags in uniform, medals and all, a somber expression on his face.

"Jake!" Lydia called out, and a broad grin abruptly spread across his face. She bolted away from the rest of us and Jake caught her up in his arms and swung her around.

The rest of us finally drew up to him, excited. There were handshakes and slaps on the back and claps on the shoulders between Jake and all the males in the family, and there was a hug and kiss between Jake and Mother (I couldn't remember the last time I had seen that happen—to my knowledge it hadn't even happened before he left for Vietnam), but there was a stiffness or self-consciousness in all of it that differed markedly from the spontaneous and unaffected coming together of Lydia and Jake. Lydia had tears in her eyes as she hugged his side and walked along next to him while Father, Ben and I carried his bags.

Jake was in the middle of us as we walked down the long halls of the terminal, flanked on the right by Lydia and Father, on the left by me, Ben, and Mother. He looked considerably older than before he left for Vietnam. He was not the middle-aged wreck of a human being that Bucky had become, maimed in body and spirit—Jake was clean-shaven and his hair, longer than it had been when he was home from boot camp, was well groomed. But he was much thinner than the last time I'd seen him. Faint wrinkles about his eyes and forehead and a certain tautness in his tanned face gave the impression he was several years older than his actual age. Older, I felt rather acutely, than I was. He walked along slowly, haltingly, with none of the swagger I'd seen after boot camp. With Lydia by his side and himself in the middle of us, Jake seemed almost happy, if happy is a word that could ever be used to describe a moment in his life.

For this reason I felt genuinely sorry for him when a pair of longhairs probably about my age called out to him as we were passing by.

"Just back from Vietnam?" the female of the duo asked. She wore a red bandanna tied gypsy-style around her head. She and her male companion were sitting hunched against a wall, knapsacks on the floor beside them.

The question froze us all to the spot for a moment. Then Jake nodded to them.

"Kill any women and children?" she asked, almost nonchalantly.

Jake stared down at them. His lack of expression as he looked from one to the other, cool, dispassionate, suggested some powerful fatality that could erupt in an instant. I was grateful it was the young woman who asked the question, although she must have sensed the same thing I did because she chuckled nervously beneath his gaze.

"You should be ashamed of yourself," Father scolded her. "That's a terrible thing to ask."

"It's a terrible thing to do," the young man bristled, coming to his companion's rescue. He gave a little shake of his long hair, which was oily and parted in the middle. Sparse curly dark hairs sprouted from his chin and above his upper lip.

"You don't know what happened over there," Father said. "You don't have any idea. What gives you the right to act as judge and jury?"

Father moved forward until he stood right above them, apart from the rest of us. He was the angriest I'd ever seen him, his face livid. As the young man stared up with a smug grin on his face, I was more afraid Father would be the one to lose control and attack rather than Jake.

Jake tugged on Father's elbow from behind. "They're a waste of our time."

Father turned reluctantly and we all began moving away, although he shot an angry glance behind him. We hadn't gone very far down the corridor when we heard the young man call out, "He never answered the question."

We continued walking. No one turned around and no one said a word.

The silence continued for some time. At last, having calmed down a little, Father said, "Jake, I'm sorry about that. They had no right to say those things."

"It's not your fault," Jake said. "But I'll tell you something… it's because of fucking scum like that that we're losing the war."

Again there was an uncomfortable silence. *Fucking scum* were not words Jake would ever have used in front of Mother in the past, yet he delivered them with such deadpan certainty, such lack of heat, they sounded almost normal. Nor did his assertion sound like the sort of thing over which an entire country had been tearing itself apart. The U.S. was losing the war because of the fucking scum opposing it. It was not an issue for debate or heated discussion in Jake's world view: it was a clear and simple fact.

I was not about to challenge Jake so soon after his return, and especially not after such an unfair attack on him, so I kept my mouth shut and walked on.

"Well, I'm sorry anyway," Father said. "But let's not let them spoil the occasion. It's great to have you back again." Father gave Jake another clap on the back.

"I'll second that," Lydia said.

Jake looked down at her and gave her a squeeze. "Thanks," he said.

"So what was it like over there, Jake?" Ben asked. By now we were in the parking lot nearing the latest incarnation of the many Ford wagons our family had owned over the years, this one dark brown with fake, light-grained metal side-paneling meant to make it look like a woody.

Jake said nothing at first, did not acknowledge Ben at all, and I wondered if he had even heard the question. Planes were taking off and landing and there was an almost constant, deafening roar above us.

Then Jake turned to face Ben and without any change in expression said, "Hot." That was all. He reached into his coat pocket and took out a pack of Lucky Strikes, lit one, and took a long drag, exhaling through his nostrils in a slow, controlled fashion.

"How long have you been smoking, Jake?" Lydia asked.

"A while. Since sometime after I got over there."

Lydia gave a nervous little smile. No one else in our family smoked (at least not *regular* cigarettes, and Lydia probably did not realize Jake and I had been smoking the evil weed for years now). "It's bad for you, you know."

"I know," Jake said. Then he looked at her and an ironic smile curled from his lips. "Some people might say Vietnam was too."

Father cleared his throat. "Well, shall we go home?" He unlocked the car doors on Mother's side, then hustled to unlock them on the driver's side where Jake and Lydia stood.

"Aren't you going to sit up front, Lydia?" Mother asked. Lydia typically sat up front between Mother and Father while the rest of us sat in the back, with me or Ben occupying the middle and Jake invariably sitting next to the door behind Father.

"No, I want to sit in the back with Jake."

Mother looked across the top of the car at her for a moment. "Suit yourself," she said. "As long as Jake doesn't mind. I just thought he might want to talk with his brothers."

Jake shrugged.

Ben and I were on Mother's side already anyway, and I confess I suddenly felt sorry for her in some unaccountable way, so I said, "I'll sit up front."

Mother smiled at me and slid into the middle of the front seat. "Thanks, Virgil," she whispered as I moved in beside her. Lydia sat in the back between Jake and Ben.

We hadn't been driving for long when Jake lit up another cigarette. Even with the windows open on this balmy summer afternoon the unmistakably foreign odor of smoke drifted through the car. Mother looked over her shoulder but made no comment. Lydia, sitting next to Jake, coughed a little and took a puff from the inhaler she carried in her purse.

"How many of those do you smoke in a day?" Lydia asked.

Jake thought about it for a moment. "Maybe two to three packs."

"That's a lot, isn't it?" Lydia said. "I mean, don't you get sick of it?"

"I don't even think about it."

"You should," Lydia insisted, coughing again as if to underscore the point.

Jake took a long drag and flicked the cigarette butt out the window.

"And that could start a fire," Lydia said.

Jake smiled a little and shook his head. "You're too much," he said, and then playfully tousled Lydia's hair.

Near home, still on the highway, Father was passing a Mayflower moving truck when we heard a loud report that sounded like a gunshot right next to us.

"What was—" Father started to say before he was cut off by Lydia.

"Jake, what's wrong? Jake? Jake?"

Jake was hunched down, his head cocked as though listening for more, his eyes narrow and intent. Lydia had him by the arm and was trying to shake him back to the present.

"It was only the truck, Jake," I said. "Some moron just turned off the ignition and restarted it. I used to see it all the time when I worked for Mayflower."

"Jake, it's all right," Lydia said. "Virgil says it was just the truck. You're home, you're with us." Her insistent tugging eventually returned the light of the here and now to Jake's eyes.

"Are you all right, Jake?" Ben asked. He was leaning forward to see around Lydia.

Jake turned to the open window again and stared out without a reply. The expression on his face was somber, reflective, as though he were ruminating on the evidence that he had just made a serious, embarrassing mistake, a mistake I knew he could not tolerate in himself.

Father was still driving and trying to pay attention to the road, a worried expression on his face as he craned his neck for prolonged glimpses of Jake through the rearview mirror.

Mother, who had turned around as I had at Lydia's first cries, now faced forward and gazed ahead impassively. She sat erect in her seat, and in profile, with her pale smooth forehead and faintly rouged cheeks she looked pretty, almost young. Only the gray in her hair and the crow's feet around her eyes—which she could no longer conceal with makeup—suggested otherwise. She never turned around again.

Back at home Lydia could barely contain her excitement. She grabbed Jake by the hand as soon as she was out of the car and led him, as planned, toward the front door, where Grandmother and Grandfather opened it on cue.

"Welcome home, Jake!" Grandfather said.

Grandmother could say nothing at first, her eyes were so filled with tears. The best she could manage was a long, tremulous hug. "Oh, Jake," she said at last, "it's wonderful to have you back again safe and sound."

The rest of us stood there grinning awkwardly as we awaited instructions from Lydia the impresario, who had planned a grand entrance for Jake.

"Well, come on," Lydia exhorted, "let's go inside!"

Grandmother and Grandfather stepped aside to allow Jake to enter first and then we all filed in after him, up the stairs to the living room. Lydia, glancing around to make sure everyone was present, raised her eyebrows in a half-expectant, half-demanding way and began the chorus she had instructed us to follow: "WELCOME HOME, JAKE!" we all shouted.

Jake stood there expressionless except for a slight tightening of his brow, as if he were trying to figure out something that didn't make sense to him. His gaze fell first upon the huge banner above the mantel that read:

TO OUR HERO: WELCOME HOME!
WE LOVE YOU, JAKE!

His eyes lingered there for a moment before he peered around at the balloons and the red, white, and blue crepe paper streamers strung across the ceiling and the vases of fresh-cut flowers that dotted the room. There were trays of cheese and crackers and bowls of fresh fruit and a sign atop the coffee table that read,

ICE CREAM THIS WAY→

(which was another of Lydia's ideas; she knew how much Jake loved ice cream). Next to the sign was an ice bucket containing a magnum of champagne festooned with a red bow and blue and white ribbons.

Jake finally turned to face us, his brow still knitted but softened now by an expression at once searching and quizzical as his eyes sought out and engaged each of us. Behind him, the grandfather clock chimed its tinny hourly melody and rang out the hour of two o'clock.

"We're all proud of you, Jake," Father said, as if in answer to some question silently posed and silently suspended in the air about us.

"That's right!" Lydia said.

Grandfather smiled and nodded his agreement, "It's true."

Ben didn't say anything but he was also nodding.

Jake looked at Mother, who bowed her head. It was difficult to tell if she was agreeing or avoiding his gaze, although her lips pursed and her eyes began to well with tears.

Then he fixed his piercing blue eyes on me and I offered what must have been a very foolish-looking smile. "What about you, Ace?" he asked with a wry grin. "Are you proud too?"

Before I could even formulate an answer he added, "Proud of the returning gook killer?"

The room went suddenly and absolutely silent.

"Jake!" Grandmother gasped.

"Jake, there's no need for that," Father said gently. "Virgil feels the same way we all do."

Jake continued to stare at me as though he hadn't heard a word. "That's what you were thinking, wasn't it?"

"I thought what those two said in the airport was terrible. It was a terrible thing to do."

"But not to think, right? I mean, you wanted to ask the same question, didn't you?"

His words hung accusingly in the air. Lydia looked at me as if I were some sort of traitor.

"Jake, come on," Father said. "This isn't right. I'm sure Virgil felt the same way we all did back there. Let's just forget about it and have a glass of champagne. The important thing is you're back with us, and I don't think anyone would disagree with that. Am I right, Virgil?"

I nodded.

"What happened at the airport?" Grandfather asked.

"Ask Virgil," Jake said with a laugh.

"A couple of punks asked Jake some questions they had no right to ask," Father explained. "But let's not dwell on them. Jake was right. They're a waste of our time."

Father smiled at Jake as he swept past him toward the champagne. "Let's have a toast." As we all moved forward Jake put his arm around my shoulder and gave me that wry smile again. "Just remember the last thing the guy said to me," he whispered, so that no one else could hear, but I didn't know what to make of this. Was he accusing me of not answering his question, or reminding me of something about himself? And if it was something about himself, exactly what was it? That he hadn't answered the question about killing? If so, what did that mean? That he was innocent? Guilty? Jake clapped me on the back, winked at me as if all were now clear, and moved over next to Lydia. He put his arm around her and rested his left hand on her shoulder. She leaned in against him.

Father popped open the champagne and poured out glasses for everyone, including Lydia. He held his own glass aloft and said, "To Jake! It's great to have you home again!"

"To Jake!" Grandfather echoed, and we all raised our glasses, clinked them together, and sipped the champagne.

Jake merely stood there in his uniform quiet and impassive and seemingly impervious to the proceedings except for the movement of his hand from Lydia's shoulder to her hair, which he stroked very slowly and tenderly, as though he were running his fingers along strands of silk.

"And to this family," Father added. "To the fact that we're all together again. May we enjoy continued health and prosperity for many years to come!"

We clinked our glasses once more, even Jake this time, who downed the glass of champagne he held in his right hand as if it were a shot of whiskey, while the fingers of his left hand never relinquished their caressing touch of Lydia's long blond hair.

Chapter Eleven

Evasion

He paused at the threshold. The golden halo of her nightlight had disappeared, at his bidding, long ago, and only a thin crack of darkness where the door had not been pulled all the way tight gave him any indication that he should enter. For the better part of two years darkness had been his sanctuary, his temple of life and death and truth, and as he stood outside her door now motionless, his ear close to that vertical line of darkness and his heart pounding as hard as it ever had in the jungle with his knife clenched between his teeth, as hard as it had the first time he had stood in this position—with the door open and the nightlight on and rage filling his heart—he listened for even the slightest sounds of disturbance within: a faint cough, the rustle of bedcovers, the whispered murmurings of a dream—anything that might suggest a reason or a need for the door to be opened, for him to go to her, but he heard only the uninterrupted rhythm of her breathing and the importunate beating of his own heart, and there in the background the distant ceaseless tick tock, tick tock of the grandfather clock in the living room. He stood for a moment paralyzed by the kind of indecision he had rarely felt in his life, listening and waiting, waiting and hoping, feeling with every passing moment the futility, the impossible absurdity of his standing here, until at last he turned from the door and left the house as silently as if he were still prowling through the jungle at night.

Chapter Twelve

Post-Traumatic Stress Disorder

Late the next morning we discovered what would turn out to be merely the first in a series of bizarre behaviors in Jake in the weeks and months to come: he was missing from the house. He had bolted from us during the night when everyone else was asleep.

We didn't discover it right away. Assuming he was tired and needed some undisturbed rest, everyone had gone about their usual Sunday morning routines. Mother, Father and Lydia went to church, Ben and I slept late (like me, Ben had quit all pretense of following the Catholic Church), and Grandmother and Grandfather, who had gone back to their own home the night before, were not due to join us for brunch until late morning. No one attempted to rouse Jake until almost noon, after Grandmother and Grandfather had arrived and brunch was ready. Even then it was against Lydia's protests. "Leave him alone, Daddy. He must be exhausted."

"He can always go back to bed later if he wants," Father said. "I'm sure he wouldn't want to miss a meal like this. The soufflé is ready and it just isn't the same reheated."

Father did not do much of the cooking in our house normally, but when he did he enjoyed it and took pride in it, especially in the soufflés he loved to whip up for Sunday brunch.

First he would deck himself out in the quilted maroon apron Mother had given him that had the word *HARMONY* in green script across the chest and patterned black measures of music all over it. Then he would put an opera on the stereo, usually something sung by Caruso, and amidst flourishes of flour and other ingredients, above the clanging din of pots and pans, he would begin what can only be described (politely, at that) as a sort of accompanying bellow. Mother undoubtedly would have preferred he pursue some other penchant—not only because of the noise he made but also because of the mess he invariably left in the kitchen. To the gourmands at the breakfast table there was never any question about appreciating Father's quirks—the meals were always delicious—but to Mother there was always a dubious cost.

On this particular morning, out of deference to Jake, Father hadn't put on any music and had refrained from any of his own mock-tenor outbursts, for which we were all grateful. He *was* wearing his apron though and he *had* made a mess of the kitchen. In addition to the shrimp-cheese soufflé that was in the oven, he had also cooked bacon and sausages, brewed a fresh pot of coffee, and whipped a bowl of heavy cream to go with the strawberry crepes he was ready to make. I was surprised the smells alone hadn't already lured Jake from his room.

With Lydia close behind him Father finally went to Jake's room and knocked lightly on the door. "Jake," he said, "there's a terrific brunch waiting for you out here." There was no answer. "It's only a few bleary-eyed steps away," he added temptingly.

Again there was no reply. "It's better than any breakfast you've had in at least two years."

"Let him sleep, Daddy," Lydia protested. "It's obvious he's tired."

"Jake," Father said, ignoring her. His voice was louder and more insistent than before. Perhaps he was beginning to remember the time Jake had run away, and the scene was becoming all too familiar to him. "Don't you want to join us?"

"Daddy, give him a break!" Lydia insisted.

"Jake, are you in there? Jake?"

"What are you doing?" Lydia complained as Father opened the door and entered the room.

"He's not here!" Lydia exclaimed. "I don't believe it!"

When Father came back out he stood there before us in the same maroon apron besprinkled with flour and whipped cream and spots of dried egg yolk and crepe batter that he'd had on when he entered the room, with the same wavy dark hair and graying sideburns, fashionably long and bushy and yet somehow incongruous on him, the same dark eyes; but the light in those eyes had dimmed, the ruddy enjoyment on his face had disappeared, and the creases on his forehead, relaxed to invisibility as he prepared breakfast, had hardened once again into tight, definite lines. It was almost as though a wand had been waved inside the room and the man who entered as an absurdly comic figure emerged as an absurdly pathetic figure.

Mother had already begun trying to clean up some of his mess and was busily flitting about the kitchen while the rest of us sat around the dining room table sipping coffee.

"He's gone," Father said to her as he stood at the border of the kitchen and the dining room. He did not look at the rest of us. "The bed doesn't even look slept in."

She was standing before the sink, where she opened the hot water faucet wide. A cloud of steam immediately began to arise from the powerful jet of water. "Do you think he got hungry again and went out for breakfast somewhere?" she said, almost casually. She glanced at him only briefly before turning to squirt Joy into the water.

"I don't know," he said, shaking his head in a sad and bewildered manner. "He knew we were going to have this brunch today. I told him about it last night."

"Where could he have gone?" Grandfather asked. "Is there a car missing?"

"No, they're both in the garage," Father said. "Wherever he went, he went on foot."

"Why?" Lydia blurted out. "Why would he leave without telling anyone?"

She sounded personally wounded, as if the "anyone" Jake should have told were Lydia herself. Her eyes began to well with tears, and as Grandmother gathered her into her arms to comfort her, Lydia broke down. "It was his first night home," she sobbed.

"I know, sweetheart, I know," Grandmother said. "But he'll be back. I know he will."

"That's true," Father said, in a tone meant to rally himself, perhaps, as much as anyone. "He'll be back soon. He's not used to all the commotion last night. We'll just have to be more aware of how different everything must be for him now." Lydia continued to sob ruefully. "In the meantime," Father continued in the best keep-a-stiff-upper-lip voice he could muster, "there's no point in letting a perfectly good meal get cold. Let's dig in, everybody."

But except for Mother's comments about how many pots and pans Father had used and what a mess he had made once again—comments which elicited none of the customary repartees from Father or anyone else at the table—the meal was a silent one.

It was this uncomfortably subdued atmosphere into which Jake entered, taking us all by surprise, just as we finished eating.

With no sound of a door opening or closing or footsteps on the stairs, he was simply there suddenly, still in his uniform, which looked remarkably unrumpled considering how many hours he'd been wearing it. If not for the smell of alcohol and the slight redness of his eyes, it would have been difficult to tell he'd been drinking all night.

"Howdy," was all he said, drawing up a few feet away from the table.

"Jake, are you all right?" Father said. "We didn't know where you'd gone."

"I couldn't sleep."

Father got up from his chair. "Have a seat. You must be dead tired."

"I'm all right."

"Please, sit down. I'll get you a plate of breakfast. Have you eaten?"

Jake shook his head and sat down.

"Where did you go?" Grandfather said.

"Nowhere. Just needed to get out for awhile."

I remembered Bucky's description of Jake as a LURP and a little shiver of apprehension tingled along my spine.

Mother got up from her place at the table and began to clear away dishes. The rest of us probably would have allowed Jake his privacy and let the subject drop at this point, but Lydia was still upset and wouldn't let go.

"Why, Jake? You had us all worried. We've been waiting for you to come home for two years, and the first thing you do when you get back is leave us again in the middle of the night?"

Father placed a plate of soufflé and crepes before Jake alongside a steaming cup of coffee and a side dish of bacon and sausages. "It's all right, Lydia. Jake just needs a little time to get used to being back here, that's all."

"Thanks," Jake said to Father as he bent nearer the plate and sniffed the steaming aromas. He barely glanced at Lydia, who pouted silently after Father's gentle rebuke. "This looks great."

For an awkward moment we all watched him eat until he said, "No, I didn't forget how to eat." Then he looked at Father and said, "Sure beats C-rats."

"I'm glad you like it," Father said.

"You had to eat rats?" Ben asked.

Most everyone chuckled, but Lydia saw the question as a more serious matter. "You idiot," she said scornfully. "If you ever did anything besides flex your muscles you'd know Jake's talking about *C-rations*. That's what they eat in the military, you know? *Rations?*"

"Excuse me, Miss Know-it-all. I've never *been* in the military, *you know?*"

"Neither has a three year old," Lydia said.

"There's no need to be insulting, Lydia," Father said.

"The only one who's being insulting is him," Lydia said, nodding toward Ben. "Eating rats," she said, shaking her head disdainfully.

Jake finished his meal, yawned, and stretched. "I think I'll hit the sack for a while."

"Go right ahead," Father said.

"Want to go out tonight, Jake?" I asked impulsively, trying, as I thought, to be helpful.

"Maybe." He went to his room and closed the door behind him.

Grandmother drew in a deep breath and let out a long, slow sigh. "I will worry about that boy until the day I die," she said, shaking her head as everyone began to get up from the table.

*   *   *

After dinner that night I asked Jake again if he wanted to go out, and he surprised me by saying yes. Occasionally in high school we spent time together at concerts of bands we both liked, but even then, I usually took friends along and Jake and I went our separate ways once the concert started. For the most part we walked in entirely different circles and hardly ever saw each other except at home. So I found myself both excited and unaccountably anxious when he agreed to join me, which made me wonder about my own expectations and motives.

"Where do you want to go?" I asked as I started up the green VW beetle I had recently bought for two hundred and fifty bucks.

"Head across the river," Jake said.

I groped for the tape box at my feet. "What do you want to listen to?" The one luxury I had allowed myself with the bug was a cheap tape deck and a couple of speakers.

"Zeppelin."

In a moment we were listening to the crude yearning voice of Jimmy Page belting out "Whole Lotta Love."

We crossed the river and the state line and Jake directed me to the parking lot of *The Cave*, a low gray building with dark red trim set against a backdrop of black, misshapen trees that overarched it. The small neon sign along the road glowed pink and blue with the emblem of a cherry and the cursive words *"Exotic Dancing."* In high school my friends and I drove by it more than once on a Saturday night, ridiculing it as the backwater haunt of rednecks and losers.

There was still quite a bit of daylight as we approached the building, but once we closed the door behind us and entered the chthonian world inside I had the peculiar feeling it was very late at night. It was so dark that it took a while to see anything at all. I just followed Jake down a short hallway that led to a single large room, where a raised rectangular stage perhaps fifteen feet wide by twenty feet long jutted out like a peninsula into a small sea of wooden tables and chairs. Maroon velour curtains with heavy folds stretched across the back of the stage. The tables and chairs, many of them empty, were pressed up to the edge of the stage and were so close together it was difficult for a waitress to maneuver around them. There was dark wood paneling on the walls and a pool table at the end of the room farthest from the stage.

"So this is *The Cave*," I said. "I always wondered what this place was like on the inside. I take it you've been here before."

"Yeah," Jake said, reconnoitering. He ambled over to a booth set back about ten feet from the stage, then slipped in and leaned against the wall. "I like to know what's behind me."

I slid in on the other side of the table. "When were you here before?"

"A few years ago."

A few years ago. "How old were you?"

"I don't know. Fifteen, sixteen."

"How did you manage that?"

Jake shrugged. "I knew someone who worked here."

A waitress came over and asked, "Something to drink?" She looked at each of us, her gaze resting upon Jake. He was wearing a gray sweatshirt and an old pair of jeans, but his hair was conventionally short and he had shaved and showered before we left. With my ponytail and granny glasses and generally unkempt appearance, I figured we must look quite incongruous.

"Southern Comfort," Jake said.

"On the rocks?" she asked.

He shook his head.

She looked at me.

"What the hell, I'll do the same," I said. I did not drink Southern Comfort often, but when I did it was with a lot of ice.

Jake shook a Lucky Strike from his pack and tapped each end of it on the table before putting it between his lips. He lit it, took a long drag and exhaled through his nostrils.

I glanced around the room. Half the tables and booths were unoccupied. The jukebox voice of some country singer crooned about "looking for love in all the wrong places."

"Is the place always this lively?" I asked.

Jake fixed me with his blue eyes and gave a little smirk.

The waitress came with our drinks and we asked her to run a tab. "When does the show start?" I asked, trying not to sound too anxious.

"In about half an hour." Jake was holding the glass of Southern Comfort just below his lips. His eyes were narrowed and he was looking at her. She was thin and pale, perhaps in her early thirties, with straight dark hair which she wore short and parted in the middle. Her hands were red and chapped, and there was a wedding band on the ring finger of her left hand.

"Do you need anything else?" she asked him.

"Not right now," Jake said.

"Just holler if you do."

As she turned and left he took a drag of his cigarette and tracked her with his eyes.

"So tell me, Ace, what have you been doing with yourself since I've been gone? Burning draft cards and protesting the war?"

"I don't burn draft cards," I said flatly, and took a sip of the Southern Comfort. Beneath the cloying sweet smell and initial taste of the drink there was a sharp bite that substantiated it as 100 proof liquor. "Though I did go to some protests."

Jake was gazing at me as though he was mildly amused by something, his gelid blue eyes, as always, unrelenting. The almost imperceptible curl of a smile at the corner of his lips and the interplay of light and shadow upon his face made his expression impossible to read.

"What do you plan to do now, Jake? Have you thought about it at all?"

Jake took another drag of his cigarette. He held it between his thumb and forefinger with his hand cupped around it as if he were trying to conceal it, or protect it from wind and rain. "Not really," he said, obviously uninterested in the question. Smoke was coming from his nostrils as well as from his mouth as he spoke. "Let's shoot some pool."

"Sure," I said.

We finished our drinks and had another as we played a couple of games of eight ball. The alcohol was beginning to have an effect on me and Jake won easily, moving about the table with a kind of fluid and unhurried mechanical preciseness that gave every shot a sense of inevitable purpose. On those rare occasions when he missed, it always came as a surprise. Most times the cue ball would lightly kiss its target, Jake would remain where he had taken the shot, motionless and bent like a jackknife, and the target ball would fall softly into the called pocket.

"So how has Lydia been?" Jake asked at one point.

"All right, I guess. I've been at school, but I don't think she's had any major attacks." Then I remembered the day before Jake arrived. "At least not until a couple of days ago."

"Hunh," Jake grunted. "She looks all right now."

"Who knows. You can never tell how she'll be from one day to the next."

Jake was looking up at the stage, where there was some movement behind the curtains. I hadn't noticed until now that *The Cave* had nearly filled up while we were playing pool.

"I guess we'd better get back to our seats," I said.

Jake nodded, but on the way back he took a side trip over to the waitress who had been serving us and ordered another round of drinks.

"You'll have me under the table in no time," I said when the drinks came. Jake just looked at me, impassive, inscrutable. I had the uncomfortable feeling that what happened to me didn't matter to him one way or the other, and it occurred to me with a jolt that perhaps the only reason I was along at all was to ferry him over here.

The air inside the room had grown thick and hazy with smoke. An expectant buzz had arisen in the crowd since the first movement of the curtains. Every once in a while a peal of coarse laughter would ring out, and I could feel my pulse beginning to throb a little faster as I peered around the room. People were sitting at nearly all of the tables now, most of them middle-aged men with sallow complexions and relatively short, greasy-looking combed hair, although there were women in the crowd also, two of them sitting with their male companions at a table bordering the stage. Men and women alike were either paunchy and overweight—bloated by years of excessive beer drinking—or bony, sharp and angular, as if having been deprived of proper nutrition. Almost none of them appeared to be my age.

The lights suddenly went off and for an instant we were plunged into a darkness that seemed utter and absolute. Then the footlights came on and loud piped-in Arabian music burst forth from the sound system. The curtains parted to reveal a woman clad in cardinal red silk pajamas and a chador-like hood that covered her hair and veiled all of her face except for her eyes. The melody was at once sinuous and raspy, as if someone had turned the volume up louder than the system could handle. The woman danced in serpentine, undulating motions meant to be in synchrony with the music, but the occasional mistiming of a maneuver, as well as her height—she was a tall woman, clearly American rather than Arabian—made her movements awkward and ungainly. This went on for what seemed like five minutes before she plucked off one of her many diaphanous veils, twirled about the stage, and finally tossed it aside with a quick disdainful flick of her wrist. She did this with several veils before anything more significant came off.

"Do it!" someone called out, prompting two or three whistles from others in the crowd.

Her hands were alternately darting above her head and back down, curling out and then beckoning in toward herself, her hips all the while gyrating below inside the red silk pajamas. The scarlet chador still covered her hair and hid her face, although above the veil her dark eyes were unwavering and mirthful and sparkled with the pleasure of taunting so many people, as if she were in absolute control of everything she saw, a puppeteer commanding the network of strings for a very large cast. Then for a moment the spell of her liquid rippling volutions ceased and her hands quickly slipped the pajamas off, revealing a sequined red bikini and long, slim, creamy legs whose exposure changed the texture of her dance entirely and elicited a few hoots and howls from the audience. The conceit of her act was now clearly the chador, and her eyes, undaunted and mocking, seemed to invite the question of what would come off next.

I took my eyes off the stage to see how the crowd was responding, and Jake was staring right at me, that faint curling hint of a smile at the corner of his lips.

"Just don't drool," he said.

I laughed, but his gaze never left me and I felt compelled to look away. Most people in the crowd had their eyes riveted on the stage, some with the sort of slack-jawed, slavering fascination I feared Jake saw in me (*had* I been guilty of this sort of fawning idiocy? the thought revolted me); some slouched back in their chairs, legs extended in a kind of practiced pose of indifference; some leaning on their tables, craning forward as though drawn by an invisible magnetic force; some continuing to hold conversations punctuated by outbursts of laughter, paying only minimal attention to the act on stage, as though all the dancer's efforts were no more significant than the fluttering of a moth.

I took another drink. In the steeping sweetness of alcohol I considered such indifference the worst form of degradation, really, and felt awash in a kind of benevolence, a warm enveloping pity for this woman with the mocking eyes who was, after all, giving something of herself to all of us. That some people had no appreciation for what she was doing—for our benefit—saddened and angered me. The very least you could do was give her your attention.

"Yeeeow!" someone yelled out.

She had stripped down now to pasties, a G-string, and the chador, the absurd conceit of which increased in direct proportion to the amount of flesh she exposed and the exacerbated jiggle of her breasts. Still, to me what she was doing was generous and wonderful, and the boors in the audience didn't deserve it.

"Face don't matter anyway," asserted a voice nearby, followed by the inevitable guffaws.

Keep it on, I found myself thinking, hoping, as though the chador were part of some bluffing game, and if she could only keep it on she would win whatever was at stake. But in a moment she lifted it from her head, twirled it around, and tossed it aside, setting loose a mane of mousy brown hair that frizzed out wildly from all the static electricity that had been built up in it. I felt a sharp pang of disappointment. Her lips, wide and very red, were set in a haughty, seductive leer, and about her face now there was a peculiar look of triumph.

But she had not finished and everyone in the audience knew it. All trace of the sinuous Arabian music departed and the only thing that could be heard now was the loud beat of drums and the occasional crash of cymbals. In perfect synchrony with the cymbals she plucked off the pasties and timed the looping swings and thrusts of her hips with the rapid drum roll crescendos and the periodic bang of the bass drum. With one last great boom of the drum the G-string flew off and she dangled it triumphantly above her head before tossing it behind her toward the curtains. Posing now with one arm straight above her head and the other extended forward, she reminded me of the rigid breathless torso of a female figure skater presenting herself to the crowd for their approval after her solo performance. But instead of a cascade of applause she was greeted with more frenzied hoots and howls and the outstretched arms of men with dollar bills in their hands. She collected the bills and tucked them into the crack of her ass, creating a tail more ostentatious than a peacock's. Then she turned so that she was mooning the crowd and, pirouetting slowly for the appreciation of the entire audience, wiggled her ass in such a way that her leafy green tail trembled. I noticed a couple of pale blue bruises on the backside of her legs.

The whistles and the catcalls continued as she snatched the money from her ass, faced the crowd again, and made a low bow. Just as she was about to wheel and depart an impulse struck her and she stepped forward to the edge of the stage not far in front of us. An expectant hush fell over everyone as she reached down to a middle-aged man seated there, took off the coke bottle glasses he was wearing, folded the temples and, just as she had done with the money, wedged the glasses into the crack of her ass. She bounced about the stage with them, swaggered back to the now red-faced owner, and using the thumb and index finger of her right hand to extract the glasses, held them at arm's length. Then she turned her head away, pinched her nose between the fingers of her left hand, scrunched up her face as if disgusted by the smell, and extended the glasses behind her to their owner. A renewed and intensified welter of jibes accompanied her as she ran to the back of the stage and disappeared through the curtains. The chador, along with the rest of her costume, lay in a heap on the floor where she had discarded it.

The man with the glasses turned as if thinking some sort of speech was expected of him and said, "I'll never wash them again," which sparked a brush fire of derisive cackles and quips.

"It was a shitty thing to do," one of the man's cohorts deadpanned.

"And we thought your eyesight stunk *before*," another one said.

I turned to Jake.

He was tracking our waitress again. As if he'd sent out a signal and she had radar she looked in our direction, saw Jake, and worked her way over to our table.

"We could use another drink," he said.

She shot a cursory look at me, then smiled at Jake and left to get the drinks. Jake shook another Lucky Strike from his pack, tapped each end of it on the table and lit it.

For some reason I found myself suddenly wanting—needing really—Jake's approval, and yet resenting the subordinate nature of such a feeling. Why should his approval mean anything to me? It was Jake who had gone to Vietnam and undoubtedly killed other human beings, not me. And it was Jake who had run away from his own family in the middle of the night, not me. Why should his opinion matter at all? And for what, exactly, was

I seeking his approval? The fact that I did *not* go to Vietnam? There was nothing to apologize for, no reason for me to feel inferior, morally or in any other way. And yet I did.

"Jake," came a voice from the moil within me, startling in its honesty and forthrightness. "Why did you ask me that question about the returning gook-killer?" His cold blue eyes bored into me. "It wasn't a fair question."

"Why's that, Ace, did I embarrass you?"

The waitress delivered our drinks. Jake winked and she smiled at him again and left.

As I was about to answer there was a dimming of the lights followed by the abruptly intense brightness of the footlights and the brassy blare of circus music. A buxom blond dressed in the sequined, iridescent garb of a circus animal trainer burst forth from the maroon velour curtains. She was fair-skinned, her face heavily made up with rouge and lipstick and eyeliner. She wore leopard skin boots and carried a whip and a chair in her hands. With her ample chest held high, she stepped imperiously about the stage cracking the whip.

I took a sip of my drink. "It wasn't a matter of embarrassment, it was a matter of fairness," I said, raising my voice above the din. I did not want to lose the moment.

He took a long drag of his cigarette. "And now's a fair time," he said, smoke coming from his nose and mouth as he spoke.

I nodded. "It's better than in front of the whole family."

Jake looked toward the stage for a moment. The woman snapped the whip and there was a sharp crack. "Hah!" he said, laughing as he turned to face me again. The humor in his eyes was like nothing I had ever seen in him before. It was a cold, wild humor, as cold and remote and joyless as the icy depths of the ocean. "So what do you want from me, Ace? You want to know how many gooks I wasted?"

There was another crack of the whip. "I want to know about your being a LURP."

A flicker of surprise faintly creased his brow. His voice was low and flat, and the blare of the circus music made it difficult for me to hear him. "Who told you I was a LURP?"

"Bucky."

"Bucky doesn't know what the fuck he's talking about. Where'd you see him?"

"He's home. I saw him in a bar one night. He said he bumped into you in Da Nang."

All the wild humor had gone out of Jake's eyes now. The only thing that remained was the cold remoteness. He took a final drag of his cigarette and mashed it into the ashtray with slow and careful efficiency, so that not a single burning ember remained. "That's a crock."

"Jake," I said, playing my final card carefully. "Bucky was in bad shape."

Jake looked at me steadily, waiting for me to continue.

"His legs were blown off by a mine. He was in a wheelchair." I paused to let the news sink in, but Jake's expression never changed. "He looked like hell, Jake."

"Fortunes of war," Jake said without a hint of emotion. If I hadn't known better I would have thought we were discussing the fate of a person neither of us knew, not someone Jake had once seen fit to defend in a brutal fight. "It doesn't mean he knows what he's talking about."

The stripper was down to pasties, G-string, and leopard skin boots now, bent over near the edge of the stage, where she was swinging her large breasts not far above the outstretched hands of several men. When a hand got too close she would rear back, thrust the chair in front of her as if fending off a big cat, then crack the whip high above the offending beast.

"So you weren't a LURP," I said.

Jake just looked at me.

The air in the room had grown stiflingly hot and steamy from all the smoke and the bodies and the musky excretions of sexual excitement. I was dripping with sweat. I took a sip of my drink. "Then what *did* you do over there?"

Jake dropped his gaze for a moment to the matches he fingered in his hand. Then he looked up at me again, his eyes narrowed not so much out of menace as out of a kind of unsparing measurement. "You don't want to know what I did over there, Ace. Do you understand? You don't fucking want to know." He enunciated each word of the last line slowly and clearly as his eyes bored into me with implacable conviction. Despite the sweltering bacchanal around us I felt a chill shiver along my spine. *He was right.* I did *not* want to know what he had done in Vietnam. Even worse, somewhere beneath the blur of alcohol and the raucous assaulting noise all around me was the sure, quiet, accompanying realization that I now *knew* I did not want to know what he had done.

On stage the stripper, glistening with sweat, had taken off everything except her boots. My stomach was beginning to feel queasy and my head was beginning to spin. "I think I need some air," I said. "I'll be right back."

Jake was not even looking at me as I started up from my chair. His attention was drawn to some sort of commotion at a table nearby involving our waitress, who was apparently contending with a disorderly customer and peering about for help from the bouncer.

"What's the problem?" Jake said, quickly moving near.

"No problem," she said, slightly abashed and still glancing nervously about her for the bouncer as the circus music grew insistently louder and faster. The stripper, finished with her routine, ran to the back of the stage where she wheeled, cupped a breast in each hand, kissed each nipple as if in thanks for its contribution to her act, and then disappeared through the velour curtains. The crowd howled in approval.

"What's it to you anyway?" said a churlish drunken voice directed at Jake. The voice came from a paunchy middle-aged man seated on the other side of the waitress from where Jake stood. A bang of oily black hair, swept to one side, covered most of his forehead. Thick black stubble sprouted from his bloated cheeks. "The lady just needs a little lovin'." He scanned his two buddies at the table and added, looking from Jake to me as he circled the waitress' waist with his fat arm, "Besides, looks to me like you already got yourself a girlfriend!"

His buddies instantly erupted in laughter, but only for an instant, because before any of them knew what was happening Jake grabbed a beer mug and smashed in the guy's teeth. There was a moment of stunned silence as everyone in the vicinity registered the fact of what had just happened, although the moaning and the blood confirmed the facts quickly enough for the guy's buddies, who leaped up from where they were sitting and tried to make their way to Jake. But they were boxed in by tables and chairs and people, and by the time they reached Jake the bouncer had also arrived, a large burly man with a walrus mustache.

The bouncer forced himself between Jake and the two enraged buddies. One of them lunged at Jake and the bouncer shoved him roughly backwards, where he lost his balance over a chair and bumped into his buddy with the broken teeth, who was still seated and cupping the lower half of his face in disbelief.

"What the hell's going on here?" the bouncer said, looking to the waitress for an explanation. He wore a white dress shirt open at the collar, with the sleeves rolled up on his thick forearms. By this time a crowd had circled around like a ring of vultures.

"This jerk," she motioned to the potbellied provocateur nursing his bloody mouth, "started giving me a hard time, and this guy came over to help me out. But he's the one that started the whole thing," she said, pointing an accusing finger at the miserable figure who had clearly received the worst of it all.

The bouncer did not hesitate. He grabbed the man by the shirt collar, pulled him from his chair, and shoved him roughly toward the exit. "Get out of here," he barked.

"What about him?" the buddies complained, gesturing angrily at Jake. They were a full head shorter than the bouncer and not about to challenge him physically, but they had not yet made a move toward the exit.

"You too, both of you. Out of here," the bouncer said, thumbing them out of the room.

"For Chrissake, he's the bastard smashed in Ralphie's teeth," one of them shouted.

"He's none of your business. Now get out of here before I kick you out on your asses."

The bouncer's withering stare broke them quickly and they slouched away, murmuring over their shoulders that they would "never come back to this fucking dive again."

The bouncer watched them until they left. "The rest of you just go back to your seats," he said. "Nothing's happening here." He made a shooing motion with his hands as if he were half-heartedly attempting to drive off a group of crows.

When the gathering had dispersed he said to Jake, "In the future, why don't you just sit tight and let me handle any problems, okay? We don't need no fucking heroes around here." He held Jake's impassive gaze for a moment before shooting a cursory glance at the waitress and ambling away to make sure the vanquished trio weren't hanging around somewhere.

"Thank you," the waitress said to Jake.

Jake nodded.

"I hate guys like that. They make you feel filthy."

She noticed Jake's glance at the wedding ring she was worrying on her finger. "I'm not married. I just wear this to keep the wolves away, but with animals like that it wouldn't matter if I wore a *sign* saying I was married."

"They couldn't read it anyway," I said.

She laughed. "I'd love to dump a beer on his head, but I can't afford to lose this job. I've got a little girl at home who needs me working. Where are you guys from?"

"Across the river," Jake said.

"Newtown," I added. "But Jake just got back from Vietnam."

Jake cast a sharp look at me.

The waitress grew solemn even as the dynamic music of the William Tell Overture began playing over the sound system and a new stripper appeared on the stage dressed as a skirted version of The Lone Ranger. She swung a lariat above her head.

"My brother was killed over there a few years ago," the waitress said.

"Where?" Jake said.

"Khe Sanh."

Jake nodded.

"What about you? Did you see any combat over there?"

"Some."

"Well I'm glad you made it home in one piece." She looked up at the stage. "I better get back to work."

"There's just one thing," Jake said.

"What's that?" she asked.

"Could you bring us another round of drinks?"

"Sure."

"Not for me," I said. "Thanks anyway." The waves of nausea I had been feeling earlier were beginning to return. I needed air.

Outside, there were no stars in the sky but the night air was cool and still, and my head gradually began to clear. I thought about what had just happened and realized I would not have done what Jake did. *Could* not have done it. Which squared perfectly with my pacifist beliefs, except that I had the troubling notion that pacifism had nothing to do with it. I would have watched the bully torment the waitress until the bouncer arrived to take care of the situation, as he ultimately did anyway, and the whole affair would have followed its natural course. The waitress would have suffered the normal consequences of duty in her line of work, the bouncer would have done what he was hired to do, the offending boor would have been rousted out—with his teeth intact—and we would all have been at least as well off. Yet this alternative scenario disturbed me in a way I could not easily define. There was something cowardly about sitting as a bystander waiting for nature to take its course. Whether Jake was right or wrong in smashing the guy's face, wasn't he at least trying to push nature along a different course, a course of his choosing rather than a haphazard one? "Not to decide is to decide" was the caveat spray-painted on campus walls across the country, and implicit within it was the imperative to act against injustice. Wasn't Jake trying to take control by acting, rather than to be controlled—or allow control to rest outside of him—by not acting? And what did this say about me?

My head began to spin again at the thought of going back inside to the smoke and the noise and the raunchy spectacle of quasi-appealing women degrading themselves. The night was still relatively young, but I felt so weary it seemed late to me. I had a powerful urge to climb into my bug and head home, except that Jake was still inside and I didn't want to leave him behind. Reluctantly, I headed back in to tell him I wasn't up for staying any longer.

But when I returned to our table, Jake was not there. I waited for fifteen minutes, figuring he'd just gone to the men's room and would be right back, but he never showed. At last I hailed our waitress and asked if she knew what had happened to him.

"He left right after you did," she said. "Didn't you see him? He cancelled the drink order and paid the tab—with a very generous tip. That's some brother you've got there."

"That's strange," I said. "I mean, I had my back to the entrance but I wasn't far away from it, and I never saw him leave. Is there another way out of here?"

"There's the emergency door over there," she pointed to a red neon "EXIT" sign, "but I thought I saw him head toward the main entrance."

"Did he say anything to you before he left?"

She looked away for a moment as though considering how she should answer the question. "He asked if he could see me sometime."

"Oh."

"He's going to meet me here when I get off tonight."

"Did he say anything else? Did he tell you to say anything to me?"

She shook her head. "Sorry."

It was between acts for the strippers and the jukebox was playing Janis Joplin's version of "Me and Bobby McGee," a song that in any other circumstance would have had me belting out with Janis, "Freedom's just another word for nothing left to lose," but at the moment I did not feel much like singing. "I wonder where he went."

"Sorry I can't help you," she said. "But I get off a little after one if you need to see him. He said he'd be here then."

"No, I think I'll head out. Thanks anyway, though."

Jake, you bastard, I thought, *where have you gone? What are you doing?* Buried beneath the anger and the confusion I felt—so far down as to be virtually out of sight—was another emotion, too dark and slippery to be dragged up into the light of full consciousness. But I knew that it had something to with envy.

It didn't take Jake long to end his dependence on others for transportation. Within a week he bought a motorcycle that he painted completely black, after which he came and went as he pleased, without notice or explanation to anyone. He wore his olive drab fatigue jacket constantly, even in the heat of summer, let his hair grow out and again grew a beard, which was no longer the peach fuzz of his first attempts—it was coarse and fairly thick, reddish brown in color. He carried a knife at all times. When he was home—which wasn't very often—he slept, if sleep is what those brief daytime interludes in his room could be called: he would thrash about or call out so sharply it seemed he was experiencing anything but sleep. Then he would emerge from his room without explanation (nor would any of us ask him for one), usually in the late morning or early afternoon, just long enough to eat a meal wordlessly before heading out for parts unknown. He was usually gone all night, and often for more than one night.

We always knew when he was home because the smell of cigarette smoke and occasionally wood smoke trailed him wherever he went. One of the most common sights that summer was Mother sniffing her way through the house with a can of Glade air freshener in her hand, stalking the invisible enemy and trying to cover it up with the cloying aromas of "forest pine" or "garden mist." One of the most common sounds was the hissing spray of these cans. Jake usually only smoked in his room—I'm sure Mother would not have tolerated it at all, otherwise—but he had a habit of flicking off his ashes wherever he happened to be, and would sometimes leave a small mound of them on the dining room table or the kitchen floor. One day as Mother was cleaning his room while he was out I heard her complain with unmitigated disgust, "We are *not* living in Vietnam here!"

The smoking was an issue for a much more serious reason as well: Lydia's health. I never heard Mother challenge Jake overtly about his smoking, but in her unending battle to keep Lydia healthy she must have been very disturbed by it—because during the summer months when I was home from school Lydia's health seemed to me generally worse than it had been in some time. I don't know if Jake's smoking—or Mother's "smoke screening," for that matter—had anything to do with it, but Lydia's allergies seemed to be constantly bothering her. She had no serious or life-threatening asthma attacks, but she was always sneezing or blowing her nose, her eyes appeared perpetually watery, and her voice sounded nasal, as if she had a cold she couldn't get rid of. She used the inhaler more often than I had ever seen her use it before. Unlike Mother, Lydia complained openly to Jake about his smoking, but she never connected its potential harm to herself—her complaints were always that the habit was harmful to him, not to her.

What Lydia did not realize, at least not at first, was that Jake had brought another habit back with him that was much more serious: getting wasted on booze or drugs, or some combination of the two, at any time of day. It wasn't as though he'd never been drunk or high before going to Vietnam—like most teenagers in the late sixties he'd had a liberal education in altered states of consciousness—but every time I saw him that summer he was fucked up on dope or acid, or numbed out of his skull on Southern Comfort and Quaaludes. I'd seen enough in my friends (and done enough myself) that the signs were pretty obvious. Jake had no qualms, either, about admitting it when I'd casually ask him what he was on: "Ludes, Ace. Fucking ludes and Southern Comfort. You should try it."

For a time I think Mother and Father, like Lydia, had no idea what was going on either. Except for the sound of the motorcycle, which announced his arrivals and departures on our quiet street as loudly as a car without a muffler, Jake came and went almost surreptitiously. He would be in his room one moment, and the next moment we would realize by the slowly receding roar of his motorcycle that he had left. He had very little to do with any of us, even Lydia, who had been so desperate for his return. She wanted terribly to go for a ride with him on the motorcycle, if only up and down our street, and Jake was willing to take her, but Mother squelched the idea with an adamantine will: "Utterly out of the question!" were her exact words to Lydia. My night out with Jake at *The Cave* was the only time we said much more than a sentence to each other that summer. He never went to any of Ben's baseball games, as the rest of us often did, rarely joined us at the family dinner table, and chose not to go to the beach at all when Father took his two-week vacation in July. Baseball kept Ben from spending the entire two weeks at the beach and my summer job kept me at home; but one or both of us would go up for at least one weekend night and would make it a point to ask Jake if he wanted to join us. His answer was always the same: "I've got things to do."

"What things?" I wanted to ask him, but I knew it would be useless.

After a while, though, even Mother and Father began to realize Jake's behavior was unusual. There was a kind of carelessness about him that he'd never shown before. He used the word "fuck"—which *no one* used openly in our family—frequently, with little regard for the listener or the context of the situation.

"Watch your language please, Jake," Mother would say with a forbearance she never would have shown to me or Ben. "You're not in the Marines anymore." If Jake chose to acknowledge her at all he might nod, but the next time he had something to say it would again be laced with profanities.

His hair would be in wild disarray whenever he came out to get something to eat in the late morning or early afternoon. One time his left eye was swollen shut and the rust-colored evidence of blood was all over his shirt.

"Jake, what happened to you?" Lydia asked. She was the only one, except perhaps for Father if he were around, who would question Jake about his activities.

"A little altercation with the fucking bedpost," he said.

"Jake, please," Mother warned.

"But isn't that blood on your shirt?" Lydia asked.

"Spaghetti sauce."

"Tell me the truth. What happened to you?"

"It was the meanest fucking plate of spaghetti I've ever seen. What can I say?"

"The truth."

"You can watch your tongue," Mother said more sharply than before.

"You should see the plate though," Jake said to Lydia.

"I'm serious," Lydia said.

"So am I."

He came home late one night belting out the lyrics to a Deep Purple song, "Hush, hush, I thought I heard her calling my name now," in such a loud drunken voice that he woke everyone in the house, or at least everyone not already awakened by the roar of his motorcycle.

One Sunday morning after Father had rousted him out of bed for brunch, Jake poured himself a cup of coffee and stood there sipping the hot brew. Everyone else had eaten and departed from the kitchen when Father came up from behind and put his hand on Jake's shoulder (Father told me later he just wanted to ask Jake if he'd like some cream cheese for his bagel). Jake wheeled and threw the steaming coffee at Father's chest. Luckily Father was wearing his *HARMONY* apron, so most of the coffee was deflected or absorbed in such a way that he was not badly burned, but the effect was almost as startling as if he had actually been scalded.

"Are you all right?" Jake asked.

"I think so," Father said as he stripped off his apron and shirt. "Why did you do that?"

"I don't know," Jake said. "Sorry."

"It's all right," Father said. "I'm sure you didn't mean it. You're probably just not awake yet. I shouldn't have woken you up before you were ready." Then he looked at the apron and the shirt and said, "I better get these in the wash right away. Coffee stains are hard to get out."

Jake nodded, poured himself another cup of coffee, and sat down at the table.

That summer one thing became clearer than ever before: Jake represented competition to Mother, competition for Lydia. She was not a competitive person by nature and would never have admitted it or defined it in such terms. Nor would she have *consciously* competed for Lydia's affection or attention—and Jake wouldn't have either. But in some ways that was what his return meant. It could be seen in apparently insignificant matters such as hair style: Mother suggested Lydia get away from the long, straight style of the day, while Jake—at least according to Lydia—said he liked it that way, so she kept it halfway down her back. And it could be seen in more important matters, such as Lydia's spending a night camping with friends. Mother and Jake actually locked horns over this issue openly—a rarity in our house even though conflict murmured through the rooms almost constantly after Jake's return.

The parents of some of Lydia's friends planned to take them to Greenfield State Park and let them set up camp for themselves for one night, then pick them up the following day. Two of the girls were Girl Scouts and had been on their own before. When Lydia asked Mother about going with them, I think she fully expected to be able to go. She sounded excited and hopeful as she pointed out that she had never been camping before and thought it would be a lot of fun.

"Lydia," Mother said, in that tone of hers that sounded so understanding and reasonable but which I knew from experience was really the prelude to disappointment, "I'm afraid you're going to have to call the girls and tell them you can't go."

Lydia looked shocked, although in retrospect I'm not sure why. Mother's response was predictable and Lydia should have been expecting it.

"Why?" Lydia said defiantly.

Mother had a feather duster in her hand and was flitting about the living room like a hummingbird. Her routine entailed lighting upon every object in the room with a quick flutter of the feather duster, then going back over everything by hand with a dust cloth. She turned to Lydia, the feather duster momentarily suspended in midair, "Because you've never been away overnight, and we don't know what could happen if you were to have an asthma attack."

Lydia was incredulous. "Is that the only reason?"

"No, but I think it's a pretty important one, don't you?"

"I haven't had a bad attack since before Jake got home."

"That's true, but your allergies have been bothering you a lot lately, haven't they? And we never know when that will flare into a full-blown attack."

Lydia sneezed, as if to prove Mother's point.

"God bless you," Mother said. And then added gently, "You see?"

"It's because of you and that stupid duster," Lydia said, her eyes beginning to water. "And all that disgusting spray you pollute the air with." She sneezed again.

"God bless you."

"Waving that around just throws all sorts of dust in the air," Lydia argued.

"And you don't think there will be dust and pollen and leaf mold and all sorts of other things to bother you on a camping trip?"

"Of *course* there will be, but I'll have my inhaler with me, and *I'll be having fun.*"

"That in itself can be a problem, Lydia, and you know it. Too much excitement, too many allergens, too little sleep, too far away from help... it's the perfect recipe for trouble."

"I *wouldn't* be far away from help," Lydia insisted, knowing she was losing the battle.

"The answer is 'No,' Lydia. You can blame it on me if you'd like, but you'll just have to tell your friends you can't go." Mother turned and resumed her dusting.

At this point Jake stepped out of his room, where he must have been hearing it all. "Why don't you let her go," he said, more as a statement than a question.

Mother turned to face her new adversary, this time looking a little shaken. She had generally steered clear of disputes with Jake—he always did what he wanted anyway—and as a result they almost never had any public disagreements.

"Jake, this is really none of your business. Please stay out of it."

"She needs to get out once in a while," Jake said. "You should start letting her go."

Mother's lips pursed and her nostrils flared as she took a deep breathe. "I will let her go when I believe she is old enough, and not before."

"When will that be?" Lydia said. "I'm fourteen now and I've never even been to a slumber party. Do I need to be forty?"

Mother gave Lydia an intense stare. "If it means you live to that age, yes."

"Oh, come off it, Mom." Lydia had been buoyed for a moment by Jake's intervention, but her resolve was beginning to wilt again. In most matters Lydia could wrap Mother around her finger easily, but in matters involving her health Mother was utterly intransigent, and Lydia understood this better than anyone.

"The answer is 'No,' Lydia. I don't care how many times you ask."

Then Mother looked at Jake. "And I will thank *you* to keep your opinions to yourself. It's hard enough raising a fourteen-year-old girl without someone challenging your authority—"

"All right, Mom, I can't go," Lydia interrupted. "You've made your point."

Mother ignored her and continued. "While you were off proving your manhood, who cared for this child when she was sick?" The feather duster trembled in her hand.

Jake stood there silently with his thumbs hooked into the pockets of his jeans.

"And believe me, she *has* been sick. Caring for her is not easy, especially when there's a battle every step of the way."

Jake remained silent but Lydia couldn't contain herself. "You're a saint, Mom. We all know it. What do you want him to do, get on his knees and pray to you?"

"You see?" Mother said to Jake. "Wouldn't it be easier to give in than to put up with this? But that's not what being a parent means, at least not a responsible parent."

"She needs to get out and live a little bit," Jake said evenly.

Mother and Jake regarded each other for a moment. "That's exactly what I'm trying to do," Mother said solemnly, "help her to live—and neither of you seems to understand that."

"Mom, life is more than going to school and reading books all the time," Lydia said, close to tears. "*You* don't seem to understand *that*. I want to do other things in my life."

"And I would like to see you do those other things, my dear stubborn baby. I pray every day you'll have a long and healthy life, and you'll live to see all your dreams come true, but not before I believe you are ready." Mother shook her head in tender sympathy as Lydia began to break down before her. She put the feather duster aside and moved to cradle Lydia in her arms. Lydia offered only a token momentary resistance before settling into Mother's forgiving embrace. "Not before you are ready," Mother whispered into the soft golden crown of Lydia's head. She stroked Lydia's hair as if it were made of the finest strands of spun gold.

Jake turned and left the house without another word.

That night I was awakened once again by the explosive reverberations of Jake's motorcycle coming down the street and into our driveway. *I'd like to scrap that noisy fucking piece of shit,*

I thought as I dozed back to sleep. I hadn't been asleep for long though when I heard the odd sounds of a woman's laughter and the jangle of bracelets coming from the living room. "Jake," I heard the woman say in a drunken giggle, "Let's do it over there, against the clock. Let's fuck Father Time." I was content to lie back and let Jake and his companion have their way with each other, but I wondered if anyone else was hearing this. Ben surely wasn't—he was snoring away. But what about Mother and Father? What about Lydia? Somebody else must be hearing this too because there was certainly nothing discreet about it. What confused me was Jake. What was he doing? Why was he here? In the past he'd never been so careless.

Then I heard Mother's voice, taut with suppressed outrage. "Jake, what in God's name is going on here?" I opened the bedroom door enough to peer down the hallway into the living room. A light was on and I could see a heavy woman with large breasts, naked from the waist up. She had black hair teased up into a sort of beehive. I could not see Mother or Jake at all.

"Who's she?" said the woman, giggling again.

"Get your clothes on and get out of this house. Don't you have any respect for yourself?" Mother's outrage was surpassed only by her unmistakable intention to end the episode as quickly as possible so that no one else—most especially Lydia—would become involved.

"Hey, wait a minute. Jake, I thought this was *your* house? Who's *this* bitch?"

"I could understand your lack of respect for me, Jake, but what about your sister? Have you no shame at all?"

"Is she your mother?"

"Jake, if you don't get this tramp out of the house *now* you'll never set foot in here again."

"Don't worry, lady, I don't like fucking in front of an audience anyway, especially when it's someone's *mother*." The woman began to put her clothes back on.

"Hurry up!" Mother said, barely able to contain her fury. "There's a fourteen-year-old girl living here who has no business waking up to the likes of you."

The woman finished dressing. Jake came into view then as he prodded the woman toward the stairs to the front door, with Mother following close behind. I could see from the expression on his face that he was present in body only. He was not only shitfaced drunk but probably tripping besides. His eyes had such a zonked out look that I wondered how he could possibly have driven home on his motorcycle. Then I realized it wasn't just driving home in such a condition—he must also now drive away.

Two days later Jake left home for good. I don't know if Mother told him to leave or not, but it came as a surprise to no one but Lydia, and perhaps to Father, although I think he was more disappointed than surprised. Ben's comment, after I described the spectacle of Mother confronting a naked floozy in her house in the dead of night, proved to be prophetic: "He's gone. Even Jake can't get away with that." But Lydia, I'm convinced, never knew what had happened and therefore never suspected Jake might be leaving soon.

She came running from his room on a sweltering day in early August and announced it in breathless disbelief: "Jake's leaving!"

Without Lydia's objections, and Father's too to a lesser degree, it would not have taken Jake long at all. He would have packed what little he owned onto his motorcycle and driven away, which is undoubtedly how he would have preferred it. Instead, Lydia followed him every step of the way, trying to convince him to stay and dogging him with questions that ranged from the pragmatic, "Where are you going to live?" (his answer: "I've got a place."), to the more deeply searching, "Why do you want to leave us, Jake?" (his answer: silence, until she repeated the question and he was forced to reply, "I need freedom, Lydia, that's all.").

"Do you have a job lined up yet?" Father asked at one point.

Jake shook his head as he swept past with a box of record albums. He wore jeans and a black T-shirt stained with sweat. It was hot enough that day that even Jake was sweating, and for once he had discarded his fatigue jacket.

"Well, why don't you stay until you find a job, at least," Father argued.

"I'll find one," Jake said as the screen door slammed shut behind him.

"Rose, what do you think about this?" Father asked.

Mother had on her cloth gloves and was trimming back a Swedish Ivy in the kitchen with pruning shears. "I think Jake is capable of deciding these things for himself," she said, clipping off a long shoot that fell to the floor. "It's not like he's never lived away from home before."

"True, but don't you think he should have a job and a decent income before he leaves?"

Mother went over to the screen door and fixed the latch so that the door would stay open. "Jake will find what he needs. I have no doubt of that."

Lydia came back inside the house with Jake. She had been haranguing him even as she helped him to pack things onto the motorcycle.

"I can't believe you're just going to let him go," she said, looking directly at Mother. Jake continued past them to his room. "He's got problems from the war, you know."

"I would love to see him stay, Lydia," Father said. "As far as I'm concerned he's welcome to stay as long as he wants. But it's his choice to leave, sweetheart, and there's not much I can do about it." Father held out his upraised palms in a gesture of futility and resignation.

"What about you, Mom? You could get him to stay if you wanted to."

"If Jake feels it's time to leave, I won't stand in his way," Mother said. "It's his life." She had resumed her trimming of the Swedish Ivy. "My, these plants grow wild quickly," she said, as she clipped another shoot that fell to the kitchen floor.

A short time later we heard three loud quick revs of the motorcycle, followed by the resounding crescendos of Jake shifting through the gears in departure.

Chapter Thirteen

The Keeper

In the daytime, asleep, it was often the same: someone would shout "Incoming!" and he would be crouching low in a hole, the heat and the sweat and the jungle rot and the exhaustion instantly gone, the only reality now the sounds of choppers and mortar fire and the pounding of his heart, and then a grunt screaming nearby "I'm hit! I'm hit!" and going forward to help but finding Jacko with his guts ripped open and shit oozing out of him and a grin on his face, and then firing his M-16 on Jacko an instant before the explosion rips his leg open in a blinding flash of red light, followed by the medic hunched over him repeating like a mantra, "You'll be all right!" and lifting his canteen to his mouth for a drink of water because he is thirstier than he has ever been in his life and finding nothing inside but the metallic rattle of shrapnel.

Or he might be watching a sapper come through the wire like a nervous twitching rat in a maze, the face nothing but a gook face bobbing up and stopping, listening, then twitching forward again, he himself watching and waiting until he knows the moment is perfect, the middle of the forehead precisely in his sights, and then the welcome release of tension on the trigger and the face transmogrifying hideously into his own before the moment of impact, which leaves upon his forehead a small perfectly formed black circle and occurs without sound except for the curious distant wail of a child, by whose cry he understands he did not hit the intended target.

The worst was the hooch going up in a wall of flame with the smell of napalm and burning human flesh so pungent as to be almost palpable, smoke rising thick and black and straight, like an offering to some warped god, himself an acolyte standing near the flame and stoking it with bodies and body parts which he pitches mechanically into its ravenous maw as if he is feeding an engine of doom, the screams and the wails and the roar of the flames merely the standard eructations of the engine operating efficiently, and nearby a grunt, impervious to the fire, entering the hooch with an empty shovel and exiting with the shovel heaped full of friable black cinders which he dumps into a bottomless chute and which fall with the peculiarly disturbing sound of creosote tinkling down a stovepipe.

The night was much safer. Awake and in control, he would drive along the dirt bike path that followed the river until he reached a spot where he knew he could stow the bike safely, no more than a few klicks away through the woods. He would reconnoiter all the way there and continue reconnoitering even as he walked the perimeter of the woods behind the house, his eyes never leaving her room for more than an instant. Sometimes when the light went off early enough and he was satisfied all was well he would circle back through the woods to his bike and cross the river to The Cave, or he would drive through the night without a particular destination except for any long straight stretch of road he happened to come upon, long enough and straight enough that he could hammer the throttle wide open and switch off the headlight to career headlong through the darkness, the wind intensifying beyond wind into sheer malevolent force, exhilarating as a kill, the road plunged into utter dark void for an eternity before resolving into a strangely luminescent ribbon cut through the black canyon of woods on either side like his personal highway to heaven, his passing the occasional random hapless motorists coming in the opposite direction—who must hear but not see what ripped past them—as startling to them perhaps as an unexpected outburst of incoming fire to a fucking new guy.

The one exception was the cop he passed hidden off the road on his side whose blue lights and headlights abruptly flashed on behind him to signal the start of a chase, a chase whose outcome was so certain in advance that to him it possessed all the drama of a mosquito buzzing about his head, the cop probably sitting there bored and awaiting any excuse for action, and he therefore intent to oblige and make it at least somewhat interesting by slowing down to a nearly complete stop, still without a light of his own, and reversing direction to wait as the cop sped closer, then slamming through the gears forward into and beyond the blinding blue strobes and the headlights which the sound of screeching tires informed him would presently be turning around behind him, as indeed they did although this time with the siren wailing out the heightened seriousness of his transgression, while he too reversed direction again and again the two flew past each other like blindly jousting knights, the cop afterwards ready for a third go, but he—having grown disdainful of the game now, with his engine off—waited silently for the cop to pass before firing up the bike and pulling out to follow the angry red and blue lights, the hunted now the hunter, until the cop slowed and he drew so near that even cutting the engine and cruising behind in neutral he could no longer remain undetected, and so simultaneously switched on his headlight and revved the engine to violent life and passed the cop to begin the chase in earnest, but only briefly, as this too soon grew tiresome and he played out the preconceived end of the drama by pulling off the road and out of sight until the cop finally passed him and disappeared for good.

On some nights he would drive to Hampton Beach and follow Route 1 to Rye and back again at breakneck speeds around the curves, surf crashing upon the rocks nearby in explosions of spray and foam, luridly white against the ebony backdrop of sea and sky. He would patrol up and down the strip on his motorcycle, past the bright neon lights of the casino and the arcades and the late-night tourists strolling the beach and the jailbait teeny-boppers out past their bedtimes hustling and being hustled by older boys, and then he would cruise the dark side streets slowly, where in the summer there was always some kind of action at night, always a party and a hole in the wall to score women or drugs if you knew how to look. On one such prowl he was drawn to the intermittent cries of a drunken woman surrounded by a triangle of three men who were poking and prodding her back and forth in the middle of the tenebrous street like a pinball in an arcade machine. Without hesitation he drove up and grabbed her by the arm and said, "Figures I'd find you trying to fuck around with somebody else," before turning to address her bewildered tormentors by saying, "I've been looking for this bitch for hours," and then dragging her roughly onto the bike. Too stunned to resist, she followed his lead until they reached the well-lit expanse of Ocean Boulevard, where he dropped her off and said, "Maybe next time luck will be on their side." He left her standing there with her shoulders slumped and her mouth agape, staring at him as if she were a hitchhiker who had just been given a short lift and dumped unceremoniously in the middle of nowhere.

He was not so lucky himself one night when he left a dive off the boulevard spaced out on acid and discovered a couple of shadowy figures trying to strip the tires from his bike. He was not even sure at first that it was anything more than a bad scene in a bad trip, but it would not disappear when he squinted and the figures bolted upright in a predictable manner at the sound of his shouts and the reckless bravado of his charge, although one of them caught him squarely on the side of his face with the swing of a chain before they wheeled and fled. The blow dropped him to the ground and nearly knocked him out. Down on all fours he sucked air and concentrated on not hyperventilating as he saw below him on the pavement a small growing pool which seemed too dark to be blood except that when he felt his cheek it was cut open and wet and had already begun to swell badly. His head spinning and his vision a nauseating blur, he got up and made his way past the wild swirling neon colors of the boulevard and the soft arresting desert of beach sand to the ocean, where he got back down on all fours and stuck his face into the breakers. The salt water stung the wound but cleansed it while the cold helped stanch the flow of blood after a time, but he could not dispose of the evidence, which remained in the form of a blood-stained shirt and an eye that swelled shut for more than a day.

Sometimes he would drive all the way to the mountains and through the notches in the deep of night when the sightseers and the tourists were gone from the highways and the road ahead did not seem to possess an independent existence, as though it were being created or invented by the single beam of his headlight slicing out a route between the rocky bluffs rising dark and enormous on either side. When he stopped and cut the engine and the lights there was an almost surreal quality of solitude and quiet and ebony darkness to the mountains, magnified and intensified to the point of bliss when he smoked a joint. On cloudless nights the stars were so prolific and the shooting stars so frequent he could no longer distinguish between what was real and what was not, unless he thought of her trapped back there in the house and how she had never seen such a night sky and maybe never would, and then he understood that an entire lifetime could blink on and off like one of those shooting stars and possess just as little reality, and that the only reality worth anything at all was what you could touch at any given moment, and that in truth none of the stars were real, or at least not real in a way *that mattered, not to him. He could do without the stars, although he also knew that if she were here she could make them real for him because they would matter to her. It occurred to him that everything mattered to her and nothing mattered to him, and that it was perhaps because she had lived so little and he had touched so much death.*

On nights when her light remained on and he felt the need to stay he would smoke cigarettes and take out a flask of Southern Comfort, and if his heart still did not slow he might retreat the short distance back through the woods to where he had set up a modest camp, out of sight but close enough that he could easily return to keep his vigil, and he might light a small fire in the clearing he had made and then do something more to ease the throbbing inside of him. The night after he had moved out he had done this and returned to find her light still on, very late, and he had waited and watched her shadow flit across the drawn shade of her window, wondering why she was awake so late and whether or not he should go to her, and then had waited more and decided, at last, that he would go to her, that he must go to her because it was no longer a matter of choice or desire now but a matter of need.

The house was dark and silent except for the normal sounds of the clock ticking in the living room and the hum of the refrigerator in the kitchen. No one else was awake when he gave her door a single short quick rap, not loud, muted by the press of his body, and waited for her to open the door for him. There was a moment of startled silence from within at first, followed by the hurried rustle of bedcovers and the creak of floorboards. When she opened the door her eyes widened only slightly. She waved him inside and softly closed the door behind him, then sat on the edge of her bed and patted a spot for him to sit next to her.

"What are you doing?" she whispered. It was well over two years since he had last been inside her room, and although she had not

grown much in that time he had the unmistakable sense that something in her had changed.

"I couldn't sleep," he said.

She gave him a curious look. "I never heard your bike."

"I can be quiet when I need to be," he said.

"But why did you come back?"

"I saw your light. It's late."

"I was up worrying about you," she said. "You didn't have to move out, you know." There was hurt in her eyes when she looked at him.

"I had to do it, Lydia."

"No you didn't. It was your choice. Nobody told you to leave, did they?"

He looked at her without speaking.

"And how do you think it makes people feel when you're never around, and even when you are you don't talk to them?"

"I'm here now," he said. He reached out and pushed the hair from either side of her downturned face, ran a hand along her cheek and down the length of her hair.

"Why?" she asked. "To make me feel worse than I already do?"

"I just wanted to make sure you were all right."

"Well I'm not, and neither are you," she whispered angrily. "You don't take care of yourself at all. You never sleep. You come home drunk. You smoke cigarettes all the time. And now you'll be gone and won't have anyone to watch out for you."

"I don't need anyone to watch out for me." He searched her eyes. "You're not having the dreams anymore, are you?"

"No. All my nightmares are about you getting killed in Vietnam." Her anger gave way to a kind of shyness. "I don't know what I would've done if you'd been killed, Jake."

He put his arm around her and drew her closer, pressed his lips to her hair. Through her nightgown he could feel the incipiently *nubile swells of her small breasts against his arm.* "You'd be all right. Better off, maybe."

"Don't say that," she said. "Don't ever say that."

Her head was against his chest and he wondered if she could hear the ferocious unrelenting throb of his heart. As he continued to stroke her hair a small sob broke loose in her and he realized she was crying. "What's wrong?" *he said.*

She shook her head against his chest. "I don't know. I just wish I could go and live with you. I think about you and worry about you all the time."

"You don't need to worry about me," *he said, studying her, but inside things were beginning to whirl and blur: her need was his need, and he was no longer certain what his need was or why he was here. He felt a twinge of something like fear.*

"I have to go," *he said.* "It's late and you need to go to sleep."

"Jake," *Lydia said to him at the door.* "I'm glad you came back."

He nodded and then closed the door quietly behind him.

On his way back through the woods it occurred to him with forceful clarity what the change was that he had sensed in her when he first opened the door: she was no longer a child.

He stopped and lit a cigarette. Her bedroom light was still on and he wondered if she might be listening for the motorcycle. But then the light blinked off and only darkness remained.

Chapter Fourteen

Moving Away

After Jake left home an unspoken tension seemed to lift from everyone. We no longer had to tiptoe around the house in broad daylight worried about making too much noise and waking him—one of Lydia's repeated admonitions, especially to Ben. And the smell of cigarette smoke disappeared, which meant we no longer had to endure the hissing sound of Mother's aerosol assaults or the pungent, cheap-perfume fragrances of air fresheners. Gone too were Jake's haphazardly deposited little piles of cigarette ashes, and we could now sleep through the night without being awakened by the cacophonous roar of his motorcycle (or by the bawdy giggles of a tart). We no longer had to be concerned about saying something—such as that Nixon was manipulating the end of the war for political advantage in his reelection campaign—or doing something—like tapping Jake unexpectedly on the shoulder as Father did—that might set him off. Mother no longer had to fear that Jake's vulgar language would defile her baby girl.

Lydia argued that Jake's behaviors were a sure sign the war had done something to him, that he needed our help; and she was correct, of course, because in retrospect Jake was clearly showing symptoms of post-traumatic stress disorder. At the time, though, the term for this condition—PTSD—had not even been invented yet, so it possessed for us no legitimate psychological or physiological reality. Even if it had, I can't help but think that, despite the correctness of Lydia's perceptions, the rest of us were relieved when Jake left. Life was just easier when he was not living at home.

After he left Jake moved into an apartment in a slummy part of Newtown and never came home again. I went to see him once before I returned to school for my senior year, partly out of curiosity and partly out of guilt, and the visit made an impression on me—especially when I learned months later that Lydia was stopping by to see him almost daily after school.

The late-summer evening light was just beginning to fade when I knocked on the door of apartment number five of a run-down brick building on Factory Street. As I stood and waited on the wooden stoop between apartments five and six, a couple passed by me on the right and entered number six. The man had shoulder-length dark hair and a bushy dark beard. He was heavyset and had an ample beer belly. The woman struck me because she was so much the reverse of the man. She appeared to be quite a bit younger, maybe only nineteen or twenty. She had long, straight, oily brown hair and was very thin and pale. Beneath her faded cut-off jean shorts her legs were long and spindly, the flesh of them a sort of translucent pasty white, like dough, upon which were faint blue bruises. I nodded to them when they approached but they passed by as if I were invisible, their blank expressions unchanging. A shoddy wooden stairway behind the door groaned with every step as they ascended. They never spoke a word.

Jake opened his door. He did not seem surprised to see me. "What's up, Ace?"

I handed him the six pack of beer I had brought along as a palliative to my own conscience. "A little housewarming present."

"Thanks," he said. "Come on in."

"I think I just met your neighbors," I said as I followed him down a narrow, wood-paneled hallway into the kitchen. "They didn't seem very friendly."

There was a cramped bathroom with a claw foot bathtub and no shower off to one side of the kitchen. Off to the other side was a bedroom with a double bed in the center and the same dark wood-paneling of the hallway. There was no living room. The floors were all linoleum and looked as if they hadn't been washed or even swept since before Jake moved in, and there was nothing but stick furniture in the kitchen and the bedroom. The kitchen was brightly lit by a circular fluorescent bulb overhead. Jake sat down at the small kitchen table and I followed suit.

"You mean that bearded dude and the skinny chick."

"Yeah."

I accepted Jake's offer of a beer and he slid a bottle across the formica tabletop.

"All I know is they live up above." He took a long pull from his beer. "And they fuck like clockwork every night. They should be starting up any time now."

I took a swig of my beer. "Are they married?"

Jake shrugged as if to say the question was irrelevant.

"So how are you doing these days? I haven't seen you in a while."

"All right."

I thought he looked like hell, truthfully, but I didn't want to say this to him. He was very thin, and with his unkempt hair and beard and the dark circles under his eyes there was a haggard, almost defeated quality to him that I'd never seen before. The Jake sitting in front of me now was a far cry from the Jake who had come back from boot camp so tanned and fit and brimming with arrogance. The thought occurred to me that he had not eaten since leaving home, but I dismissed it quickly because weeks had passed since then.

"What have you been doing with yourself? Have you been able to find any work?"

Jake finished his beer and took another. I could hear movement from up above, as though the bed had spontaneously begun to start some mechanical operation or exercise which caused its springs to creak in protest. "I started at the Gillette plant about a week ago."

"How's that going?"

"It isn't."

"Why?"

"Ever been inside?"

"No."

"It's a noisy fucking squirrel cage. And the stink of Right Guard could cover up a fucking dead skunk."

"So what happened? Did you quit?"

"The foreman thought I should be paying more attention to the cans on the line. When I did, he didn't think it was the right kind of attention."

"Were you fired?"

Jake just looked at me and took another drink of his beer.

"What kind of attention did you pay the cans?" I asked, smiling. Above us the creak of bedsprings had taken on the unvarying one-two, one-two rhythm of a rocking chair moving rapidly over a squeaky floorboard.

"I got bored watching thousands of Right Guard cans click by without a hitch and get sprayed with this fragrant white shit, so I rigged the line to provide some entertainment."

I was smiling broadly now although Jake was still expressionless. "What did you do?"

"I jammed the machine that drops the stems down into the cans, then pulled up a seat to watch. I paid real close attention when the cans started falling off the fucking line. Every time a line of cans reached the jam there'd be a jerk and the cans would start falling backwards like a fucking row of dominoes. Cans were clanging on the floor and the white shit was coming down like jets of milk from a cow's tits all over the fucking floor and forming pools, like fucking pools of white blood, like the Right-Guard-stinking blood of Gillette. I don't know how long this went on—I was tripping and lost track of time. Then the foreman comes over with this look on his face like he's just seen someone shitting on his mother's grave. He shuts off the line and says, 'What the fuck's goin' on here?'

"I said, 'I'm watching the line like you told me.'

"'The fuck you are,' he said. 'Clean up this fucking mess and punch your card. You're through, asshole.'

"'I guess we just didn't understand each other,' I told him. 'Maybe next time you should be a little clearer about what you want.' Then I walked away and left him standing there."

Jake took another long pull of his beer. His expression hadn't changed during the entire story even though it was probably the longest I'd ever heard him speak at one time. I wondered for a moment if he might be feeling lonely, but his eyes had a numbed out look to them and I realized his talkativeness was more likely due to whatever drug he was on at the moment.

"That's a great story, Jake," I said, laughing. It was classic Jake—doing something I'd never do myself even though, like Walter Mitty, I loved to imagine myself doing it.

Above us the creaking continued without interruption, rhythmic and unvaried, and with no sound of a human voice.

I nodded toward the ceiling. "Do those two ever get a coffee break?"

Jake lit a cigarette and tossed the match carelessly on the floor. I noticed other burned out matches on the floor along with ashes and a few filterless butts not much longer than a fingernail. There was an ashtray on the table but it was already stuffed with mashed butts.

"Don't knock it," Jake said, closing his eyes wearily. "They're better than valium."

I felt a sharp twinge of concern. "Are you all right?"

Jake opened his eyes. There was a glassy, vacuous quality to his gaze. "I'm fine."

"No, I mean it. Are you all right?"

He nodded with exaggerated slowness. "Perfect. Thanks for the beer, Ace."

Was I being dismissed? I couldn't tell by the look in his eyes. It was almost as if he were not seeing me anymore. Then I noticed movement off to one side. A cockroach, camouflaged against the like-colored background, twitched along the paneled wainscoting near me.

Jake followed my gaze. "They're very quiet and they don't eat much," he said. "Not that there's much to eat around here anyway."

I took off one of my sneakers and squashed the chitinous vermin against the wall. Its hard shell made a crunching sound before it fell to the floor.

"I used to do that too," Jake said. A faint smile curled from his lips. "Squash them like gook heads. But then I realized they're tough little fuckers, survivors. They've been around a long time, long before us, and they'll be around a long time after we're gone."

Jake appeared to be looking at the spot where I had smashed the cockroach, but I had the feeling he wasn't seeing anything at all in this room. The sounds from above which had seemed interminably and disagreeably persistent only moments before abruptly ended, leaving a far more terrible silence.

"Is that it?" I said impatiently. "Are they done? Without even one 'Oh God'?"

Jake came back from wherever he was and turned to me with a look on his face that was partly beatific and partly inane. "I guess the earth doesn't move for those two."

I shook my head, feeling a sudden inexplicable anger. "Only the bedsprings."

"Thanks again for the beer, Ace." Jake toasted me before swigging the rest of the bottle.

This time there was no doubt in my mind that it was time for me to leave.

No one else except for Lydia ever went to Jake's apartment, and initially her going was probably my fault—before leaving for school I made the mistake of mentioning I'd visited him.

She was instantly attentive. "How was he doing?"

"Surviving," I said, not wanting to lie to her.

"What does that mean?"

"He was getting by."

"But what did he look like? How did he seem to you?"

I remembered the cockroach and hesitated.

"Come on, Virgil. This isn't twenty questions."

As always, I had a hard time denying Lydia what she wanted, but I refused to give her all of it. "To be honest, I don't think he looked very good. He seemed thin, and I wondered if he was getting enough sleep. You know how he was living here."

"That's what I was afraid of," she said, shaking her head angrily. "I knew he wouldn't take care of himself. He never has."

"Why do you say 'never'? He might not be taking care of himself right now, but I've always thought of Jake as the most independent, self-sufficient person I know."

"In some ways yes, in some ways no," Lydia said cryptically. And then she added, as if it were a command to herself, "I've got to see him."

Lydia had recently started school as a ninth grader at the junior high and she walked to school on nice days. Mother thought some regular, not-too-strenuous exercise would be good for her, although on questionable days Mother drove her to school in the mornings and picked her up in the afternoons. The day after I spoke with Lydia about Jake was questionable, with drizzle falling when school got out. Mother had told Lydia to look for her after school, but Mother sat parked in the usual spot for more than half an hour with no sign of Lydia. Finally she went inside the school and found no one there knew any reason for Lydia to be late, so Mother drove home following the route Lydia would normally have walked. Still no Lydia. Mother's confusion escalated into worry as the afternoon wore on, and I found her sitting in the living room nervously waiting for the phone to ring when I arrived home from my summer job.

"Even if she had some school function nobody knows about she should be home by now," Mother said as the grandfather clock chimed five times. "She's never been this late."

I remembered my conversation with her about Jake. "Could she be at someone's house?"

"It's possible, but whenever she's done that before I've known ahead of time and cleared it with the friend's mother. This just isn't like her." Mother shook her head. "Still, maybe you're right. Maybe it's something simple like that. I'll just give Becky Stuart's house a call and see if Lydia might have stopped by there. Becky's her closest friend."

Becky confirmed that Lydia had been in all her classes that day, but she had no idea where Lydia might have gone after school. The call did nothing but make Mother feel simultaneously more worried and more of an alarmist. "Now I've got Becky and her mother all upset," she observed ruefully after getting off the phone.

"Should I call your father? He'll be home soon but maybe I should call him anyway."

I had just about decided I would tell her that Lydia might be at Jake's—I could not get out of my mind the cockroach and the sound of the bedsprings—when we heard the slowly advancing thunder of a motorcycle.

We both went to the living room window to look outside. Jake was coming up the driveway with Lydia behind him on the bike, her arms around his waist and her cheek pressed against the back of his leather jacket. Neither one glanced up toward the house. We watched until they disappeared from view behind the garage.

Mother did not know what to do with herself. She paced to the head of the stairs as though going down to meet them, then apparently thought the better of it and paced back into the living room where she dropped down heavily into the overstuffed chair and waited. She looked at me but never said a word. The worry in her face had been replaced by anger.

Lydia was on her way up the stairs when we heard the idling bass rumbles of Jake's motorcycle rev into the sound of departure, followed by a resounding blast that ripped the uneasy quiet in the house.

"Hello," Lydia said to us as the sound of the motorcycle gradually died away.

"Hi, Lydia," I said.

Mother regarded Lydia in silence, her fingers lightly drumming on the arm of the chair.

"Where have you been, Lydia?" Mother said at last.

"I went to see Jake," Lydia said simply.

Mother considered this for a moment before answering. "Did it occur to you that no one knew where you were?"

"I knew where I was. Jake knew where I was."

"Don't be impertinent, young lady. You know what I mean. I checked with the school and nobody had any idea where you could have gone."

Lydia didn't say anything.

"Did it never occur to you that I might worry when I went to pick you up and you weren't there? Or that other people might worry when I started asking if they had seen you?"

"I thought about it."

"You thought about it and you didn't find it necessary to say anything to me?"

"No."

"Why, Lydia?"

"Because you would have told me I couldn't go over to see my own brother."

Lydia's words hung in the air resonating with hard truth, and for a time Mother seemed incapable of responding. Then she said, "In the rain, Lydia? Given all the problems you've had with your lungs over the years? Of course I would have said no."

"That's not what I meant," Lydia said.

"Well, what did you mean?"

Lydia bowed her head. "Let's not talk about it any more."

"I think we need to talk about it," Mother said. She seemed to be regaining a sense of control—of herself, at least, if not of Lydia. "We need to talk about why you were on Jake's motorcycle when you were strictly forbidden from ever riding on it."

"Should I have walked home in the rain then instead?"

"If you'd called I could have given you a ride. Instead you compounded the first mistake by making another just as bad. And both could have been avoided with a simple phone call."

Lydia was not ready to give in. "Why didn't *you* try calling *Jake* to see if I was there?"

Mother had no immediate answer and Lydia pressed the attack. "It's not far-fetched to think I might have gone to visit my brother, is it? I bet you don't even know he has a phone. I bet you haven't even talked to him since he left this house."

Mother got up from her seat and held out her arms in a beseeching manner. "Lydia, what's wrong? You're always so angry these days." She began moving toward Lydia.

"Don't," Lydia said.

"What's the matter?" Mother said, stopping short. Her voice was tinged with real concern, and perhaps a little fear.

"I just don't want to be touched right now," Lydia said. She turned and retreated down the hallway to her bedroom.

At that moment we heard a door slam shut downstairs followed by the sound of Ben whistling (off-key as usual) what sounded like the Stones' "Under My Thumb." He came bounding up the stairs two at a time—none too quietly for an athlete supposed to be light on his feet—then like a bongo player gave his characteristic drum rap on the flat-topped newel post.

"Why the glum looks?" he said when he saw us in the living room. "Somebody lose a friend?" He looked from Mother to me. I raised my eyebrows apprehensively.

"It's nothing," Mother said, distracted. She was looking down the hall toward the closed door of Lydia's room. "Nothing that I haven't been through three times already."

I wasn't so sure about that.

She glanced at Ben and then me and said, with forced cheer, "You would think I'd be an expert at it this time around, wouldn't you?"

This incident between Mother and Lydia was merely a prelude to what followed. There had been disagreements in the past, some quite intense, but they nearly always centered around Lydia's health. In less significant matters Mother usually gave in without much of a struggle. If Lydia wanted to go to the movies, Mother would take her. If she wanted cinnamon toast for breakfast, Mother would sprinkle on the cinnamon. If she wanted a transistor radio or a new board game or a gilded copy of Tolkien's *Lord of the Rings,* Mother would oblige.

But Lydia was growing older and I think Mother was having a hard time accepting it. In another year Ben would be off to college—he was already getting scholarship offers for baseball—I would be *finished* with college, Jake was Jake, and Lydia would be moving up to high school, then off to college herself not long after. The chicks were rapidly leaving the nest, and the last one, the smallest and weakest and most defenseless, the baby, was beginning to flex her wings. Lydia was still smaller and younger looking than other girls her age, but she was fourteen, she was in the ninth grade, and she was growing, even if not dramatically. I probably saw this more clearly than others because two or three months would pass between my visits home from school, and my perceptions of change were not blurred by the myopia of daily living.

The most important changes I saw though were not physical—they were changes in attitude. Lydia wanted new freedoms, some of which had little to do with health. She wanted to be able to wear makeup and miniskirts, she wanted to make tie-dyes for herself and listen to the Grateful Dead, she wanted to go to junior high parties and see movies of more complexity and sophistication than *Swiss Family Robinson*. As a result she and Mother were constantly arguing, which I witnessed for myself whenever I came home but also heard about at school through letters and phone calls. Lydia once wrote to me that Mother had caught her smoking a cigarette in her room and had "thrown a fit." Her door was closed and she was smoking next to her open window, listening to Janis Joplin's "Ball and Chain" when Mother burst into the room and grabbed the cigarette from her hand. Mother began "ranting and raving" about how smoking killed people and how an asthmatic like her was especially susceptible and how stupid Lydia was for trying such a thing and how it "never would have happened if Jake hadn't come home from Vietnam with the fiendish habit" and how smoking was just the beginning, the first small step toward drinking alcohol and using drugs. Mother wanted to know what had happened to her "baby" who had sung so sweetly and innocently at folk masses and now listened only to trash like *Light My Fire* sung by "a confirmed drug-user and exhibitionist." I felt for Lydia through all of this because Mother was harder on her than she had been on the rest of us. Instead of being beaten down by all the battles and tests of will in raising three boys, Mother seemed intent to make one last desperate stand over her little girl, no matter how much that little girl resisted.

I felt for Mother too. After Lydia visited Jake's apartment I talked with her about where Jake was living—without delving into detail. Mother knew the area and said she would never go there herself, let alone permit Lydia to go there. "I don't know why in God's name he chose to live in such a neighborhood," she said, "but it doesn't mean Lydia needs to follow him. She can ask him to come home if she wants to see him." Mother had visions, I'm sure, of Lydia walking past the crumbling wooden tenements and the abandoned brick mills with their broken windows and boarded up doorways and being assaulted before she could even reach Jake's apartment. To be honest, I shared some of her fears, although my own fears were not so much of what might happen *outside* the apartment as of what might happen *inside* it. I did not want Lydia exposed to the filth of cockroaches and the vulgar sounds of mechanical and loveless fucking.

Still, Mother's fears and diatribes and threats meant nothing to Lydia, who absolutely refused to stop going over to see Jake after school. One time when I called home they had just had another argument about it and Mother was at wit's end, so I asked her to put Lydia on the line. The connection was poor and Lydia's voice sounded small and distant through the static.

"What's going on between you two?" I asked.

I had a hard time hearing her answer clearly, but it almost sounded as if she was surprised by the question. "Nothing. What makes you think there's anything going on?"

"Mom just told me you two had been fighting again."

"Oh, that. Well, she's right."

"What happened?"

"Same old thing. She's afraid I'll fall off the earth if I don't go directly home after school."

"She's worried about you, Lydia."

"So she says."

"You don't believe it?"

There was a crackle of static on the line. "I believe it. But what about Jake? He gets these terrible headaches and nobody seems to care. She certainly doesn't."

"Why do you say that?"

There was a pause. The static started up again as soon as she spoke, as if her voice were somehow activating the interference. "For obvious reasons."

"She may not even know about the headaches, Lydia." I knew nothing about them myself, and felt as though I was defending myself in defending Mother. "He doesn't say much to anyone about what he's feeling."

Lydia did not respond.

"So how are you able to help him?"

"I just get him to lie down and relax," she said through the static. She seemed hesitant. "And then I give him a massage all around his temples and his forehead. He says it helps."

"It's kind of a rough neighborhood though, isn't it? Couldn't you meet somewhere else?"

"You mean like here?"

"There. Wherever."

"Sure, Virgil. He could come over here and Mom could give him the massage. Then we could all sing 'Happy Trails to You.'"

"No, seriously. I've been over there. It's not a very nice place where he lives."

"Seriously, he needs my help. And I don't care where he lives."

"Okay, okay. Just try to understand where Mom is coming from. She's not an ogre."

"I know that."

"Okay. Then just be careful. Tell Jake I said hello, and I'm sorry about the headaches."

"Sure, Virgil."

"Bye, Lydia. Take care of yourself."

The static grew louder and I could barely make out her voice saying, "Goodbye, Virgil."

In the early spring of that year the arguments grew so heated between Mother and Lydia that Lydia actually tried to stay at Jake's one night. Her health had been deteriorating for some time, to the point where she was having frequent asthma attacks that left her struggling for air. She was also missing school. Mother was very upset by this and aggressively sought new ways to control Lydia's environment. One way was to forbid Lydia—categorically—from going to Jake's. Mother believed Jake's smoking, in the confines of his apartment and in Lydia's presence, was the principal reason for Lydia's poor health. This injunction had already been in place for months, but Lydia had been ignoring it; so to enforce it Mother threatened to call Jake and ask him—for Lydia's own good—not to allow her into his apartment.

Lydia was outraged by this and went directly to Jake's after school the very next day. True to her word, Mother telephoned Jake's apartment as soon as Lydia did not come home at the usual hour, but there was no answer. Lydia told me later she had disconnected the phone from the phone jack—a trick she had learned from me—and hadn't said anything about it to Jake.

At some point that evening she called home and told Mother where she was and that she'd be staying there for the night. Mother wanted her home immediately and asked to speak to Jake. When Lydia refused, arguing that Jake had been having a rough time and was asleep, at last, and she would not wake him, Mother said she was going to drive right over.

"I only called to let you know where I am and that I'm all right," Lydia complained bitterly. "I should have known you'd be this way about it. I shouldn't have even called."

According to Lydia, shortly after the phone conversation she heard a sharp rapping at the door—"It reminded me of the SS coming for people in the night, I felt like Anne Frank"—and knew instantly that Mother had not been bluffing about coming over. The sound woke Jake, who bolted up to answer the door.

Lydia followed along trying to explain, "It's Mom, Jake, it's Mom. She's come to get me but I don't want to go."

It was warm that night and Jake, wearing only a pair of old ripped jeans, was shirtless and barefoot when he opened the door. Lydia stood behind him in the hallway. His hair was all matted and disheveled, his eyes glazed over with the disoriented look of someone roused from a deep sleep. When he saw Mother standing there he threw the door open and invited her in, but she only glanced at him in a cursory, scornful way and continued standing there on the stoop, staring at Lydia with an expression of immutable will, her red lips set in a line so tight it seemed words could not pass through them.

"You need to come home now," Mother said. Behind her there was a loud squeal as a car peeled rubber and accelerated down the street. She winced but did not turn around.

"I don't want to," Lydia said.

"You don't have a choice."

"What do you mean I don't have a choice? Of course I have a choice. I want to stay here. Jake has been sick, he needs me."

"Wait a minute here," Jake said. He held his hands up defensively, as if someone had pulled a gun on him. He looked at Lydia. "I'm fine," he said. "She's welcome to stay," he said to Mother, "but I'm fine."

The tire-squealer turned around at the end of the street and began peeling rubber again in the opposite direction. Mother waited for the noise to pass.

"Well she is *not* fine. I'm sure she wouldn't tell you this but she's been having one attack after another and has missed a lot of school. I asked her to talk with you about it…obviously she hasn't. It's not good for her to come over here. Smoke is one of the worst things for her. We talked about it just yesterday and decided there would be no more visits to this apartment."

"*You* decided there would be no more visits. I never agreed at all."

Mother ignored Lydia and said, "I can see this is all news to you, Jake."

Jake nodded dumbly, turning to Lydia.

"I didn't want to make you feel bad," she said, wounded, before she shot a baleful look at Mother and added, "the way *she* is right now."

Jake's eyes were fixed inward as he appeared to be weighing all he'd heard. "You better go home, Lydia," he said at last in a toneless voice, his face revealing no emotion.

"Come, Lydia," Mother said. "It's getting late." She started down the stoop.

"Jake—" Lydia said. The expression in his eyes was so blank it terrified her. "Mother, can't you see?"

"See what, Lydia?"

"That he needs help?"

"What I see most clearly is that you need to be home to control the attacks."

"Attacks! Attacks! I'm sick of hearing about attacks. I'm sick of worrying about attacks. Sometimes I wish I'd never been born, then you wouldn't *ever* have to worry about attacks."

"Lydia! That is the most selfish—" Mother began.

"It's time to go," Jake said, cutting her short.

Lydia regarded him carefully. "Just promise me one thing."

"What's that?"

"You'll call me when you need to."

"I won't need to."

"Promise me."

Jake looked at Mother, who was jangling her keys. "All right."

"Remember," Lydia said.

Jake nodded.

"And take care of yourself."

"Always."

"Goodbye, Jake," Mother said.

As they drove away Lydia looked back to see that Jake had already shut the door to his apartment. A shiver ran through her and left her wondering what would become of him.

Although the accounts of that night varied depending on who told the story—if Lydia told it, Mother was an unfeeling witch; if Mother told it, Lydia was a headstrong child lacking all common sense—one thing was consistent: Jake was unaware of how serious Lydia's condition had become until Mother showed up on his doorstep and confronted him with it. I can only speculate about the effect this had on him—possibly it had none and his leaving the area was just a coincidence. After returning from Vietnam he'd been unable to do more than land a series of low-paying, menial jobs which invariably resulted in his quitting or being fired, and he may have grown tired of this. He may have decided a change of scenery was the best remedy for someone as short on funds as he must have been. Or he may have found that after nearly two years in the jungle he could not live in the midst of civilization: he needed to surround himself with woods, not cars and people. Whatever effect that night had on him, the undeniable fact was that soon afterwards he moved from Newtown for good. Without notifying anyone until just before he left, and without leaving an address where he could be reached, he moved to a small town up north not far from the Canadian border.

Lydia took it extremely hard and placed the unequivocal blame for it on Mother. "He wouldn't have left if she hadn't forced him to," she argued.

"There were undoubtedly other things involved," I said, implying that Jake had his own reasons, though what I really had in mind was Mother confronting a spaced-out Jake and a half-naked hooker in her own living room. "The truth is never what it seems."

"As if you know what the truth is!" she said caustically.

"I'm not suggesting I *do* know," I said, believing I certainly knew more than she did. "I don't know why Jake left. Maybe that night had something to do with it, maybe it didn't. All I'm saying is there's usually more there than meets the eye."

"You can believe whatever you want," Lydia said, "but I *know* why he left."

During the remainder of that school year Lydia continued to have frequent serious asthma attacks. Even her grades began to suffer. In the past she was such an exceptional student that despite excessive absences every year she could easily keep ahead of her classmates. During the last part of ninth grade, however, except for English—which was still a strong subject for her because of her extraordinary reading and writing skills—she had great difficulty. Algebra began to confuse her; biology revolted her because of the dissections, particularly the dissection of the frog; history was taught by a man who believed our mistake in Vietnam was not dropping the atomic bomb on North Vietnam early in the war, and who dealt with discipline problems amongst the boys by slapping them in the face; Latin seemed to her an utterly dead and useless language. Her report card for the last quarter of that year showed a straight line of C's, with a blip for the A in English. Mother and Father were shocked. Lydia was unmoved, apathetic.

When they first began to realize there was a problem, Mother and Father attributed it to poor health and a degree of absenteeism inordinate even by Lydia's standards. Mother was sensitive to the fact that Lydia no longer argued with her about clothes or makeup and that the usual badinage Lydia instigated with Ben had disappeared from the house. She also noted with quiet alarm that Lydia wanted to be driven to and from school all the time now, and showed no interest in walking even on the nicest spring days. At home, Lydia exhibited a disturbing lethargy and lack of confidence. She would stay in her room with the door closed reading books like *Wuthering Heights* and *Jane Eyre* and leave only for dinner or to make a trip to the bathroom; and she wouldn't accept a challenge of Scrabble from anyone for fear of losing. Mother noted all of these things, as well as the slumping grades on work Lydia brought home from school, but refused to believe Lydia was experiencing anything more than a temporary setback. Eventually, Lydia would right herself and things would return to normal.

By the time Mother and Father saw the depth of the problem reflected so graphically in the report card—Lydia had *always* been a straight-A student—they understood something serious was happening to their baby girl, something real and threatening and more than just temporary. When the doctor who had been treating Lydia since she was born insisted her problems were not asthma-related, they believed him. What they had trouble accepting was his further diagnosis: Lydia's main problem was not physical.

Chapter Fifteen

A Loss of Faith

This time his leaving was like a door slamming shut with such loudness and force the reverberations set off an incessant ringing in her ears, which suffused each attempt at communication so thoroughly a kind of detached distance developed and she heard nothing clearly enough for it to be of much interest. At home the voices of her mother and father and brothers droned on about her health. At school the voices of her teachers droned on about the necessity of their subjects and the increased importance of good grades, ninth grade being the first year of high school and therefore the gateway to college, good grades being the vehicle to transport her through the gateway and beyond, and wasn't she, stellar pupil that she had always been, concerned about the way those grades were falling? In the hallways her classmates droned on about who was dating whom and in study hall whispered to each other and passed cleverly folded triangular love notes that detailed the latest gossip about parties, to which she had been invited for a time until it became clear the invitations were being wasted: she was never allowed to attend parties. She was aware of all the concerns swirling about her but only in a detached and peripheral way, unmoved by any of them.

She had learned to detach herself from him too over the years, when his need to touch and be touched turned him into someone— or something—she did not understand, a creature of enormous silent pain and yearning, which she felt through his touch like a kind of electricity, shocking, unnerving, sending her out of her body to a place somewhere up above it all where she could observe his writhing pain conjoined to her own without being touched by either at her core, as though her body were a garden with a gate around it and she could choose to open the gate and depart at any time, or as though she were two people, one of whom was corporeal and subject to pain, the other insubstantial and ethereal and capable of drifting above the world at will as an unattached spectator, surprised at the image of herself below whose eyes would sometimes well with tears. He would begin to do whatever he must and she—fearful of the force of his need, the sheer consuming torment of it that overpowered and controlled even him, who controlled so much—would depart and remain outside until it was safe to return. And return she would, always, because from an early age she understood without understanding why that his need for touch was more than just physical, and that in a way which she also did not understand she was saving him from something.

But in truth she returned for herself as well because without any mention of her illness and with no allowances made for frailty or disability, he took her to places where she could not go on her own, which to her was as vital and replenishing as her inhaler and certainly more generous than what anyone else in the family would do for her. When he took her out on the motorcycle and drove her away from Newtown to the country and then along rural winding roads at high speeds and she felt the force of the wind on her face and blowing wildly through her hair, when she felt the tight controlled arcs of the bike banking through curves so near the ground she could almost touch it, and heard the engine roar like an angry beast beneath them, all of it—the speed, the sound, the power, the danger—controlled by him, harnessed and tamed by him, when he took her out and she felt these things she felt also a kind of terror rivaled only by the most serious asthma attacks, and yet welcome because it was terror not of the absence of air, the helpless slow constriction of herself from within and the wheezing struggle for breath as she felt life being choked from her, but terror of the opposite, of too much air, of air rushing past in such excess and with such speed it was dizzying, intoxicating, and made her wish she could somehow draw upon its plenitude forever. In these moments which occurred all too rarely in her life she believed that as surely as she was saving him from something he was saving her from something, though what it might be or how and why he might be doing it was just as vague as the reasons for her own self-sacrifice. Which did not matter, really. It was enough that she possessed such faith, whether she could explain it or not. Even when he ran away so many years ago, and more recently when he spent two years in Vietnam, she did not believe he was gone for good, did not doubt he would return and save her from... whatever. And so when he left again this time and she found herself feeling lost and helpless, abandoned, believing for the first time in her life that he might not return, believing with a conviction as intense and unshakeable as any she had ever possessed, she began to understand that what she had wanted him to save her from all along was the absence of a future.

Chapter Sixteen

Dissolution

When I graduated from the university in late May of 1973, the whole family, except for Jake, came up for commencement. I viewed it as a day of duty and obligation, but for my family— like countless others present for the occasion—it was a day of pride and excitement and celebration; and, under the warm sun and blue sky, with flags and pennants waving and students and faculty in their caps and gowns, adorned like peacocks with their colorful tassels and hoods, it was a day rich with the golden promise of prosperity.

Cheerful scenes abounded of families brightly clothed in spring attire, shooting pictures and hovering around their graduates like clucking birds. My own family was no different, with beaming parents and grandparents making much ado about what I considered nothing, and Ben, laughing with good-natured derision, firing barbs about "eggheads" becoming "flatheads" and how well such a look suited me.

Only Lydia failed to be moved by the occasion. She was dressed gaily enough in coral-red culottes and primrose blouse, but she was quiet and subdued throughout the day, as she had been for weeks now. Her eyes teared constantly with all the pollen in the air, and a tissue was never far from the reddened nares of her nose. Aside from the worry I felt for her, I recalled with vivid clarity the effort and emotion she put into Jake's homecoming celebration, and the contrast between her disposition then and now wounded me with unanticipated force.

I only remember her saying one thing to me that day, apart from perfunctory courtesies: "If I ever make it to college myself I plan to be an English Literature major too."

"That's great, Lydia," I said, taking it as a compliment, although it might have been intended as a taunt of sorts to Mother, because it clearly had that effect.

"Why would there be any question about your making it to college?" Mother asked.

Lydia shrugged and covered her nose with a tissue. "You never know," she said.

I couldn't tell if she was trying to bait Mother or genuinely doubted her future. "Well, we don't need to worry about it right now," Mother said, "but when the time comes, if you decide you want to major in English, I think it would be a wonderful thing for you."

Lydia's eyes had grown teary again and she took another tissue from her purse.

"I do too, Lydia," I said. "You've always been such a strong reader and writer... it would be perfect." But Lydia merely continued daubing at the corners of her eyes with the now balled up tissue and said nothing.

The luster of day, which I did not realize I cared about until then, was suddenly gone.

After graduation I moved home again, unsure about what I wanted to do with my life. I had been leaning toward law school ever since one of my professors pointed out that the most common undergraduate major for law school was English Lit. That came as a surprise to me at the time, but it made sense. Being able to make and defend a point in writing; construct logical patterns and sequences of thought; understand shades and subtleties of meaning in language; read sophisticated text carefully and critically; uncover truth by digging beneath the surface of things and peeling back layers of facade and deception, all of these were skills I had honed in my four years at school, and all would be directly relevant to studying law.

In those days I was deeply suspicious of institutions. Kesey's *One Flew Over the Cuckoo's Nest* was, ironically, a sort of bible in this respect, and I believed fervently in the inherent corruptness of "the system" and the inherent integrity of the individual. It was therefore easy to imagine myself in a courtroom fighting for the rights of individuals oppressed by institutions and disadvantaged by "the system." I envisioned myself as a passionate defense attorney, the modern day version of Perry Mason.

Not until years later, after I'd had a taste of public defense in the courtroom, did I understand the blissful ignorance of my thinking back then. The accused I found myself defending, contrary to the Perry Mason image, were nearly always guilty— of crimes ranging from the incomprehensibly stupid to the outrageously feral. These were not the wrongfully accused, clean-cut denizens of the middle-class seen on TV—nor the noble downtrodden poor, the "there-but-for-the-grace-of-God-go-I" souls of honest conviction and simple conscience abused by the injustices of life and the power of the wealthy ruling class—that I had romanticized all through adolescence and early adulthood. With numbing regularity I found myself defending repeat DWI offenders—many of whom had killed, or maimed for life, innocent people; dealers pushing drugs to school-age kids; rapists and child molesters; and some of the worst bullies imaginable—unrepentant liars guilty beyond any reasonable doubt of mine.

Two cases in particular served as a watershed for me. The first involved a man who had coached Ben in baseball. Henry, the coach, was charged with aggravated felonious sexual assault of a minor when a former player of his made the accusation after years of private suffering. Through counseling the boy had come to understand the only way for him to begin true healing was to bring Henry to justice. After he came forward two other former members of Henry's teams made similar formal accusations. It fell to me to defend Henry.

Henry had a wife and children of his own, and he looked like everybody's favorite uncle. He was medium height and a trifle overweight, with a modest but visible potbelly. Grey-haired at the temples and balding slightly on top, he had the sort of ingenuous blue eyes that always had a cheerful twinkle in them. He knew a lot about baseball, and the kids really liked him. I know Ben did—he was as shocked as anyone when the news broke in the local paper.

What I have never forgotten about the case is not that the system went wrong and justice was never served: Henry was found guilty and sentenced to several years in prison—not as much as he should have received, perhaps, but a serious punishment nevertheless. What I will never forget as long as I live is a conversation I had with him before going to trial.

We were sitting at a table talking about the case and he was leaning back, smoking a cigarette. He had admitted to me from the outset that he was guilty, and had no apparent qualms about admitting it. We were discussing how if he pled guilty and fell upon the mercy of the court, showed willingness to undergo counseling and to rehabilitate himself, he might be able to get a reduced sentence. He agreed with the strategy but immediately grew quiet and pensive. I remember wondering if he was sitting there regretting what he had done and rehearsing his words to the court, when he said to me in a wistful voice, as if I were his friend and confidant, "You know what I'll miss the most, Virgil?" The cheerful light twinkled in his blue eyes.

"What?" I asked, expecting him to say his family or sunny spring days on the ball field.

"That soft young ass. There's nothing like a young boy."

I think I almost gagged, wondering *What the fuck am I doing here? I wanted to shout at him, Don't tell me this shit, I don't want to hear it!* But somehow I swallowed my revulsion.

"I hope you won't say anything like that in court."

"Oh, of course not," Henry said.

"Good. Because I don't think it would go over too well with the judge."

Henry nodded agreeably.

What I understood in those few moments was that Henry was addicted to children, he was far beyond hope, and I could not fault the system; nor was I in any conscionable way advancing the cause of justice by seeking a reduced sentence for him, which would put him back near children sooner rather than later. Despite the axiom that a client be forthright with his attorney, it would have been better—for me—if Henry had been a little less than candid.

The second case involved defending a twenty-three year old psychopath, Norman, who had driven up from Massachusetts with three of his scumbag buddies for a joyride through Newtown. At a stoplight he pulled up next to the car of four Newtown high school students—two couples—out on a date, and started harassing them. The students, from all reports, tried to ignore the lewd taunts and jeers but grew terrified when Norman's band of misfits in the wildly swerving, horn-honking vehicle that followed them kept falling back and racing ahead to ram them from behind. The kids then made the mistake of heading to the home of the boy driving, instead of to the police station, and were horrified when their crazed pursuers pulled into the driveway right behind them and slammed up against their bumper with headlights blazing.

Norman got out of his car and challenged the manhood of the two boys on the date, then smashed in the drivers' windshield with a baseball bat. A fight ensued involving not only the four hoods, all armed with chains or bats, and the two boys on the date, but also the father of the driver. One boy had his teeth knocked in and was left unconscious; the other had a broken arm and severe contusions all over his body; and the father had cracked ribs and kidney trauma serious enough to warrant a lengthy stay in the hospital. One of the girls tried to help and received a blow to her face that required stitches, caused the entire side of her face to swell, and left her with a black eye for days afterward; the other girl had the clothes on the upper half of her body ripped off her. Fortunately, the mother of the boy driving had called the police immediately or they might all have been beaten to death or raped.

The four joy riders had been drinking and were high on PCP, or "magic dust" as Norman liked to call it, and believed they shouldn't be blamed for actions induced by alcohol and drugs. "I mean what the fuck," Norman said to me, "the fucking magic dust is what did it, man. That's mean shit." Of course, he was grinning as he talked about what had happened, especially whenever he mentioned "magic dust" and what "mean shit" it was, as if he possessed a kind of perverse reverence for its power to create havoc and inflict brutal damage upon innocent people.

When I pointed out the likelihood of a guilty verdict and tried to explain the merits of a plea bargain to him, it was as though I spoke a foreign language. He could understand the concept of plea bargaining—with his long and sordid criminal record he understood that sort of legal parlance all too well—but he could not grasp at all the concept of causality, the causative, culpable connection between his act of inhaling "magic dust" and the "magic" that resulted from it. He had no problem recalling in vivid, gory detail the sequence of events or admitting his participation in them, but he could not fathom the possibility that responsibility could lie anywhere but in that "mean shit," as if he were just an innocent victim himself.

"It's amazing how much in life is beyond our control," I said to him.

"Fucking right, man," he said, without a hint of understanding the irony.

Equally far beyond him was any capacity to feel remorse for the people he had injured. Which, I suppose, contained a certain warped logic: if you saw no causal connection between yourself and your actions, why should you feel any remorse about the outcome of those actions?

I got so sick of dealing with the Normans of the world in my short career as a criminal defense lawyer that at times I wanted the prosecution to win. I wanted to *be* the prosecution.

These two cases, Henry's and Norman's, sent me off for good in the direction of civil law, where the contests are much more interesting because they're much more nebulous, where guilt and innocence blend and blur, and the question of culpability is like a watercolor left out in the rain. They also helped to crystallize another realization for me: there were things in life I didn't want to know anything about.

While I was living at home, working and applying to law schools, I saw Lydia gradually come out of her depression. Her asthma attacks occurred less frequently, a sanguine pinkness came into her cheeks and replaced the pallor that had been there for months, she actually seemed to grow a bit, she regained her affection for school, and the sharpness of her tongue returned. At the same time Mother began allowing Lydia more freedoms. As a sophomore Lydia was now attending the high school, where she was allowed to remain after school hours for meetings of the Latin Club or the Debate Team. I'm sure Mother was pleased to see Lydia becoming involved in school again after the disastrous end to the previous year, but it must also have been difficult to watch the child she loved so well, the last and youngest of the family, the child who had always been so dependent on her, beginning to grow up and move away. With Ben off to the university, the house must have seemed very empty much of the time now for Mother.

None of us ever heard from Jake after he left, not even Lydia. "How's Jake doing?" neighbors or friends would occasionally ask. Those who hadn't seen the family in a while would often add, "He got back from Vietnam all right?"

Mother's response became the standard family reply: "Yes, he came back and stayed with us for awhile but he's living up north right now." Since Jake never wrote, we had no idea what he was doing, so it was easier to offer brief, polite replies than try to explain what none of us really could explain.

We knew he was living somewhere up in the Pittsburgh area, but that was about all we knew. Lydia tried writing to him several times immediately after he left, but she never received a response from him and the post office never returned any of her letters.

"Are you still writing to Jake?" I asked one time when I saw her writing in her journal six months or so after he had left. I remember thinking she finally seemed to have made peace with his absence, and this was perhaps partly responsible for her recent general improvement.

"Once in a while," she said.

"I thought maybe you had given up by now."

"I'll never give up," she said defiantly. "He wants people to believe he doesn't need anyone, but I know it's not true. He was really messed up when he left here."

The "messed up" part I had no quarrel with, but I seriously doubted how much he needed—or wanted—people near him. "It must really bother you that he doesn't write back."

"Doesn't it bother you? He's your brother too!"

"It's just Jake, Lydia. It's who he is." Her brow was stern and unconvinced. "I try not to take it personally," I added gently.

Her expression softened at this and tears began to well in her eyes. "I don't understand him," she said, her voice breaking.

I sat next to her on the bed and put my arm around her. She felt like a small child, not a sophomore in high school. "I don't either. I don't think Jake even understands himself."

Her head was bowed and she gave a little sob. "I wish I could take your pain away," I said, though I felt trite and inadequate saying it.

Lydia raised her head up. "Well I won't stop writing," she said with sudden anger, as if she hadn't heard me at all, "whether he ever writes back or not."

One of the freedoms Mother had finally consented to allowing Lydia was going out on dates—not with older boys who had cars but with boys her own age, fifteen, who needed to be driven somewhere. Lydia never would have admitted it but she wanted very much to have a boyfriend, though her suitors did not exactly line up at our front door, and on those infrequent occasions when she did go out something always seemed to go wrong: at the movies one time she spilled a drink on her date's lap; another time, at a school dance, her date left her standing alone half the night while he "waltzed away" (those were Lydia's words) to dance with another girl; once her date took her roller skating and she fell and cracked her head on the floor.

I'll never forget her first time out on a date, a Friday night in October. I had agreed to drive because Lydia thought it would be less embarrassing than having a parent do it.

She spent an inordinate amount of time getting ready before finally emerging from the bathroom in jeans and a sweater, although she wore makeup and it was the meticulous attention to that, I suppose, which took her so long. The makeup was also a recently won freedom, and Lydia worried over it as if her very life depended on its being applied perfectly. She applied it with incredible slowness and patience, as though she were painting the most delicate lines on one of those tiny collectible porcelain figurines.

The result was that she almost looked her age, although there was still nothing she could do about her size—Lydia never grew to be more than four feet nine inches tall—or the flatness of her chest. Size didn't matter much on this occasion, however, because her date, Tucker Williams, couldn't have been much more than five feet tall himself.

Tucker had shoulder-length dark hair that had the effect of making him look even shorter than he was. He wore granny glasses with coke-bottle lenses, and sitting in the back seat of my green VW bug he never answered my questions with more than one or two words. I feared him right from the start. I figured he was probably an incredibly horny little bastard who couldn't wait to get to the football game and spirit my baby sister off into the woods nearby.

"I'll be parked over by the swimming pool after the game," I said as I dropped them off near the ticket lines. "Be good," I added jokingly.

Tucker just looked at me with unemotive brown eyes twice the size of normal behind those thick lenses. Lydia, by contrast, was beaming, so thrilled to be out on her own at last (I don't think it would have mattered if she'd been with the class golden boy instead of Tucker) that she even abandoned her normal sense of irony. "We will," she said with ingenuous cheer.

As it turned out, I wasn't too far off in the old-fart paternalistic intuitions I'd had about Tucker. After we'd taken him home, Lydia told me he'd been "a real pain." He hadn't wanted to stay in the stands where her friends were, but instead wanted to buy popcorn and go off for a walk with her. She kept refusing the offers to walk and he kept buying popcorn, which left them apart during much of the game but left Lydia and her friends well supplied with popcorn.

She told me she wasn't interested much in going anywhere with him again (at this I merely nodded) but had a great time anyway and couldn't wait to go to the next home game, maybe this time with a couple of her school friends rather than on a date.

The next home game happened to be the following week, and I drove her once again. The other girls walked to the stadium so Lydia was my only passenger. I dropped her off with the same instruction to meet me at the swimming pool after the game. Unlike the week before, however, when Lydia and Tucker had shown up promptly at our rendezvous point, Lydia was late by nearly half an hour this time, and when she did show up she was being half carried by a girl nearly a foot taller. I didn't recognize the lurching shadowy shape the two of them made until they emerged from the darkness of the overarching maples and stood illuminated by a streetlight. Then I saw a glint of light on Lydia's golden hair, pressed tight to the midsection of the girl she leaned against, and I grew panicky. *Was she having an asthma attack?*

"What's wrong?" I said, bolting from the car.

I could smell the answer in the pungent odor of alcohol and puke as I drew near. "She...she wanted to turn herself in to the police," the girl said hesitantly.

"The police? Why?"

"I don't know," the girl said, sort of pushing Lydia forward toward me at arms' length. When I received Lydia into my arms the girl began to sidle away and said, "I've got to go."

"Okay. Hey, thanks," I called after her.

Lydia was a small, semi-conscious bundle of pliant human clay in my arms. "Lydia, wake up. Come on, we've got to get you to the car. Can you do it? Can you wake up a little?"

Her head rolled but she followed my lead, leaning against me the whole way.

"How are you feeling," I said as I helped her into the passenger's seat.

"Not so great," she mumbled, eyes closed. Her head lolled to one side.

I fired up the bug and began driving around. "We've got to sober you up somehow," I said, but she had either passed out or fallen asleep.

At some point as I was driving along trying to figure out what to do, she startled me by blurting out with a sardonic drunken laugh, "She had bonny children," a line I recognized from D.H. Lawrence's "The Rockinghorse Winner." Then shortly after, in slurred susurrations, "She can't know about this, Jake! Promise! She mustn't ever know!"

"It's Virgil, Lydia. You're with me, Virgil."

Then she said again, in a sorrowful whisper, "She mustn't ever know. No one can ever know," and started whimpering softly.

I realized then that she wasn't even awake. She was drifting around in that limbo region of remorse and sentimentality we fall into sometimes when we've had far too much to drink.

"I promise, Lydia," I assured her quietly, and began thinking again of how best to get her out of this predicament.

After driving around for a while longer, I came up with a plan I thought might just work. I would call home, purportedly from a pizza joint, and explain that Lydia and two of her friends had been hungry after the game so I had taken them out for pizza. When they were finished, I would drive the other girls home. It might be late, but there was no need to worry or wait up.

Mother was a little surprised when I called, having expected us home already, but she bought the story completely. "Just make sure you don't keep them out *too* late," she said. "They're only sophomores, you know, and Lydia especially needs her rest."

"I'll have her back by daybreak."

"Very funny," Mother said. "It's nearly eleven now, so be back by midnight, Virgil."

"Consider it done. I'll tell them the score right now."

"Good night, Virgil."

"Good night, Mom. And thanks. I'm sure Lydia will appreciate it."

When she comes to, I thought as I hung up the phone.

As I drove I would jostle Lydia's shoulder every few minutes and prod her with words. She would straighten up a bit and murmur something semi-intelligible, then sink back down into her stupor. This went on for some time, the car all the while reeking of alcohol and vomit, which Lydia had managed to get on both her sweater and her jeans. Not knowing the effects of alcohol on an asthmatic, I was mostly concerned about her condition somehow precipitating an asthma attack. But her breathing seemed regular and unimpaired, and I realized after a while that the most pressing problem, assuming I couldn't rouse her, would be to get her into the house and out of her foul-smelling clothes without being discovered.

A strange kind of nostalgia came over me as I killed time cruising the outskirts of Newtown and passed some of the old parking spots I'd had when I was not much older than Lydia was now. She still seemed a child, not old enough to do the things I'd done, and yet the fact that she sat next to me in the car sotted with alcohol gave compelling testimony to how deceptive those feelings were. I also thought about how bizarre the situation would appear to someone who didn't know us, like the police, if they were to stop me for some reason. Twenty-two year old sober male with fifteen year old (albeit *eleven* in appearance) schnockered female passed out beside him. Wouldn't look good at all.

The thought made me wonder about Lydia as a sexual human being, and again she seemed too young, *much* too young, to have experienced anything more than a kiss, and even that I had a hard time imagining given the lack of opportunity in her life. She seemed to me perfect in her Lilliputian beauty, barely on the faintest cusp of womanhood and incapable, as yet, of leading a sexual existence; still, as I drove through the night along the dark, winding roads of Newtown's outskirts with her passed out beside me, I found myself mourning something lost. It may have been as simple a thing as her innocence. Which is to say, her fall from childhood. That inevitable fall from the realm of brilliant clear light into the one of dimly lit shadow-shapes, the adult world of relationships and politics, of complication and confusion. The evidence that her fall had already begun was inescapable—it permeated the car and rested indisputably on her clothing. It was evidence I felt an overwhelming need to suppress from Mother and Father.

When I reached home it was just after midnight and Lydia was still out cold. I switched off my headlights and cut the engine, coasting as silently as possible into the gravel driveway. The outside lights were on, as were the foyer lights, but the rest of the house was dark. Trusting.

"Lydia, we're home," I whispered, leaning close after opening her door. "Do you want me to carry you in or can you make it on your own?"

"I'm fine," she mumbled with a roll of her head, and then made no effort to get up.

"Come on, we've got to get you to bed."

I managed to drag her out of the car and hoist her limp body onto my back.

"I just want to sleep," she slurred.

"Shhhh," I said, muting the car door as I closed it. Even as dead weight she did not weigh very much on my back, and I was able to carry her silently to her room. The only sounds at all were the normal clicks and pings of a house fortifying itself against a chilly autumn night.

I laid her gently back upon her bed and pondered what to do next. "Lydia, I've got to get your clothes off. Can you help me?"

She shook her head with an exaggerated roll back and forth. Her eyes never opened.

Her pale yellow sweater, reeking and spotted with bits of puke, came off easily, and I rolled it in upon itself to contain the evidence. Underneath, she was wearing a pink turtleneck which crackled with static electricity when I pulled it up over her head, her hair fanning out and clinging to the garment and to my hands as if it had a life of its own.

"I don't want to," she said with absurd anger, from another world and time.

"Shhhh."

The bra Lydia wore seemed a kind of tokenism borne more from a debt to her chronological age than from any actual need.

She wore no belt around her jeans, which were fairly snug around her midsection, so I unsnapped and unzipped them before trying to wriggle them down the sides of her legs. As I did this Lydia began to whimper again softly, as she had in the car. "Careful, Jake, please be careful," she pleaded in a whisper. Her eyes never opened.

"Shhhh. It's Virgil, Lydia. I'll be careful."

At that, even in the dark, I could see her eyes startle open. "What—" she started to say, and then seemed to understand all that was happening. "Oh God, Virgil, I feel so yucky," she said, and I could hear the small sounds of her crying. Her eyes, closed once again, were brimming with tears. "I wish I were dead."

"Shhhh. You'll be all right in the morning."

I finished tugging off her jeans and rolled them around the balled up sweater. Lydia's diminutive legs and dainty panties gave me the absurd feeling that I was undressing a doll.

"Thank you, Virgil," Lydia said as I helped her under the covers. "I'm sorry, I'm sorry."

"It's all right. Go to sleep now," I urged her, but there was no need. She was asleep again already.

In my room I realized that the smell, the evidence, was on my own clothing as well, and as I thought of how I would have to wash them too, of how desperately I wanted to withhold the evidence of the evening from Mother and Father, it occurred to me that I wanted to do the same for Lydia. And even—it struck me in a moment of wishful insight—to do the same for myself.

*   *   *

Eventually I was accepted into law school in Virginia and moved away from home. Years went by, during which my only contact with Lydia and the rest of the family was on the major holidays and, if I could manage it, for a week of summer vacation at the beach. Ben finished college and went to Georgia to play baseball for a major league farm team in hopes of someday cracking the big leagues. Lydia finished high school and began a year at Smith, but she grew homesick five or six weeks into the semester and returned home for good. In the meantime, as far as anyone knew, Jake continued his cryptic existence in the godforsaken reaches of northern New Hampshire, although no one really knew this for sure. Father, like Lydia, never gave up hope that Jake would get back in touch one day and, if not return home, at least resume some form of contact with the family.

Little did he know he would provide the reason for Jake to return, at least for a few days, and for all the family to gather. And as good and decent a man as Father was, as much as he loved his children and his family, I do not think he would have chosen to bring Jake back by losing his own life without ever seeing Jake again. Father died of a heart attack just shy of his fifty-third birthday, and I can honestly say *everyone* mourned his loss, including Jake. It happened on a brutally cold day in the beginning of February while he was driving home after getting out of work late, as usual. It was a massive attack which came on so suddenly he lost control of the car and plowed through a snow bank before finally coming to rest about thirty feet down an embankment. No one saw it happen, and it was several minutes before anyone realized that below the broken snow banks was a car. It was several minutes more before rescue personnel could reach the scene, but according to the doctor who pronounced him dead as well as to those who worked on him in the ambulance, there was no chance of reviving him even if they had been there when it happened. There was just too much damage to his heart.

And there was too much damage to the hearts of everyone in the family. Grandmother and Grandfather turned ancient, it seemed, overnight. Grandfather grew silent and grey, his face the color of ashes, and I heard him say once to Mother that he had lived too long. Grandmother lamented to everyone she saw at the wake and the funeral that it was against nature for a mother to outlive her own child.

Except for those moments when Mother was being more solicitous about Lydia than she had been in years, terrified perhaps that such loss might push Lydia into an asthma attack that would take her away also, Mother wore a blank, numb expression on her face. She wore her makeup and her red lipstick as always, but it was as though a plug had been pulled from her, sapping her of some vital life force that imparted facial expression.

Ben took to reminiscing about the times we had gone camping and Father's singing in the rain after losing at strip poker, while Lydia seemed angry about everything: Ben's reminiscing, Jake's postmortem visit, and especially Mother's heightened concerns about her health.

For my own part, I listened to others and tried silently to understand and make peace with this man, and the memory of this man, who had been my father. He was a man whose greatest strength was also his greatest weakness: he wanted always to believe in what was best about his family, to the point where he was never able to accept anything about his wife and children that challenged his idealized image. I am certain he saw work— the seemingly unending hours of it week after week and year after year—as not only his responsibility to the family but also his greatest contribution, his greatest gift and sacrifice to us all. That we would have preferred less sacrifice and more of his presence in our lives presented a paradox, a contradiction to his work ethic that he never truly understood. Or maybe he did. Perhaps it was this contradiction between the ideal he wanted so desperately to believe in, to work for, and the reality that he lived with that ate away at him in secret and grew too much for his great heart. I do not know. But I believe the heart recognizes things the mind will sometimes not acknowledge, and it is the conflict between this knowing and not knowing that causes the heart finally to succumb to its own private grief, its own final expression of sorrow and protest at being ignored too long. Whether or not this is what happened to Father is a question I will never be able to answer, but my heart has its own kind of certainty.

Jake was present for the wake and funeral because of Lydia's insistence that he *must* know and that he *must* be a part of such final ceremonies for his own father. After years of no communication with Jake and given the voluntary nature of his seclusion, I would have been inclined to let it continue that way. But Lydia sent a telegram to him the day Father died. She *knew* he would attend if word reached him, and the fact that he did merely underscored how much more clearly Lydia understood Jake than I or anyone else in the family did.

Jake was still lean, and despite the lines on his face that bespoke more years than his actual age, he looked much healthier than the last time I had seen him—in his apartment. He still had a beard, and kept his long hair tied back tight to his head in a ponytail. For the services he wore a gray suit which fit poorly, as though he had borrowed it from someone. It struck me as an absurd irony that I was the one who had once had the long hair and scruffy appearance, while Jake had been the clean-cut patriot; yet here I stood now as the quintessential American professional with my close-cropped, stylishly cut hair, tailored dark suit and expensive cologne.

During the Mass the priest spoke words that had little or nothing to do with my father, using the sort of platitudes that I know Father would surely have tuned out. He had only continued attending church through the years out of respect for our grandparents, and out of a desire to set a good example for his children. Which was, I suppose, vintage Father. If it meant supporting his children, he had no trouble overlooking his personal convictions.

The ringing of the *Kyrie eleison* bells during the funeral Mass snapped me back to those days when I was a seven year old altar boy and rang those bells myself. It was Father who used to drive me to church in the blue-black darkness and chill of October mornings, or in the dead of winter, so that I could serve the Mass, who would sit there among the assembled faithful beaming with pride at his beautiful young son, me. And in the deep respectful quiet of the Mass the ringing of the bells—the issuing of those clear high-pitched tinkling notes from the golden bells I held in my hand—was a proclamation of love and faith, an act which carried a meaning about the harmony of my life and world that I could surely not have defined in those days but felt coursing through my body like an elixir of joy.

Standing and kneeling next to Jake, who observed the rituals of the Mass with impassive propriety, I could not help but wonder what he was seeing and thinking about Father. Jake had never been an altar boy, as I had, and could certainly never have known that powerful sense of rightness with the world that I had known, with Father so close by, at the ringing of the bells. But with the exception of Lydia, Jake had no greater booster in life than Father, and I wondered if he understood this, if he appreciated what he had lost with Father's death.

He may have, because at one point during the Eucharist I noticed out of the corner of my eye that Jake had his head bowed, and he murmured something to himself that sounded like, "He was a good man," as if he were at that moment making his own personal peace with Father. And then again at the gathering back at the house Jake was standing near me talking with one of Father's coworkers, who apparently made a comment about how often Father had spoken of his children at work, and I clearly heard Jake say, "He cared a lot about his family." He never said anything like this directly to me, though, nor to anyone else in the family so far as I know. The face he presented to us was the face he had always presented to us. There were no tears, no hoarse broken words, no moments of being suddenly overcome with emotion. Nothing but the normal impassive equanimity which he nearly always wore on his face. It occurred to me that I could not remember Jake *ever* crying.

The day after the funeral Jake returned to his frozen north country, and Lydia, distraught over Father's death, offered little resistance to his leaving. With a sense of ominous and inexplicable sorrow, I wondered if I would ever see Jake again.

Chapter Seventeen

Inferno

It was full dark in the early evening of a December night, had been dark for hours, when he heard the crunch of snow beneath the wheels of a car pulling up outside and had the immediate unreasonable thought that he knew who it was. There had been those letters, to which he had never responded despite the dire tone and the insistent forewarnings that she would come up to see him, and although she did not know where he lived and he had neither seen nor talked with her since the funeral, he believed he knew. It would not be Mossback, not at this hour. Mossback would already be well into the moonshine stupor he had witnessed each time he had been to the sometimes garrulous sometimes cantankerous old coot's hooch in the evenings to ply the secrets of trapping from him. And the sound was not the rattle and sputter of Mossback's old pickup but the slick clean purr of a well-kept modern engine. Unless some hapless idiot had lost his way on a cold December night and wandered far afield, it could not be anyone else. And yet for it to be her there would have to be an equally unlikely conjunction of circumstance—or need. The thought turned his innards liquid in a way he had not felt since Vietnam.

He opened the door and she stood there for a moment in her pink parka small and shivering against the cold, her hair cut above the shoulder, shorter than it had been since she was a baby. A new Toyota Corolla idled fast but smoothly only a few feet behind her, headlights on, its newness alien to this domain and its engine sending billows of frozen exhaust into the air behind her, making her appear more a pale surreal apparition than a creature of living flesh and blood. Until the apparition spoke.

"Jake!" she said, her eyes registering at once recognition and surprise. With his hair tied back in a ponytail and his beard grown full and bushy, flecked already, prematurely, with gray, he must look very different to her than when they had last seen each other. "I can't believe it. I've found you!" She was in his arms before he even realized he had opened them to receive her, his hand reaching without conscious volition to the truncated locks of gold.

"What happened?" he said.

"Did you get any of my letters?"

He nodded, although he had not read most of them.

"Mother thought it would make me look 'older and more mature.'" Her voice turned sarcastic in imitation, "Maybe then I'd be able to find a good job and get invited out on dates."

He pressed her head against his chest. The top of her head still did not reach his shoulders and he thought with grim humor: there's nothing she can do about that.

"Better turn the engine off," he said, the exhaust continuing to swirl about them, "and come inside." He released her and waited in the open doorway. "Yours?"

She shook her head. "Mom's."

He watched the diminutive pink form that seemed too small and young to drive move around the car and slip incongruously into the driver's side to extinguish both sound and light, and the impossibility of the situation, the inescapable certainty of what he had known since before he opened the door, since before the letters and since long before even that, since that time more than half his life ago when he ran away, struck him again with sudden force and clarity: they could not (even more: they should not) be together.

But she was already moving past him through the doorway, a small luminescent blur, when the engine began the pings and clicks of rapid cooling on a sub-zero winter night.

"It's cold in here," she said after she had removed her parka. She drew her shoulders in tight to her body and rubbed her arms.

"Sit over here," he said, indicating a chair near the small woodstove in the center of the room, where he invoked a whoosh of air when he opened the door of the woodstove to stir the coals and add some wood.

"The fire feels good," she said, sitting down. "It's really cold tonight. It wasn't anywhere near this cold when I left Newtown."

"It's always colder up here," he said, adding a couple more pieces of wood to the stove. He closed the door and opened the damper a little and the fire began to crackle. Then he pulled up a chair opposite her and waited for her to speak. He did not have to wait long.

"I wasn't sure I'd ever find you," she said. "Someone gave me directions but this road seemed to wind around forever. I felt like I was getting farther away from where anybody might live, and I kept thinking, 'What if the car stalls or I go off the road? It's freezing outside and I don't know where I am and I haven't seen a house for miles.' Then finally I came to your driveway. But I was really beginning to worry…"

He watched her pause and reconnoiter the pelts and the traps and the guns hung on the walls and suspended from the ceiling joists, her face betraying nothing more than curiosity without judgment, then watched her take a deep breath as if to gather herself for her next words, which she delivered with careful restraint. "Why haven't you been in touch with anyone over the years, Jake? And if you've been getting my letters, why haven't you answered any?"

Despite the fact that she had not grown much she looked older to him now in the lamplight with her hair cut short, her eyes shadowed with makeup and her lips frosted pale with some sort of glossy lipstick. Her voice, too, had deepened a little, although the forthright tone had always been there with him, a thing he had always resisted and admired. Still, this version of Lydia who sat near him did not square at all with the image frozen in his memory.

"Never been much of a writer or talker. That's your bailiwick."

"But not even a word in more than five years? If it hadn't been for the funeral I wouldn't have known you were alive."

He shrugged and withdrew a cigarette from the pack he kept in his shirt pocket, leaned forward to strike a wooden match against the stove and waited for a moment for the sulphur to flare off before lighting the cigarette.

"Weren't you interested at all in what was happening to any of us?"

He took a long drag of the cigarette. "You're in college now," he said, emitting a thin exhaust of smoke along with each word.

A shadow of doubt and fear flickered in her eyes. "And still living at home."

"You're only twenty."

"You were in Vietnam when you were my age."

"So what."

"So I should at least be able to live away from home."

She looked at him with an impassioned and almost accusing earnestness, but the look wilted and fell to the floor before his steady gaze. "I tried, Jake. I really did. I went off to Smith last year with every intention of making it work—I mean, the school is only two and a half hours away. But the second weekend there I had Mom come pick me up and bring me home. A few weeks later I came crawling home again for good, like a terrified first-grader. It was pathetic." She continued looking down at the floor as she shook her head and repeated, "pathetic."

"*The thing is, I don't want to be living at home—Mom and I fight all the time about nothing. Believe it or not, on those rare occasions when I'm out late she still gives me grief about what time I come in. And I certainly don't want to be going to a local college like Saint Anne's for my education. I liked it at Smith. The classes— at least the ones I went to—were wonderful. But I would get so afraid sometimes I couldn't even step outside my room. I'd stay in bed all day and get ahead on my reading assignments, but then I wouldn't go to my classes. The more classes I missed, the more afraid I was of going to them. My roommate kept asking if it was my asthma and if I needed to go to the infirmary. She even offered to go with me if I couldn't go by myself, but every time she asked I'd tell her I was feeling a little better and maybe all I needed was one more day of rest. Eventually she stopped asking. She must have thought I was crazy. It got to be very uncomfortable whenever she was in the room.*"

Her shoulders were drawn in as she finished speaking and she was hugging herself, stroking one shoulder as if she were cold or scared this moment. "What were you so afraid of?"

"*I don't know, really. I've thought about it and thought about it and can't seem to come up with an answer. Failing is part of it, I know that. I'm afraid of trying something because I might fail at it. So if I don't try a thing then I can't fail at it. But in the meantime, by not trying anything I'm failing at the most important thing of all—living my own life.*"

A shiver convulsed her and she huddled more tightly into herself. "Sit closer," he said, stuffing out his cigarette on the ashlip of the stove. "I'll get you a blanket."

"Thanks," she said when he returned and handed her the blanket. She sneezed as she wrapped it around her shoulders. "Oh Jake... sometimes I get so scared all I want to do is crawl into bed and die. I think about the future and I literally have trouble breathing. One time when I was very young I climbed inside the toy box we used to have and Ben, as a joke, sat on top of it and wouldn't let me out. That's what it feels like now, like I'm inside a box. It's completely black inside and I'm afraid if I move around too much I'll use up what little oxygen there is. I feel like there's nothing I know how to do, no place for me anywhere. I feel helpless, stupidly, stupidly helpless."

"You can write though, can't you? I've still got that poem you wrote."

"That was easy. I thought about you being in Vietnam and how much you were sacrificing, and how much I missed you, and I just wrote it. It's not that simple most of the time." She stopped herself for a moment as if reluctant to continue, but then looked at him and said, "It's always easier when I think about you. You've always helped me to be less afraid."

Things were beginning to snap into focus for him now—their conversation, her presence here tonight, the tone of her recent letters—and what he saw gave him a sharp premonitory stab of that old fierce conflict which he thought he had left behind, and with that a sense of something beyond what he could see, moving him out of control. "Does anyone know you're here?"

She flashed a puzzled look at him for the non-sequitur before sneezing again. "No, why?"

He shook his head. "Nothing."

"I told Mom I was going to a friend's house for the night."

"Why didn't you tell her you were coming here?"

"She would have told me it's too long a ride to make by myself and if you'd wanted visitors you would have asked for them."

"So why did you come?"

"I had to. I couldn't stand being where I was any more." She paused a moment before she spoke again. "And there's another reason."

He waited.

"I wanted to ask if I could stay with you for awhile, just until I figure out what I want to do with my life."

The sense that things were moving beyond his control was throbbing inside him now as if he were standing next to a Bouncing Betty which he knew was there but could not quite locate. One false move and...

She sneezed again and drew the blanket tighter around herself as he considered his answer. "You're still cold," he said.

"It's probably more allergy than cold," she said. "I'll be all right. But I'd take a tissue if you have one. I seem to have used up all the ones I had in my purse."

He retreated to his room and returned with an old handkerchief, which she gratefully accepted. "What do you think, Jake?"

He could find no words adequate to all the pulses of thought and memory and need that ran through him, all the half-formed superstitions and the inarticulate longings and the nameless sense of doom when he measured the possibility against the unreplete peace of solitude that had been his for the past few years. It came almost as a surprise to him when he said, "You're better off somewhere else."

Her look was not so much of disbelief as of confusion, as if she did not quite understand what she had heard. "What do you mean? Do you want me to leave right now?"

"No."

"But after tonight?"

"We can talk about it in the morning."

"Why wait until the morning?"

"We both need time to think about it," he said, although he had thought about it as much as he needed or intended to. Once the words had been uttered, even though he had not known what they would be before he said them, he knew they spoke the truth: she was

better off somewhere else, which she would perhaps see more clearly herself by sleeping on it.

"So you won't give me an answer now?"

He shook his head. "You're tired and cold, and I've got to get up early to check my traps. We'll talk about it after I get back."

She daubed at her eyes and blew her nose into the handkerchief he had given her. He could not tell whether she was reacting to allergy, cold, or sorrow.

"Could I use your bathroom?" she asked.

He gestured toward the door where she had come in and said, "It's out that way. I'll get you a flashlight." Then he pointed to a toilet seat hanging on the wall. "You'll need that too."

"The bathroom is outside?"

"It's not a bathroom."

He left and returned with a flashlight.

"Where do you wash?"

He nodded toward the crude kitchen area behind him where there was a hand pump mounted on a counter next to a tub. "Nothing fancy here."

She shivered and zipped her pink parka up to her chin. "I guess not."

As he stood in the doorway and watched her cone of light forge its way through the darkness, aware of the intense cold himself but aware of it mostly as a thing malevolent to her, he believed he knew with certainty that his answer to her was the only one possible.

When he awoke in the cold-black morning he checked the thermometer: twenty-five below zero, and wondered if she would be all right. He had forewarned her he would be leaving early to check his traps and would be gone when she awoke, given her explicit instructions about the stove and what to do if she were cold. Yet he could not shake the uncomfortable sense which he could neither *define nor dismiss that something was awry, although it might have been the mere fact of her presence that made him so uneasy. When he had left Newtown he had left with no plans of returning, and the years of early rising in the cold, of running the trapline in deep snow, of killing trapped animals and skinning and fleshing and stretching the pelts to cure them had become a kind of ritual, and through ritual a continuous exorcism of those forces which had been so powerfully a part of his life before. To open the door and find her standing there outside had been, at once, exactly what he expected and a shock to the ritual certainty of his life.*

For her sake he could have decided to set out later than usual, when it was not quite as cold and she was awake, but it was better right from the start, he thought as he loaded the woodstove, for her to see his routine, for him not to alter anything because of her. He did not want an animal out there longer than it needed to be, especially if it were alive but even if it were dead—other critters might corrupt its fur and destroy its worth before he reached it. Near a beaver bog along his line he had recently seen the tracks and scat of a large lynx, and he did not want to have the good fortune of trapping such a fine and valuable animal only to see its worth diminished because of an omission or mistake on his part.

As he assessed the rectitude of this thinking it struck him with astonishment: Right from the start? *More than the frigid black morning cold the thought sent a chill along his spine. He could not be thinking that way. Better almost to follow last night's cowardly impulse and sneak off to find a telephone—nothing would put an end to it sooner or more finally than one call—but he knew now as he had known last night that he could not do such a thing to her, or to himself.*

After a quick breakfast of coffee and toast and adding on the layers of his wool trapping clothes he was set to go, his trap pack ready as always, strapped to the second-hand snowmobile he had bought two years ago out of necessity—his trapline had been growing longer each year—though it still had the feel to him of luxury, a little like having a motorcycle to ride across the snow in winter. But there was already enough snow on the ground to warrant snowshoes, and the line stretched out at least ten miles now through deep woods that crossed the Canadian border in places and traversed territory so remote as to be nearly inaccessible, territory where the tracks and evidence of the human animal were seldom to be seen.

The engine fired up right away despite the intense cold, and after revving it to insure the flow of gas he let it rumble into the normal syncopated rhythm of its idle. Even with the leather mask on his face he could feel the hairs of his nostrils become icy pinpricks of cold each time he inhaled. Above him the northern night sky with its myriad stars set against the jet black void had not yet begun to lose its daily battle against morning. He switched on the powerful headlight and moved slowly away from the house and into the woods, following the trail he had blazed with the machine more than a week ago after a heavy snow. There had been no snow since then and the weather had been clear and very cold, though this night had been the coldest yet, perfect for furbearers like lynx that would be hungry and on the prowl. And his sets were ready.

As he entered the woods heading east he had the vaguely confident expectation, as he always had in matters of hunting and guile, that he would be successful. He had been successful at both through most of his life. Given enough time and patience, which he knew he possessed in abundance, there were only three other qualities needed: knowledge, the skill to deceive, and luck. Knowledge he had been acquiring all his life, the knowledge of the ways of wild animals representing merely the most recent and by no means final or complete addition to his store. The skill to deceive had been with him for as long as he could recall; it seemed to him inborn since he had no idea where it came from. Luck was a beast of a different kind, a beast which no amount of patience or time or knowledge or skill could ultimately master: each in sufficient measure—especially patience and time—might result in trapping the beast, or at least believing you had trapped it, for a while. But there was no controlling it, never any controlling it. Luck had taken him through Vietnam mostly unscathed and helped him survive countless other battles, and there were those in his life who had wanted to define him as lucky—in Vietnam his reputation for luck was so strong there were grunts who gave him the kind of fearful sidelong glances reserved for freaks or gods—but he possessed no illusion that luck would always be with him, or that he had any real power to lure it to himself.

Still, he had made money trapping over the years, had been successful and lucky at it, and this morning especially the feeling of luck, the belief that today he would discover what he wanted in one of the cubbies he had set near the beaver bog, grew stronger all the time. The more distance he put between himself and the dilemma he knew awaited upon his return, the more his uneasiness and confusion diminished, and the more clearly he could visualize the great night-roaming cat in his trap: back arched as it shrank down in a low crouch, one of its front legs held tight just above an outsized paw, the whiskers flaring prominently away from its wide blond face and the tufted black-tipped ears flattened back in a kind of deceptive look of humility or submission, only the fierce yellow-green dilated eyes, riveted upon his every move as he approached, betraying the contained fury lurking inside it and the sense of violation at this loss of its wild freedom, for it was a beast as jealous of its freedom as any in the northern woods, a beast at once curious and habitual and therefore easily trapped if you knew what you were doing, and at the same time utterly unpredictable and contemptuous of humanity, living only in the deepest and most remote woods in the coldest of climates, as far away from civilization as possible. He saw it in the light of early morning since the sun would have broken the horizon by the time he reached it, saw himself approach without hesitation to dispatch the beast with the merciful quickness of a twenty-two through the skull just above the eyes, the quickness particularly important to him with this magnificent animal which he respected above all others for where and how it lived. It was his regard for the animal, perhaps, along with a sense of kinship, which even more than the value of its pelt and the belief in his own prowess lured him to this vision as unerringly as the animal itself was drawn to the baited and scented trap.

But he did not increase his speed as he traveled, having learned more than once that to hurry out of anticipation or fear often led to disaster—he had seen it all too many times in Vietnam where the fucking new guys especially would move too quickly and die too quickly, or have their legs blown off by a mine. Instead he proceeded at his customary steady pace, stopping only long enough while it was still dark to inspect his sets right from the snowmobile with the beam of a powerful flashlight he carried with him. If the sets looked untouched he continued on, maintaining as great a distance from them as possible. If he saw a set had been altered or the glistening eyes of a trapped animal, he strapped on his snowshoes and remade the set or killed the animal and then remade it, careful in all he did to avoid leaving his own scent.

The first several sets he checked were untouched, and after an hour he had only a raccoon to show for his effort. An hour and a half later, after he had drawn nearer the stream that flowed down from the beaver bog and had added a mink and a red fox, both of which were in good condition and would fetch a pretty fair price, the expectation of a successful day mounted in him once again. The fox was undoubtedly the one he had been seeing signs of and had been trying to trap for a couple of weeks now.

Above him the deep black north woods sky had softened into the dark blue of early morning and then into that pale blue that is nearly indistinguishable from gray except for the lingering evidence of a few tenacious stars and the pink glow of dawn in the east. It would not be long before the sun broke the horizon and with its growing light snuffed out those few remaining stars as it began to create the illusion of warmth above this frozen land.

He made his way unhurried to the first of the sets he had made for the great cat, a tree set just to the side of his snowmobile trail. Knowing of the cat's penchant for curiosity to distract it from its natural wariness, he had set the killer trap there hoping the lynx would follow the trail. But the trap was untouched when he came upon it, and finding no new spoor in the area he slowed down but did not stop as he passed by it. With the morning light increasing by the moment, he saw from a distance the next two sets were also untouched and continued past these too without much thought, except for acknowledging in passing them that he was at least drawing closer to the cubby set near the beaver lodge that he had been envisioning all along.

He had made the cubby teepee style using some of the sticks and logs from the beaver lodge itself and forged a snowshoe trail which ran from the snowmobile trail directly to the opening of the cubby. Before he could even draw adjacent to the site, however, from a hundred feet away, he could see that something was wrong, the trap had been sprung and there was no animal in sight; even more, the cubby had been partially torn up by whatever animal had sprung the trap, and the log used as a drag was on top of the snow several feet away. He accelerated a little, his own curiosity piqued now by the scene and the story unfolding before him.

There were patches of dark fur and blood on the snow, bright red frozen spots of it around the trap, and in the trap itself was the black severed foot of an animal. Fisher, he realized when he drew close enough to identify it. It was a good and valuable animal in its own right, ferocious and brave, its pelt worth a fair amount of money, and under most circumstances he would have been pleased to have such an animal visit his trap. But now it represented an impediment—a loss of the more valuable lynx and a delay which meant he must not only strap on his snowshoes to find it and kill it, but also remake the set for the lynx.

The trail was not difficult to follow in the snow and the fisher had not traveled far, no more than a quarter of a mile, before finding shelter beneath the partial obscurity of a hemlock bower. By the time he reached the fey creature there was not much life remaining in it. The fisher lifted its head and bared its teeth in a feeble snarl but made no attempt to rise from the death curl its dark body had assumed in the wake of injury and cold. He took out the stick he always carried with him on the line and gave the fisher a sharp rap between the eyes to stun it, then positioned his foot behind the foreleg and administered the merciful kick which collapsed the animal's lungs and brought about a quick death. He put the dead fisher into his trap pack and returned to the snowmobile, where he added the corpse to the others in the crate. With the cold slowing his efforts and the amount of repair needed to the cubby set, it took him another twenty minutes before he could get back on the snowmobile and continue along the line.

There were several more traps to check in the area around the beaver bog, three of which were set specifically for the lynx, but the expectation of finding it today in one of his traps had diminished with the discovery of the fisher. He knew such mistakes were inevitable: if you had enough traps out and trapped long enough you were bound to have smaller, non-target animals stumble into a trap too large for them, but he did not like to see it happen and tried his best to avoid it. The fact that it had happened today, when he was anticipating a scene so much different from what he found, made *him feel vain and foolish, as if he himself had been caught in a trap he learned long ago to avoid: counting on good fortune.*

His new presentiment about the lynx proved correct—the remaining sets were untouched—and the arc of his line now swung him sharply away from the beaver bog to the northwest, where he traversed a ridge that afforded an extensive overlook west and south toward the valley from which he had come. He stopped for a moment to consider the view, allowing his engine to idle, as he often did at this point along the line when the weather was clear.

The sun was high enough now to be lighting up the western landscape, although the advancing line between sun and shadow had not yet reached the area where he knew his house to be. He could not see the house itself—trees and the slope of the land concealed it from view—but he knew precisely where it lay and with his binoculars he could see the plume of gray-white smoke rising from his woodstove. He wondered if she were awake yet and whether or not she had grown cold in the night. If so, he had given her instructions about the stove and he would be there in less than an hour himself, but for now there was not a thing he could do about it.

It occurred to him almost with surprise that missing the lynx again today was still bothering him, as much—if he were honest about it—because he had been counting on trapping it as because the fisher had suffered. Through all of his adult life and most of his younger life he had tried to avoid depending on anything or anyone, to excoriate from his soul the expectation that he had control over anything but himself, and here he had fallen prey to that same credulous optimism he viewed with contempt in others.

And yet as he stood gazing out over the cold and beautiful landscape below him, the dark green coniferous trees predominating over the gray hardwoods, the hills and the white slopes of the frozen land stretching expansively to the horizon, sharply defined beneath the clear arctic blue of the sky, all of it utterly soundless but for the insistent idle of his machine, he felt again the enormous sense of wild freedom that had years ago drawn him to this merciless northern clime. He realized with mounting satisfaction that he was where he belonged, he was free, and he had, after all, met with a degree of success he had no right to diminish: he had already taken four fine animals from his traps, three of them of great value, and he had no right to expect more. If the morning had not gone exactly the way he had hoped, then the problem was not with the animals or his luck— because the dead animals behind him clearly testified that he had had luck—but with the hoping itself, the hoping for more. All any living thing had a right to hope for was the freedom of continued survival, and these animals had lost that freedom, had had it taken from them for the benefit of his own survival. He had no right to feel cheated or misused.

The balm of this justly reasoned satisfaction accompanied him all the way along his descent from the high ground to the deeper woods below where he began following the remainder of his line. He took another raccoon farther along the line and considered himself—with five animals now—richly rewarded for his morning's work, the raccoons providing not just their skins for sale but decent meat for meals. He wondered, with a kind of grim though not mean-spirited humor, how she would take to the idea of having roasted raccoon for dinner—that might be enough in itself to disincline her from her own proposition of staying with him.

It was only when he drew within half a mile of his house that the smell of the smoke—even before the sight of it—alerted him to something being wrong, and in the very instant he understood what that was he opened the throttle wider than he had ever opened it in the woods.

From the beginning she had difficulty falling asleep. The familiar night sounds were absent: the regular quarter-hour chiming of the *grandfather clock, the intermittent firing of the furnace and its subsequent drone, the metallic pings of the heat registers expanding and contracting, the hum of her alarm clock beside her bed, all gone, replaced by dark quiet and stillness as if they had been nothing but the surface sounds of excess stripped away by this harsh Spartan existence of his. Even when she did manage to drift into a light, restless sleep for an hour or so, she kept waking. His bed was comfortable enough (he had insisted on giving her the only bed in the house), and with the several layers of blankets he had heaped upon her she managed to stay reasonably warm, but her allergies plagued her relentlessly through the night. Her eyes teared without surcease, her throat felt as if an animal hair from one of the pelts that seemed to be everywhere had somehow gotten lodged there and was tickling her, her nose continued to run long after she had turned his handkerchief into a useless wet rag and had exhausted the supply of toilet paper she had taken with her from that godforsaken, vile-smelling pit outside (which she would not return to through the murderous cold merely for the paradoxical benefit of a few more shreds of paper for her nose). And she most certainly did not want to rouse Jake to let him know of her discomfort, thereby confirming herself to him as the pitiably whining and dependent creature she believed herself to be, and detested. The reason she had come here in the first place and asked him if she could stay was to change that— to get distance from her mother and prove to herself that she could live away from home, away from the insidious allure of having someone regulate your life for you—and she did not want to undermine this on her first night here.*

So she passed the night in a fitful netherworld that was neither true sleep nor true wakefulness, and heard his cautious rustling inside the house and the squeak of the woodstove door twice before she heard the muted clinking sounds of metal as he went about his preparations somewhere at the other end of the house, followed by the much louder rumbling of the snowmobile he had forewarned her about last night. Only after the last muffled reverberations of the machine receded back into the dark stillness did she feel free to get up and try to alleviate her distress, for it had become that while she endured the night. She was beginning to have trouble breathing.

She withdrew from the warm cocoon of her blankets carefully and got up to find a light, groping about in the dark for the pull chain she had noticed last night—there were no switches in this room. After finding it at last she took the inhaler from her purse, quickly formed the necessary rictus around it with her lips, and inhaled a couple of puffs as deep into her lungs as she could. The effect was almost instantaneous, the relieving sense of freedom, of widening and expanding, as if the thick tight feeling inside her were a kind of snow or ice being melted away by a benevolent warm mist. If only she could do this with her life, she thought as she switched off the light and returned to the still-warm refuge beneath her blankets—take a puff from some magic inhaler and pull greater freedom down into the recesses of her being, shrink away her fears and open up the latent possibilities of her character.

When she awoke again she did not know what time it was but she could see through the one east-facing window in the room that the first faint light of morning was beginning to dawn in the sky. Last night she had been too intent on Jake and her request of him to be much aware of the house, so she took the opportunity now to get up, wrapped tightly still in a blanket, and explore her surroundings. It was a small house, not new from the aged look of the wood, but not finished either, with all the rooms—five of them—on one floor. There was uncovered pink insulation between the studs in many places, and in those places where the insulation was covered it was covered with plywood more for the apparent purpose of providing a surface to nail into than for any conceivable aesthetic reason. Aesthetic concerns were clearly nonexistent in this house, while *function was apparent everywhere. The house was not so much cluttered as it was made use of. In the room at the far end of the house, where she had heard him rummaging around in preparation to leave, was a latched wooden door on the northwest wall which connected the house to an outdoor shed, a workbench and rough wooden shelves covered with tool boxes, and one plywood wall with so many traps and spools of wire and other trapping supplies which she could not even name suspended from the countless nails knocked into it that it functioned like a floor-to-ceiling pegboard.*

One of the rooms she hadn't seen at all last night startled her and sent nervous tingles of sudden, inexplicable dread up and down her spine when she flicked on the light switch inside the doorway. Before her were the pelts of animals: foxes, raccoons, muskrats, even a large coyote that she thought at first was a dog, stretched out and nailed to triangular-shaped lengths of wood that looked something like an artist's easels, except that animals nailed to wood in this way reminded her so forcefully of crucifixes that she felt sickened, queasy with doubt. She felt cold and disheartened. The possibility that staying here with Jake was a misguided and foolish idea from the start, the invention of a pathetic and desperate mind, began to work its way from the pit of her stomach to the core of her heart, where it coiled and tightened like a constrictor. There was, too, the knowledge of what he had always needed from her in the past, which she had until this moment stuffed so successfully into the darkest recesses of her soul that she had not thought of it in years, not even while driving up here, but she thought of it now and knew it was a thing, his need, that she could no longer accommodate.

She made her way to the woodstove feeling suddenly so cold that she shivered, so cold that she could not seem to get close enough to the stove to stop shivering. She found herself wishing absurdly that she could get right inside it for a moment to thaw out. There was wood he had left for her nearby in a woodbox, and as she took some to load into the stove she remembered his instructions and his cautions of the night before clearly. The black iron door squeaked in complaint when she opened it wide, and in the same moment she saw the glowing red coals and the white licks of flame she also felt the outward rush of heat and lingered there for a few moments before adding more wood, lingered again after that to watch the wood begin to smoke and then ignite into flame. She closed the door and opened the damper wider, as he had instructed, planning to wait there by the stove, by the heat, for the ten minutes or so he had suggested until it was time to damp the stove back down. But even being this close to the heat could not melt the chill she felt spreading inside her.

She was having trouble breathing again and got up to retrieve her inhaler, which was in her purse next to the bed where she had slept. The tightness in her chest increased as she went, her breaths coming now—as she had once explained to Ben when he appeared to have no concept of what it was like to struggle for air—with all the difficulty of trying to inhale through a pillow pressed tight to the face. With every step she took it seemed her breathing grew more labored, more impossible, and she knew even before she circled her lips around the inhaler and took two slow ineffectual puffs from it that she was in serious trouble.

She sank down to a sitting position beneath the window, her back pressed against the wall below it, and closed her eyes, tried consciously to slow the racing of her heart and the swelling suffocation in her chest, tried to visualize, as she sucked on the inhaler a third time and again a fourth time, the quelling effect of the vapors working through her clogged bronchial tubes and expanding them ever so slightly, dilating the grapelike alveoli sacs and seeping into the tiny capillaries beyond, delivering to the innermost core of her being life itself, but the effort failed, and she felt herself finally, with a sense of relief, slipping into darkness.

She never heard the spontaneous sound of combustion when the stovepipe, grown cherry red, ignited the wood surrounding its flashing into flame.

The scene of smoke and flames and incipient destruction that confronted him when he arrived at the house was of a magnitude he had not encountered since his time in Vietnam, since the days of napalm and firebombing, and he knew without thinking it into words that the house was already gone, had been gone from the moment it caught fire, but if she were still inside (he got off the snowmobile and made a quick reconnaissance outside, looking and shouting, but she was nowhere to be seen and he heard nothing but gusts of wind and fire shooting from blown-out windows), if she had stayed low enough, she might still be alive.

He moved to the doorway and opened his way into the inferno beyond it with the reflex speed of one who has no thought of danger to himself, with the only thought at all running through his mind the thought that he must find her, on his knees groping through the blinding suffocating smoke and the roaring oven of heat and the ravening flames, guided by feel alone in the absence of sight and hearing, the stench of burning hair from the pelts filling the air: find her, *crawling and feeling blindly along to his left into the living room and then along as much of its perimeter as was not already in flames, shouting her name between convulsions of coughing, moving to the kitchen and by feel finding nothing there either, and then on deeper into the house to the equipment room that connected to the shed, the fire not having reached here yet but the smoke as thick as everywhere else, thinking* maybe through there *but finding the door to the shed still latched and bolted from the inside and again finding nothing in the room, thinking* where then? where? *as he began to circle back clockwise to the curing room and then all around inside it knocking over the wooden stretchers with their drying pelts, shouting and calling her name and hearing nothing but the sound of the fire and the clattering fall of the stretchers, the awareness of her choice dawning fully on him now as he made his way to the only room remaining, his own room: outside into the arctic cold or inside amongst the searing flames and either way hope for rescue, and with the awareness the question arising inside him with a kind of fury upon remembering he had seen it outside:* why not the car? *but even that question snuffed out quickly by the imperative that drove him:* find her, *and then he did, his hand bumping into her inert form slumped along the floor beside his bed. She was covered by a blanket and lay directly beneath the only window in the room. He picked her up wrapped in the blanket, jackknifed his body around hers, and bolted away through the wall of flame blocking the open door through which he had entered.*

Outside, he placed her in the cab of his pickup and took off layers of his own charred clothes to wrap around her, then turned the key in the ignition and listened to the engine whir sluggishly against the cold before at last turning over. He sought her wrist to check for a pulse and found her fingers still tightly curled around her inhaler. There was no pulse in her wrist so he placed two fingers on the carotid artery of her neck and pressed his cheek close to the blanched lips, but he could not feel even the slightest quiver of life beneath his fingers, and upon his cheek there was not the faintest whisper of breath. He pressed his ear hard against her chest as if to force life into it, and for a deceptive instant thought he heard something, until he understood that it was nothing but the echoing sound of his own blood throbbing inside him. Then he backed his pickup out of the driveway and began the journey toward a pronouncement that he had already heard in the deepest chambers of his heart.

Epilogue

The official cause of Lydia's death was "smoke inhalation," although Mother refused to have an autopsy performed. There was no justifiable benefit to what she saw as the further violation of her child. The fire itself was determined to have originated when the woodstove in Jake's house overheated and caused the wood around the stovepipe to combust, but no one has any explanation for how this came about. Why didn't Lydia control the fire more carefully? If she had been aware of the problem—as it seems she must have been—and was overcome by smoke while trying to combat it, why did Jake find her in his bedroom instead of in the living room? And if, recognizing the situation was beyond her control, she had time to flee to Jake's room, why didn't she instead leave the house for the safety of Mother's car? I have no answers to these questions, only doubts and confusion.

Immediately after Lydia's death the adrenaline of disbelief and sorrow managed to get Mother through the wake and the funeral with the semblance of her continuing, somehow, to function. Although she wore a black dress and hat with a veil lowered constantly over her face, her clothing was always impeccably neat and pressed, and beneath the veil she wore makeup that had been applied—I saw her doing this at home—with the same meticulous care she always took in her appearance. Only her swollen eyes, which she could not hide, betrayed the evidence of her enormous grief, and only once, at the wake, when she was at the kneeler in front of Lydia's open casket, did she publicly break down into tears, requiring that

Ben and I, at each elbow, help her up and guide her away. Otherwise, the image she presented to the world was of courage, and stoic endurance.

But at home, in the days and weeks that followed the funeral, Mother neglected herself completely. She would sit in the overstuff chair that she and Lydia so often used to curl up in together, and she would gaze dully into space for hours, unmoving, sometimes remaining there through the night. She often refused to eat or to otherwise take care of herself, and without food, without any of the makeup she had always been so fastidious about, she grew pale and gaunt, and I began to fear for her. It was all she could do just to put on clothes each day, and even that, I suspect, required assistance from Grandmother, who along with Grandfather mercifully came to stay with her for some time after Lydia died. It had only been two years since Father's death, and Grandmother knew all too well how much Mother was suffering, how devastating it was for a parent to lose a child, how important it was for her to subordinate her own grief over Lydia's death to the greater need of helping Mother through the daily struggle of simply enduring.

In time, Mother's stubbornness and her will to remain independent arched up in her, and Grandmother and Grandfather returned to their own home. It was enough, after that, for me to stop in and check on her two or three times a week (the given reason was to join her for lunch, which I would sometimes bring with me, though more often than not she would prepare it). I had moved back to Newtown about six months prior to Lydia's death to start up a law practice with an old friend, so it was easy to stop in and make sure Mother was all right.

Nowadays Ben also stops in regularly to see her. Unfortunately, he never made it past double A baseball, and after a few years of "kicking around in the minors to chase women," as he puts it, he came back up north to live. He works as a life insurance salesman now, and although Mother has hinted to both of us more than once in recent years that she would love to have grandchildren, neither of us seems ready for that sort of commitment anytime soon. Ben and I still see each other often and manage to keep up the banter we've always had in our relationship, but it seems hollow at times, as though just on the other side of our words and our laughter is an edge of meaning that would cut us to the quick if we ever truly touched it.

Mother has never been the same since Lydia died. Eventually she got back to her lifelong passion for volunteer work, for helping others, and in time she began tending her gardens again, but to this day, especially during the coldest cold snaps of winter, she lapses into bouts of depression during which she dwells upon what she sees as her own absolute culpability for Lydia's illnesses and death. Nothing I say during these times can loosen the fierce grip of her guilt, and I have learned over the years the fine art of listening without comment or judgment, while waiting for something—perhaps an incident at the homeless shelter where she works, involving someone she perceives as less fortunate—to call her away from herself. It has always been curious to me that she has never once implicated Jake at all in Lydia's death, even though it happened in his house. "Jake has his own crosses to bear," she said to me one time when I was wondering aloud if we would ever see him again.

The last time I saw Jake, over ten years ago now, was during those days of ceremony and sorrow following Lydia's death. He did not talk about what had happened, and as always, he revealed nothing about what he was thinking or feeling. The only comment I remember him making to any of us was the one he made to Mother as we were walking out of church after the funeral, delivered in that curt tone of his which seemed both analysis and judgment at once: "She was afraid of living." In her grief, Mother simply nodded. No one asked him what he meant by that.

At the wake—even in the face of so many people kneeling before the open casket, gazing for a few final moments upon Lydia's seraphic beauty, and leaving in tears, as both Ben and I did—the stony impassivity of Jake's expression never changed. He went up too, kneeled and bowed his head, but when he turned around he seemed to me completely unmoved. I wanted to say to him, "Don't you ever feel anything, Jake? Don't you know that she loved you, that she was crazy about you?" But I said nothing, and I realized as I thought about him that there was inside of me no true understanding of him, no real sense of kinship or connection to him, no... love for him. And in that moment it occurred to me that there had never been any love for him. A kind of grudging respect, maybe, as well as a fascination amounting, at times, almost to reverence, to awe. But never any love, never any warmth. I realized then that if I did not see Jake again in my life it would not matter to me in the least.

As for my questions about what happened to Lydia and to our family, I have no true answers. Why did she go to Jake and not to me on that fateful night? I lived right there in Newtown in an apartment that had plenty of room for her to stay in if she felt the need—as Jake stated to the police—to get away from home for a while. Why did she feel so compelled to drive two hundred miles north to find a brother who had deliberately taken himself out of contact with the world, when she had a brother who was living comfortably *in* the world, right nearby, and who was completely willing to do anything he could for her, anything she asked? What does that say about me, and about who Lydia saw me to be?

I wish I knew. I only wish I knew.

About the Author

Tim Barretto teaches writing, speaking, and literature at the University of New Hampshire's Thompson School of Applied Science. He and colleague Kate Hanson co-founded the Community Leadership program at the school in 2001 as a way of helping students interested in becoming activists and community leaders to find and develop their voices. His creative work includes *Searching for Joy*, a novel; short stories published in literary journals; and a one-act play about bullying that was performed at several schools in New Hampshire's Strafford County. He has spent most of his adult life pur-  suing ways to eliminate child abuse, and in that pursuit has served as a passionate advocate for children. When he has free time, he loves to spend it outdoors fishing, hiking, or skiing with family and friends. He lives in Dover, New Hampshire, with his wife, Mary.